Road of a Paragon

Rise of Shadow • Reign of Light

Volume I

L.R. Knight

NOTE: If you purchased this book without a cover, you should be aware that this book is stolen property. It was reported as "unsold and destroyed" to the publisher, and neither the author nor the publisher has received payment for this "stripped book." No part of this publication may be reproduced, stored in a retrieval system, or transmitted, in any form or by any means, electronic, mechanical, photocopying, recording or otherwise, without prior written permission from the author or publisher.

ROAD OF A PARAGON

Copyright © 2020 by Dr. Luc Niebergall (L.R. Knight)

All rights reserved.

Editor: Lorna Albert

Cover Design: Todd Toews and Life Designs + Media

ISBN: 9798631485495

Printed in Canada

I dedicate this book to my father, Scott, for teaching me the value of creativity and imagination. Thank you for always being such an affirming, strong, and consistent anchor in my life.

Road of a Paragon

"The rises and falls which occur within an individual fascinate me. There are moments when our confidence soars above the highest mountain peaks. In flight, no thought is too lofty, nor dream too folly. Then, in the descent is where insecurity triumphs. There we hide in the deepest of caves, too unsure to show our faces. There, we become immersed in fears and uncertainties, a constant tension raging within us. From high to low, from warrior to coward. This tension sharpens us. It moulds us. For as we ascend and descend, a certainty begins to take shape within the foundation of who we are. We must decide who we will one day be. Though both pride and insecurity veil the truth, a true warrior will not stop seeking until they know the answer to the question ringing throughout their soul like an echoing of bells:

"Who am I?"

- Dolan Thain
Heart of the Brave

Chapter One

A Fallen Legend

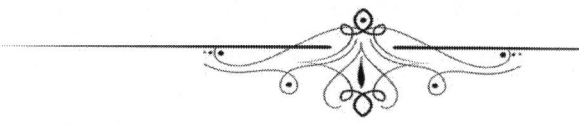

Kaldon watched the billows of smoke wafting into the sky. The weather chilled his hands and feet, but he was warmed by the crackling fire before him. Encircled by a crowd, they watched as scarlet flames consumed the great Warrior General's lifeless body upon the burning pyre.

Light rain, fitting for a funeral, descended. The heavy grey sky contrasted with the billowing orange flames. Kaldon watched the rain run down the Warrior General's corpse, face, and beard like tears. As those around him wept, he felt a sting of sadness.

With the exception of the sound of sobs and sniffling noses, the crowd was silent as people reflected upon the death of Dolan Thain. The somber silence was interrupted by an occasional person speaking forth a memory of the General, or a song of musical eulogy. Kaldon mused that many musical compositions would now be written in tribute to the General. His memory would live on as legend.

Kaldon knew the stories of Dolan Thain's tremendous feats. How, on numerous occasions, he led tens of thousands of soldiers into battle. He was a genius in war tactics and a Philosopher. The man wrote countless books on the topics of war and the nature of mankind. He was brilliant. The General's death was unexpected, as it often is with those carrying such influence. In the small city of Rundle, a minor plague broke out, lasting several weeks. The plague claimed a dozen or more lives. The General had been born in Rundle and, despite his fame, came back every few years to his humble beginnings. Kaldon supposed that people often feel a deep connection to where their stories began.

The dead General had been a mountain of a man. He had won thousands of battles and wars and had not expected to be affected by the plague upon returning home. When he fell ill, the mayor called in the most skilled healers from the surrounding regions, yet nothing could be done. Dolan Thain was one of the pillars of safety for Agadin; he brought order to the land. Now, he was gone, felled by mere sickness.

The rain drenched Kaldon. It matted his auburn hair and beard, soaking his travelling clothes. He had never ventured beyond his hometown. He wore travel clothing for their function and durability. The forest-green cloak about his shoulders matched his moistened, emerald eyes. As the heat from the fire licked his cheeks, his tears cooled the warmth. Watching flames consume the lifeless body of a legend, his thoughts drifted inwards to a childhood memory hidden deep within his heart.

It was the morning of his tenth birthday. Kaldon's eyes snapped open in anticipation. Arriving at your tenth year of life is distinguished as a monumental time for a child. Today was his day, and he knew his mother had a surprise she wanted to give him. Many of his friends would visit to congratulate him on stepping into this new stage of life.

Traditionally, on the day a child turns ten years old, they are affirmed by their father. It is a rite of passage as a child steps into their second decade of life. Having never met his father, Kaldon didn't know what to expect from the day.

Coming into the kitchen, he saw his mother sitting at the table. Her chestnut hair looked copper as the summer light streamed in through the windows of their home. Looking up at him, she beamed with pride and motioned young Kaldon to the seat beside her.

Tears brimming in her eyes, she lovingly reached out and clasped his hands. "Kal, today is your day to be affirmed into your next stage in life."

She swallowed hard, then continued. "I have something for you, dear."

He noticed a rather sophisticated-looking book sitting on the table. It was of a mahogany colour, trimmed in gold. Reaching for it, he held the book before him. He had never seen a book so luxurious in all of his life. His brow furrowed, thinking his mother must have paid a fortune for it. Knowing how scant they were for coin, he was speechless.

Giving him a moment, his mother spoke tenderly to him. "I know you must be disappointed that you have never known your father, and therefore he can't give you the affirmation you deserve on such an important day. The book that you are holding right now is no ordinary book, Kal. This was written by your father."

He looked up at his mother with widened eyes as her words sank in.

"We have never spoken of him, but you are old enough now to know the truth. Your father left me shortly after you were conceived. To this day, I still don't understand why he left us. I suppose he wasn't ready to take on the responsibility of raising a family. Kal, you should know that your father is no ordinary man. He is a genius, a Philosopher. He not only wrote this book, but he also penned many books on the topics of war and the art of how people think. Your father is the renowned Warrior General. Your father is Dolan Thain."

Confused, Kaldon looked around the room, trying to grasp what his mother was saying. The stories he heard of Dolan Thain raced through his mind. He recalled boys at school excitedly telling of the armies he led and of the battles he'd won. His mind thundered with images and impact. His gaze rested upon a large crack, spiderwebbing up the central wall, along the ceiling above them. His scrambled thoughts came to an abrupt stop, one question ringing louder than the rest. "How could a man of such renown leave him and his mother with hardly enough to eat and living in a house that was always cold?" The land of Agadin may have needed a Warrior General, but he needed a father.

Kaldon's mother slowly pulled the book from his hands, breaking his train of thought.

"Your father is not a bad man, Kal. I don't understand all of the reasons why he was not here with us, or why he isn't here today to affirm you. He is a good man. He has helped countless people. I want to read you something from this book."

Opening the royal-looking book, she skimmed through a few pages to find what she was looking for. "Ah, here it is," she said with her finger pressed upon the text.

"Kal, I want you to close your eyes. Your father may not be able to affirm you himself, but his words can. I think this paragraph is fitting for a day such as today."

Moments after Kaldon closed his eyes, his mother began to read over him words from his father's book.

"The calling over your life is far too precious to be sold in exchange for the approval of others. Your destiny was never fashioned to fit within the parameters of other people's expectations of who you should be. For some, greatness is merely a distraction people dream about in order to escape their reality. The truth is that to walk in greatness is a choice. To live in purpose is a choice. Life and circumstances will try to crush body, soul, and spirit, but you were never meant to be caged. Never allow yourself to be the victim. You are the victor. Do not crawl. Soar."

The affirmation came to an end, and Kaldon could feel the words going down deep into his soul. Opening his eyes, he saw something he did not expect. His mother was holding a necklace with a bronze-like pendant hanging from it. The circular pendant was simple in design. There were two circles—an inner and an outer. From the inner circle were five points that began in the middle and penetrated outside of the outer circular wall. It reminded him of *a compass. The pendant hung in the air before him, catching the sunlight.*

"This is the only thing I have of your father's," his mother said. "He left it behind the night he left me—left us. I've kept it for you. You are old enough to have it now."

Reaching his hands forward, his mother thought he was reaching for the pendant. Yet, he wasn't reaching for the pendant at all. He was reaching for her. Leaning into her, he wept into her shoulder.

He spoke through sniffles and tears. "The words were moving, momma. Thank you for reading me my affirmation. The most meaningful part of it all wasn't the words or the pendant, it was that you care enough about me to be here with me on such an important day as this."

Together, they cried.

Coming out of the memory, Kaldon rolled the circular pendant between his finger and thumb. As he did so, he could feel each of the five points pressing into his skin. The pendant was precious to him and never left him. For the very first time in his life, he was standing before the man it originally belonged to, the father he had never known. As Kaldon tinkered, his eyes were caught by what looked like an eagle soaring in the distant skies. Its caws filled the morning air, joining the mounting cries and wails of the people mourning Dolan Thain.

Just then, twelve city officials of Rundle approached the burning pyre, each holding a single lit candle. As each found their place in a circle around the fallen hero, a female's voice ascended from the crowd of people. The soprano voice and song echoed through the rain-filled sky as she sang of the Warrior General's fame. Kaldon's mouth began to twitch as he forced himself to maintain composure. He saw his mother's face in his mind and wondered if she and his father were together now in death as they should have been in life. He wished she were still alive and could be with him at this moment.

The sting of emotion quickly dissipated as something caught his eye. Through the company of men and women filling the funeral court, he saw a man watching him. Everyone else in attendance either had their eyes closed in reverential mourning or was gazing into the fire; yet this man's attention was focused on Kaldon. The man looked to be in his late thirties with salt and pepper hair and a beard. His eyes were like a hawk's, peering at him from beneath a burred brow. This was no ordinary man. The man wore a black cape with dark-tailored boots and a charcoal breastplate. From his hip hung a large sword, held in a decorative sheath. Next to him were two others with identical clothes and swords. Kaldon knew exactly what they were, although he had only heard stories of the men clad in black, travelling in threes. He had begun to believe they were fables made up to entertain children. Now he knew they were real. They were Knights of Agadin. It made sense to Kaldon that such men would be there to honour his father.

He uncomfortably ran his hand through his wet hair, trying not to fold under the man's penetrating stare. Kaldon was used to feeling invisible in crowds. He had no clue why a Knight of Agadin would take interest in him. Most might assume that this man of nobility was trying to intimidate, yet he could tell that his expression revealed him to be more curious than threatening. The Knight was trying to figure him out.

Cutting off his own train of thought, he told himself that the reason the Knight was giving him unwanted attention didn't matter. His mother told him years ago that no one knew he was Dolan's son. Even though he was a Thain by blood, he took his mother's last name, *Wendal*. That was how people knew him; as Kal Wendal. He preferred it that way. He lived life on the sidelines. He was left alone.

Tired of the stare-lock with the Knight, Kaldon broke eye contact. Focusing on the ceremony again, he knew the funeral was stirring emotions which had lain dormant for much of his life. Memories were being provoked from deep within him.

Feeling the weight of the death and the pressure of the Knight's continuous scrutiny, part of him wanted to run and hide. He rejected the urge, looking for the first and last time at the man now burning on the pyre. The man who should have played the role of a father in his life, but never did.

Chapter Two

Rundle

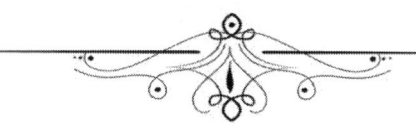

The small city was uncharacteristically hectic. Normally a lowly and slow-paced place to live, Rundle was humming with people. Vendors vigorously tried to entice potential customers, as street musicians and dancers performed zealously to draw attention. They would all likely be doing so long into the night, attempting to make a decent wage. Young children scampered through the streets, playfully trying to get a glimpse of the many tourists. The varied attire of the people from surrounding cities splattered the drab city with vibrancy.

Rundle was generating more wealth in the few weeks since the General's funeral than it had seen in an entire decade. The motels were booked solid. Commoners in town were renting out spare rooms in their homes. Even though the funeral was almost two weeks past, the city was still swarming with people. Such things never happened in the small city. Still, it wasn't for little reason. The passing of Dolan Thain was no small occurrence.

"Kal! Come on, hurry!" Claude bellowed. The stocky man shook his balding head in frustration as he rushed down the street.

Kaldon shook his head in return, laughing. "You know, Claude, even when I work at my fastest pace, you are never satisfied."

Claude grunted in response. Claude was the owner of the Templar's Well. There were a few taverns in the city, but his was known as the best around. Kaldon had worked at the tavern for a few years now, helping Claude run it. On this day, Claude was especially anxious because some of the nobles in town had reserved the entire bar the following night for a get-together.

"You do know we still have a full day until the gathering, right? You honestly have no reason to be so concerned," Kaldon said, hoping to ease the tavern owner's nerves.

Claude spun, turning to him. "That's what you said about the McGregor's retirement party. Do you remember what happened that day? The tavern wasn't prepared in time, and Betty was so nervous she burnt her famous sausage and hash. She never makes a mistake with that meal." Betty was Claude's wife, who he had married a few years after starting the tavern.

"Oh, I remember," Kaldon said, frowning. "That may have been one of the worst things to ever touch my mouth."

"Exactly!" Claude said with his finger in the air to make a point. "So, you'd be wise to listen to me then, wouldn't you?"

Before he could respond, the stout man went scurrying back towards the tavern to prepare. Trying to keep up with Claude's pace, Kaldon took in the city. These streets were more than common roads to him. They were, in many ways, his home. They were a place that once offered him routine and familiarity in a way the circumstances of his life had not. He was quite well-known throughout Rundle, especially in the downtown core – if not by name, then at least by appearance. When his mother died shortly after his tenth birthday, the streets adopted him. He was known as the boy who wasn't born an orphan, but became one. He was no longer that boy; now he was a man.

After his mother's death, the stone ground was where he laid his head to rest at night. These streets were now a symbol of what he had risen from. Where he was once one who others pitied, now he was somewhat respected. Kaldon was by no means wealthy or successful by others' terms. However, he had not fallen victim to his lot in life, as many had.

Many years ago, he'd overheard someone of importance quote something his father had written. "Your circumstances are not what determine whether you sit stagnant or move forward. It is your perspective." Kaldon chose to live by those words. His life was by no means easy, but he was determined not to allow circumstances to dictate his path in life. The streets he walked may have once been his home; now they were a part of his history.

Working at the Templar's Well was one of the things that helped him get off the streets. The tavern provided work, decent pay, and a room to call his own on the upper floor of the building. Kaldon was on the taller side, but not a large man. He was average in build. During the years he lived on the streets, he had slimmed down quite thin. Working for Claude allowed him to feast on Betty's cooking every day. This built him back up, keeping him healthy and fit.

"Kal, take a look at that!" Claude shouted, pointing at a group of men who were pushing wheelbarrows towards the city hall. There were at least a dozen wheelbarrows.

The city hall wasn't exactly large, but it was enormous for Rundle's standards. Built with detailed craftsmanship, the building was the seat of government in the city. Considering most of the city consisted of smaller homes and a handful of shops, it was a prominent piece of architecture.

Each wheelbarrow was filled with an assortment of books of varying sizes and colours. He hadn't seen so many books in his entire lifetime. Books were rare and more expensive than most people could afford.

"Do you think those are all books Dolan Thain wrote when he was alive?" Claude asked.

Everyone knew his father had written hundreds of books, so the question wasn't too farfetched. Even though Claude was one of his closest friends, he had no idea Kaldon was Dolan's son. No one did. Until his death, Dolan was considered the smartest man alive. Kaldon's mother had warned him never to confide in anyone who his father was. Who knows what trouble could have stirred if people knew he was from the Warrior General's lineage? He could very well have been taken away from his mother, or there could have been threats to their lives if others had known. More likely, no one would have believed him. His claim would have been dismissed as a desperate cry for attention or evidence of insanity.

"I wouldn't doubt it, Claude. I've heard they are setting up a memorial at the city hall in honour of the General. It should be open for viewing tomorrow," he tried to state casually.

Claude nodded. "I've heard that whenever he was in Rundle, he spent most of his time in a smaller library in the city hall. Word is that the city officials will be filling the library with Dolan's writings, so it can be set up as a memorial for his life. Considering how pricey those books look, there's no doubt it will be supervised by guards."

It was rumoured the General spent nearly all his time in the city hall while visiting, so it made sense that it would be there where his books were put to rest. Considering how regal the books looked, the General's writings seemed out of place in Rundle. Seeing the bright ensemble of colours brought Kaldon's memory back to the contrasted black attire of the Knights of

Agadin. Ever since the funeral, the Knight's daunting gaze and bright hazel eyes had played through his mind. Thankfully, he hadn't seen that man again. The entire city was talking about their being at the funeral. Many didn't even believe in the existence of Knights until that day. It was likely that the three had already begun their journey back to their unknown home. Considering the rarity of seeing such men, they must have travelled from far beyond Rune Forest.

In the Southeast of Agadin, there were a few small cities and towns, such as Rundle. The rest of the Southeast was filled with forest. Rune Forest was the largest of them and surrounded much of Rundle. Beyond the forest were the Mountains of D'aal. Beyond the Mountains of D'aal, Kaldon didn't know how far Agadin's landscape stretched. He hadn't travelled past Rundle. He had never needed to.

It wasn't long before they reached the Templar's Well. Swinging the wooden doors open, Claude stepped into the tavern. His agitated eyes fell on two workers sitting at a table playing a game of Quibb. The workers laughed and hollered as they rolled dice, trying their luck.

"Get up, you lazy sluggards!" Claude shouted. "The gathering is tomorrow!"

Both men hurried to their feet, one knocking over a chair while rushing to work. The men, Perry and Neil, were newly hired by Claude and didn't have the leeway Kaldon had earned. Betty could be heard in the back cooking furiously.

Before even giving himself time to settle in, Claude was in a frenzied state of cleaning. Looking back at Kaldon, seeing he was standing by the door, Claude shouted out at him.

"Great Divinity, go and grab a mop!"

He couldn't help but laugh at how Claude, who was usually as steady as they came, became an anxious mess whenever he had to entertain people of importance.

Reaching for the mop, he complained. "I can't believe those nobles scheduled such a big event with so little notice."

"Boy, it's just ridiculous," Claude said. "They come into our city and demand the world. I am going to make a killing off of tomorrow night, though. If they want to reserve the whole tavern on this short notice, you had better believe I will charge them through the ceiling for it."

Betty popped her round face out from the kitchen. "Claude, I am hearing a lot of talking and not a lot of table wiping."

Claude balked out loud. "It's amazing how I built this tavern from the ground up, yet this woman acts as though she is the one in charge."

Kaldon smiled. He knew Claude secretly liked it when Betty poked fun at him. She brought stability to how the tavern was run. They made quite a team. Not to mention, their constant bickering resulted in endless entertainment for guests in the tavern.

Even though Claude was his boss, the years had formed a deep trust and friendship between them. As a younger man, Claude was a part of Agadin's Southeast quadrant of the army. After a few years of serving in the military, he came home to Rundle and discovered he was quite entrepreneurial. He started the Templar's Well nearly twenty-five years ago and watched as it grew into a thriving and sustainable business. The tavern was now a prominent part of the city.

The tavern was much of what one would expect. Wooden tables and chairs were spread out within the confines of mahogany walls and ceilings. Along the left wall was a staircase leading upstairs to the bedrooms for the staff. In the centre of the main room was a grey-stone fireplace, providing warmth to all on a winter's eve. Above the fireplace was a silver inlaid shield with a rouge border, adding character to the tavern. The place felt like more than a tavern to most. It was a place of safety and a place to belong.

In spite of Betty's interjection, Claude persisted in being his chatty self. "You know, Kal, I was surprised to see all of the tourists sticking around. I figured most would leave immediately after the funeral. Not that I am complaining at all, I'm making quite a profit with all of the guests. But when I heard about the sightings, it all began to make sense."

"Sightings?" Kaldon questioned.

Claude continued, "You haven't heard? Ever since the General's death, there have been rumours of dangerous and mysterious beasts in Rune Forest."

The two other workers flinched at the news, but kept working so they wouldn't fall subject to Claude's scowl once again.

Intrigued, Kaldon began questioning the rumours. "Who spotted these creatures? What do they look like?"

"Word is the city guards have been seeing whatever those things are. It seems they are trying to keep it secret, so no one knows what they look like. All I know is I've heard they are as dangerous as they come."

"Are you sure this is true?" Kaldon prodded, "I mean, people have a tendency to spin tales around what they fear is true. Could that be all that this is? People making up stories?"

Claude twisted his face in thought, weighing the theory.

He continued, "I also know some who are younger have been foolishly travelling where they shouldn't be. Could it be that the guards are making this up to keep people from going where they shouldn't? Rune Forest isn't somewhere inexperienced travellers should go, whether there are creatures around or not."

Claude grunted, saying, "One of the guards lost his life to one of those beasts. The mayor has been trying to keep that little tidbit hidden. Word is that he tripled the city guards since this took place."

Kaldon's brows lifted in surprise. That bit of information was startling.

Perry, one of the younger workers, piped up in fear. "Are you serious?! Why are we here cleaning for a party if those things are about?"

Claude quieted him with a glare. "Even though it was only two weeks ago, things have changed since Dolan Thain's death. There have been numerous accounts of these creatures being seen. Many of the roads leading out from Rundle are no longer safe either. Apparently, there are thieves about. I have already heard of merchants being attacked and robbed, left nearly for dead. They were lucky to still have the clothes on their backs."

Kaldon noticed both Perry and Neil were unusually quiet – they were scared out of their wits. He was still unsure. He trusted Claude when he said something, but he also knew how people got once a rumour was floating about. All someone needed to do was to say a mouse was running loose in the city, and in a matter of time, peddlers could turn the tale into news of a lion lurking in the shadows.

Claude could tell that his mentioning of the creatures was putting Neil and Perry on edge. Wheels of fear were spinning in their minds, which he knew would slow down their work.

"Come on, you sluggards. Enough chat!" Claude bellowed. "The night is drawing close, and this tavern isn't going to prepare itself."

The staff cleaned and prepared through much of the night. Not a table was left without being wiped down, and not a speck of floor was left unswept before each retired to their private rooms on the upper floor.

Such a busy day of preparation would normally leave Kaldon exhausted, yet he found himself lying awake. This was becoming quite common in recent nights. The wooden pine bed beneath his back, he gazed up at an oak ceiling obscured from view in the black of night. In pensive thought, he considered his life. He considered the sudden occurrences in Rundle. He pondered his father's death. Although he had never met Dolan Thain, he almost felt orphaned all over again, left more alone than he already was.

From the Knights of Agadin, to the rumoured creatures, Kaldon's thoughts flitted about, trying to find a place to land. The recent occurrences seemed as though they were ancient tales that had come to life. They reminded him of stories his mother had shared with him before her passing. Men and women of legend and myth who had supposedly walked the land of Agadin thousands of years ago. She shared stories about those who could command creation. He remembered the story of a man being chased by an entire army of men. In order to escape, the man dove from a mountain's edge to be caught by the wind, as though he were the one controlling it. There was also the lore of a man who never fought with weapons, but manifested fire to devour his foes. His favourite stories were of Dawntan Forlorn. Dawntan was known for rescuing all of Agadin nearly four thousand years ago. Myth said darkness and evil had once covered the land to such an extent that even the light of the sun appeared dim. Dawntan was able to dethrone the evil to the point where light once again could shine upon the land.

Kaldon knew the stories were completely illogical. Yet, for some reason, they comforted him now, just as they had when he was a child. They made him feel as though there could be more to his life; more than the running of taverns. More than Rundle.

Disrupting the still eve, he was jolted by a sudden noise. From beyond his window, in the distance, it sounded like a faint whimper or a far-off cry. It couldn't be the cry of a child, because the sound was far too shrill. It also couldn't be the sound of a woman in danger, because the tone was higher than what a human could produce.

His eyes snapped open. The distant shrieks filled the hollow air. His state, reflective a mere moment ago, was now fused with adrenaline. His heart thudded against his chest. Rising from his bed, he peered out the window in the direction of the cries. Stars shone, faintly brightening the night. Beyond the city, Kaldon's attention rested upon the far-away sea of trees that made up Rune Forest.

Above the landscape of the mighty forest, he saw some of the stars quickly dim as though something was flying in front, blotting out the light. The small dark blotch in the already darkened sky released a screech filling the silence of night with its lamenting woes. Though too far away to distinguish its features, the creature Kaldon thought was only a rumour now became all too real. What was once only a story suddenly became reality.

Chapter Three

A Glimpse of Divine Fire

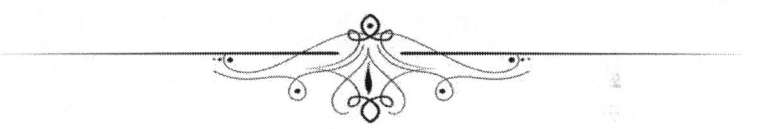

The sun's rise peaked past the skyline, and foot traffic throughout the city was scarce. Vendors weren't yet open. Buskers were still asleep. Morning came quicker than Kaldon had hoped. Pushing off the fog from the late night, he knew the task at hand required his full attention.

Walking to his destination in the still of the morning, the creature's shriek from the night before still rang throughout his nerves. The nocturnal bellowing had caused him to twist and turn through the night until sleep finally took him. His thoughts turned to Rune Forest. The mystery of it intrigued him. Now, with strange creatures suddenly about, all the more so.

There were two items he never went anywhere without: his pendant necklace and the blade he carried since his youth. The short sword was a dependable weapon. It wasn't flashy, but that was how he preferred it. His hand gripped the brown-leather hilt hidden underneath the shelter of his forest-green cloak. The familiar touch calmed him.

Arriving at his destination, he stood in front of city hall, taking it all in. The grey stone walls towered before him. Today, Dolan Thain's memorial would open to the public. The official revealing wouldn't take place for several hours yet, but he knew most of the guards at City Hall. Many were regulars at the Templar's Well, and he'd determined to convince them to let him in early. In his mind, he had every right to see the memorial before anyone else. It was the least his father could give him.

"Kal, I didn't take you for an early riser," the guard teased.

Tom spent many nights at the Templar's Well. He was glad it was Tom on shift instead of some of the more hardened guards.

"I wanted to come early and show respect for everything the Warrior General has done for Agadin," Kaldon said casually, trying not to give away that there was a deeper reason for him being there.

Tom's eyebrow raised. "Mayor Wade would have my head for breaking protocol. You would have to make things a little interesting for me to do so, considering the risk and all."

Kaldon hid his smile. He hoped Tom would be in a bargaining mood. "How does a night of free drink at the tavern sound?"

Tom scoffed. "Bah! One measly night? Come on, Kal. I'm putting my neck on the line here! You'd best give me at least four."

"Three is the most I can do, Tom. Can you imagine the scolding I'll get from Claude for even offering that?"

A smirk spread over Tom's face. "And?" the guard pressed.

"Fine, I'll see if I can convince Betty to cook you up a free meal," Kaldon said, trying to close the bargain.

"Deal," Tom said with finality.

Kaldon didn't really care about the cost. He *needed* to see the memorial. He knew he'd be working many overtime hours for what he just did, but it was worth it to him.

Following Tom, he entered the building. Strolling between the cobblestone halls, he noticed the subtle elegance of the place. Still, it was less profound than he thought it would be. As a boy, it looked like a palace to him. He'd felt pride that Rundle possessed such a regal show of architecture. Now grown, his perspective was different. Walking through the building, he realized it was merely that—a building.

"The memorial is just around this corner," Tom motioned.

Turning the corner, Kaldon froze. At the end of the hall was one of the men in black clad. The Knight of Agadin was talking to one of the guards, his back towards them. Kaldon couldn't tell if it was the same Knight watching him at his father's funeral. Whether it was the same Knight or not, he knew he wanted to keep his distance. He couldn't fathom why the Knights would stick around a place like Rundle for as long as they had. Men such as these must surely be accustomed to castles, not rundown cities. The Knight began turning around.

Tom opened the door to the memorial, giving Kaldon a chance to slip in before the Knight could spot him. Instinctively, he wiped his forehead, realizing he had been sweating.

"Those men make me feel uncomfortable too," Tom said, clearly seeing his discomfort. "I don't like it one bit that they are here. There are troubles in these lands. You've heard rumours about the creatures, haven't you?"

The night prior, Kaldon had experienced more than rumours; however, he kept that bit of information to himself. The shriek he heard the night before still gave him goosebumps.

"I've heard the rumours. Why do you think those Knights have stuck around so long?" he asked, quickly changing the subject.

"Beats me," Tom said, shrugging his shoulders. "All I know is that things are changing. I can't help wondering if it's all connected somehow. Since Dolan's death, nearly everyone is out of sorts. All of Southeast Agadin seems shaken."

Kaldon nodded in thought.

"Anyway, I'd best leave you to the memorial. You can't be here for too long," Tom said, knowing he should get back to his post. "If anyone sees you, both of us will be in for it. If that's the case, you'll need to convince Claude to give me a room to live in instead of only a few nights of free drinks. Got it?"

"Got it," Kaldon consented.

The door closed. He was finally alone in the memorial. He scanned the room as the morning light streamed in through a skylight in the ceiling. This was the place where his father spent most of his time while visiting Rundle.

Books of every colour and size filled the room. Many of the books were written by the Warrior General. Most that weren't penned by Dolan were at the very least written about him. The rest seemed to be books he studied earlier in his life. From ground to ceiling, each wall contained built-in bookshelves, except for a stone fireplace built within the main wall. The only furniture was a single leather chair directly in the centre of the library.

He chose to be here rather than be with me. Kaldon pushed the thought aside, rejecting the emotions that came with it.

He took a seat in his father's chair. It was hard and stern, befitting the type of man he assumed his father was. In the private library, he felt as though he were bathing in knowledge, engulfed in a sea of his father's writings. His eyes fell upon a double crescent axe hanging above the sturdy fireplace. Dolan's genius was only one aspect of who the man was. He was not only a

Philosopher, he was a General; not only a distinguished intellectual, but also a savage warrior.

Kaldon stood, removing the mighty axe from its resting place. The wooden handle was worn, rough in texture. Its weight was heavier than he preferred in a weapon. Growing up on the streets, he'd grown accustomed to weapons. You needed to be if you wanted to survive. He preferred swords, since they were more subtle and precise. The weapon in his hands had likely killed thousands of men. Visions filled his mind of his father's barrel arms slaying his enemies.

Sitting down again, he rested the axe on his lap, taking in the blade. Even though it was a well-used weapon, it shimmered in the light. Those who staged the memorial must have oiled the axe to give it a cleaner look. In the face of the axe's blade, he was taken in by his own reflection. As thoughts and emotions entwined, the pain of past memories pulled him in.

Kaldon could still hardly believe his mother was gone. It had been one year since her depression led her to the addiction which stole her life. It had been an entire year of him living on the streets of Rundle. At the age of thirteen, he was responsible for nothing but surviving.

Roaming the streets, his main chore was finding food for himself. Usually, this wasn't a daunting task; however, with winter sweeping in, rabbits were becoming scarce. There were times he would come across a kindhearted vendor who would offer him fruit and nuts he could eat, but the economy was down. Merchants were more hesitant to part with what could make them profit.

It was growing late, and he knew being out past dark could be disastrous. There were street gangs he tried to avoid by any means necessary. Bumping into a gang member resulted in one of two things: they would either beat him or try to recruit him. Neither was enticing. Being in a gang offered a daily meal and, at times, even shelter; however, Kaldon didn't condone what they stood for. Murders were not common in Rundle, but when they did happen, the gangs were usually involved. Scethane, the drug that took his mother's life, was also catching on in the different gangs. That was reason enough for him to keep his distance.

Right as Kaldon was about to give up looking for some form of meal, he saw a family in the distance. The father, mother, and son were shopping from merchant to merchant. He remembered what it was like to feel like he belonged. Pushing through a pang of sadness, he had reached a point of hunger where he was willing to cross a line he had never crossed before. He always told himself that he would never beg for coin or food, but it had been days since he'd eaten. As humiliating as it was, he walked up to the family and stood behind them, waiting for them to notice. They didn't.

"Excuse me," Kaldon said quietly. The family kept going about their business. He figured they didn't hear him.

Summoning every bit of courage, he spoke louder. "Excuse me!"

Each member of the family turned around. As they did, Kaldon was surprised to see he knew the boy. His name was Jeremy. He had known Jeremy from school and even spent a few afternoons playing with him. When his mother passed away, he had no choice but to stop attending school. He hadn't seen Jeremy in over a year.

The two boys stared at one another, not knowing what to say. Jeremy's voice hesitantly broke the lingering silence. "Kal? Is that you?"

Kaldon stared at Jeremy. He looked up at his old friend's parents and saw the pity in their eyes. He was suddenly aware of how he looked. He hadn't had the opportunity to look in a proper mirror since he left home. The only time he saw his reflection was when he walked past a shop with windows. He had worn the same clothes for a full year. He had lost a significant amount of weight from not eating properly. He was covered head to toe in dirt. As the family speechlessly looked at Kaldon, shame draped over him. For the first time he could remember, he hated himself. Not knowing what else to do, he did the only thing he could. He wouldn't be able to speak without sobbing, so he turned around and ran. He ran as fast as he could without looking back.

Tears streaked down his dirt-caked face. He passed houses and darted between people. Though he had no food, he knew where to find shelter for the night, a hiding place from the condemning eyes of others. He discovered the place only a few weeks after he was orphaned – his secret place.

In a dark alley, on the outskirts of the downtown core, there was a manhole leading to the sewers. The manhole was hidden under a wooden dumpster. Since he was small, he had just enough room to sneak under and squeeze into the manhole. Kaldon's chest scraped over rocks as he slid under the wooden crate. He dropped into the hole leading below ground.

Reaching his private enclave, relief flooded in. People often overwhelmed him. Even though the sewer was dank, it was the only place he truly felt safe. He was thankful for it. In fact, this was where he found one of his most favourite possessions, his sword. He didn't know much about swords, but when he saw the weapons the other boys had, he knew it was a good blade. He had no clue who had left it there, but when he first discovered the secret place, the sword was resting against the cement wall. He liked to believe it once belonged to someone like him. That it belonged to someone who had no home or family. He liked to believe someone left this place and sword for him on purpose to give him a chance to survive.

Resting his head on the cement floor, he exhaled deeply. Often, he would gather leaves to lie under his head. The leaves softened his sleep, but he didn't gather them this night. He was too tired. His body ached. He tried not to think about the look Jeremy and his parents gave him. Kaldon sometimes bumped into people he knew before his mother's death, but now it felt different. It felt as though these people thought they were above him, better than him. Maybe they were.

Looking up, he could see through the sewer drain. In the dark and dank sewers, the drain was like his own private window. It was a reminder that he wasn't destined to live below ground forever. The moon shone over all of Agadin in perfect alignment with the scope of the drain. Stars gleamed around it. The moon's glow pierced the darkness of the sewers, offering light to a dismal place.

Suddenly, a small flash of fire glimmered in the skies as though something clothed in flames was flying before the great moon. He was transfixed by the reds, oranges, and yellows flitting through the night sky. As he laid, he watched what looked like fiery wings stroking the wind. The fire in the sky began to spark a fire inside his heart.

Peering at the mysterious soaring fire, bravery began shaping itself inside of him. The judgmental eyes of others began to melt away from his mind. The bravery he felt emerging was not necessarily for his external circumstances; it was for the internal battle stirring in his soul. There was a war taking place inside his heart. The light of the moon and flames shining in his fortress of shadowed sewers gave him strength to believe he could live for greater things. Moved by the moment, he began to speak aloud. What he said was more than a statement; it was a declaration.

He said, "I was created for more than the depths of the sewers. One day, I will soar among the stars. One day, I will be someone great."

Looking at his own face in the reflection of the axe, Kaldon saw a man who had matured in appearance. He was no longer that scared young boy in the sewer. Yet in his eyes, he saw something broken. He was physically strong, but he knew there was something shattered inside his soul.

He recalled the fire in the sky and how it blazed through the night. He still didn't know what it was, but the thought of it moved him. Despite his inner brokenness, he felt a welcome fire burning in his heart. Tears dripped onto the blade, upon his father's axe.

Glancing around the room through the blur of his tears, something caught his attention. At the bottom of one of the bookshelves, engraved in the wood, was something that looked familiar to him. Placing the axe aside, he got on his hands and knees to get a closer look. He ran his fingers over the engraved wood. He realized why it looked familiar. Kaldon pulled the circular-bronze pendant out from around his neck. In all his life, he had never seen the symbol that made up his pendant anywhere else. Yet, there it was, engraved in a bookshelf in his father's personal library.

Running his fingers through the five grooved points that extended out from its centre, it struck him. Not only was it the exact same symbol, but it was the exact same size as his pendant.

"Could it be a key?" Kaldon murmured under his breath. Placing the pendant into the engraved wood, he heard a snap. To the right of the symbol, a small wooden drawer popped open from the bookshelf.

The secret drawer wasn't big; in fact, it was rather small. He looked inside hesitantly. There was a book inside. He had never seen a book so ancient. Carefully lifting it out from the drawer, he held it out for a better look. The book was a smokey-grey in colour, with his pendant's symbol inscribed on its face.

"What could this mean?" Kaldon whispered, thinking aloud.

The old book opened with a creak. Skimming through, he quickly recognized that he couldn't understand much of it. The book was written in *Old Agadin*, a dialect used centuries ago and long forgotten. In Southeast Agadin, to his knowledge, everyone spoke the present dialect, *High Agadin*. Although the dialects overlapped every so often, they were quite different. He had never even met anyone who spoke the ancient tongue.

Flipping through the book, he watched as a piece of paper spilled out from between the pages. Picking it up, he felt the roughness of the paper between his fingers. He saw scribbled writing on the note. Thankfulness washed over him as he realized the penned words were written in High Agadin. He read the note aloud.

"If you are reading this note, I am gone. I have travelled much of Agadin, enduring hardships that most should never face. What I have learned is this: we are not safe. Shadow is rising in Agadin. Make no mistake, this book holds significant secrets. Secrets written within can dethrone Shadow and bring order back to the land. Use it wisely."

- Dolan Thain

Kaldon let the book drop to his side, taking in the words of his dead father. He wondered what it meant for Shadow to be rising in Agadin. Was the creature he saw the night prior part of this danger his father wrote of? He wished the Warrior General had elaborated on the threat he referred to. Kaldon knew that him possessing the key to the hidden drawer meant his father could have written the letter decades ago. Maybe the threat was already passed? On the other hand, this evil could have drastically progressed. Looking again at the words written in the ancient book, he grew frustrated. What good was a book that could help keep Agadin safe if no one could read it?

Cautiously examining the book more, he noticed its interior was much older than its cover. He supposed that made sense. Older books would need to be rebound a few times over if they were to last. Turning the book to its side, the title on the spine was penned in High Agadin, the present dialect. It had definitely been rebound.

Reading the spine, he began to sweat even more than he had in the presence of the Knight of Agadin. Based on his father's letter, he knew this was a book of great importance; perhaps the most important in his father's library.

The title boldly read, *The First Paragon*.

Chapter Four

The Gathering

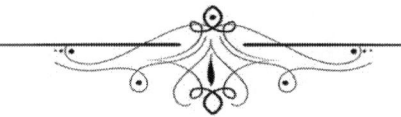

Kaldon rolled the pendant between his thumb and finger, running through his mind what he'd found earlier that day. He had no clue what a *Paragon* was, but the word pulled at him. He felt the book's weight inside his cloak pocket. He knew the book belonged to his father, yet Dolan couldn't have accessed it without the key. Likely, no one knew the book existed other than him. Why was it locked away, hidden in that secret drawer? Was his pendant the only key? Every question brought more questions – and with the General dead – where could he find answers?

Guests were already starting to arrive at the Templar's Well. The tavern clean, there wasn't much left to do but wait for everyone to arrive for the gathering. Kaldon hadn't had time throughout the day to share with Claude or Betty what he'd seen or heard the night before. Even if he had, he would have kept it to himself. Not only did he not want to frighten them, but he simply preferred to think things out on his own before sharing his thoughts.

"Kal?" Betty probed, snapping her fingers to get his attention.

Before he could answer, she crammed a spoonful of her sausage and hash into his mouth. If her incessant beckoning didn't get his attention, the savoury mouthful of meat certainly did.

"I need to have this perfect for our guests. Is it any good?" Betty asked directly.

Furrowing his brow in thought, he affirmed the woman. "It's actually the best I've tasted."

A wide smile lit up her circular face. "Well, I'm glad to hear it."

Over the span of an hour, nobles spilled into the tavern. Their exotic and colourful dress made the tavern vibrant. As Claude and his workers served them, Kaldon kept to himself at the back of the pub, watching. He preferred to be on the outskirts of such social chaos.

When Mayor Wade Stauva and his wife Chandice entered the bar, Claude looked at Kaldon, raising his eyebrows in surprise. The mayor didn't often visit local businesses, let alone set foot in a tavern. Kaldon immediately knew that Claude would use this to market the tavern. He would probably find a way to convince the entire city that the Templar's Well was the mayor's favourite tavern, although he had only stepped foot in there once.

The mayor and his wife sat up at the front, dressed as though they were attending a ball. Wade was a shorter man with a wide girth and thinning hair. His wife, Chandice, was tall and slender. Her blonde hair cascaded down her back. They couldn't have looked more opposite. Claude's eyes darted around at the different guests, obviously not knowing how to host those of a certain prestige. This was a significant gathering.

Once the guests had drinks and a plate of food, they sat around wooden tables waiting for the evening to begin. Kaldon, Claude, and the other workers had finished their work for the time being. Now, they could take in the evening as well. They each took a seat at the back of the room to be around in case anyone needed anything or something went awry. Considering the nature of this gathering, they would have found a way to listen no matter where they were in the tavern. It wasn't every day that such people gathered together.

Right as the evening looked like it was about to begin, the entrance door creaked. As it did, there was a flicker of black cloth. At the sight of black clothing, Kaldon inched back closer to the wooden wall, his hand nervously clenched around the hilt of his sword. The wood rafters cast shadows. From behind their shelter and comfort, he watched the three Knights of Agadin step into the Templar's Well.

The city was whispering about the three Knights. Men such as these did not go unnoticed in a small place. Kaldon was relieved the mysterious guests didn't take notice of him. He was still confused. Why was one Knight intrigued by him at his father's funeral? Based on what he had heard of the Knights, he was sure he didn't want to know.

Moving cautiously, Claude stood up to usher the Knights to a front table next to the mayor and his wife. After giving people a few minutes to settle in, the mayor and his wife stepped up in front of the fireplace, facing the guests. Chandice took the lead, as she usually did. Wade recognized his wife's gift with words, so he often let her do most of the public speaking. Even in council meetings, she often spoke on his behalf.

Standing elegantly by her husband's side, they patiently waited for the calm. With roughly eighty guests, various voices and accents filled the tavern. A quiet hush began to sweep like a wave through the room, and once there was silence, she began.

"It is our honour to host so many men and women of importance from throughout Southeast Agadin. You have all been gracious guests, waiting here in our humble city for this meeting. To think we would host representatives of different cities throughout Southeast Agadin is still a wonder to me."

From her side, Mayor Wade nodded his head in adamant agreement.

She continued, "We all know changes are occurring throughout Agadin. My husband and I could try to communicate what they are; however, there are some here who are better suited to articulate such important matters."

The mayor took a step forward. Knowing how soft-spoken he was, people leaned in with expectation.

He began, "There are men here who have travelled much of Agadin. They have been to places holding names my ears have never heard. My wife and I have spent much time with these men in the weeks since the Warrior General's death. They have been beacons of clarity to us. They have shone a light on current events and have made clear to us the seasons and times we are living in."

Rubbing his hands together, a nervous tick of his, the mayor found his thoughts and continued. "My friends, we have been living in ignorance of the peril surrounding us. We have entered into dire times, and it is my honour to introduce to you a man who can better illuminate what it is we are facing."

The mood in the room was darkened by the somber tone of the mayor. This was clearly not the type of meeting anyone expected.

The mayor held out a hand, prompting his guest to come forward. "I present to you, Medric, Knight of Agadin."

The man who stood was the Knight who had taken interest in Kaldon at his father's funeral.

Adorned in onyx, Medric stood before the fireplace, replacing the mayor and his wife. In most gatherings, a guest of importance was greeted with clapping or cheers. The seriousness of this meeting made such a response inappropriate. The room held a forced stillness.

Medric stood with authority, his presence commanding attention. "The time of peace and order has ended," he said calmly. "Whether you are warrior, or butcher; whether a general or farmer, now you are called to rise for the sake of Agadin. You are called because we are at war."

Whispers began flooding the silence as tensions rose. The mayor placed a hand on his wife's shoulder to comfort her. Medric continued, cutting off the mounting panic. "Many of you think peace is now threatened because of Dolan Thain's death; however, war has been taking place throughout Agadin for years. This is the very thing Dolan Thain was fighting. He was a symbol of order throughout our land, but now, darkness is rising to take advantage of his absence. Such things are mere rumours in these parts south of the Mountains of D'aal. Luckily for all of you, the mountains have acted as a barrier, protecting you from the violence and darkness beyond your borders. However, having travelled extensively beyond those mountains, I can assure you, it is very real."

Medric's words spun through Kaldon's mind. What his father wrote in his note was true. Such talk was completely foreign in Rundle. He had read about wars and heard stories of his father's bravery, but hearing from someone who witnessed such things filled him with a sense of awe. He'd never met anyone who had been beyond the Mountains of D'aal. In fact, he had only met a handful who stepped foot near them.

Medric continued, "Many of you may have heard of the sightings of creatures in Rune Forest. I assure you these are not fabricated tales. They are called *Kreel*. Beyond the Mountains of D'aal, these beasts are well known and feared. They have torn apart entire cities, preying on the innocent. Rundle and other regions on this side of the Mountains have been sheltered from the realities that Agadin's Northern quadrants are facing. The war taking place is not only made up of men and swords. This war extends beyond what our eyes can perceive. Greater realities are at play, having to do with realms many refuse to accept as real. Even the plague that took Dolan Thain's life was a part of this war. Plagues of all kinds are infesting towns and cities throughout the land. Even though we do not know the cause of the plagues, they are, without question, part of the war we fight. Corrupt individuals are waging war on Agadin, forcing the masses into subservience. These individuals wield dark powers. All of this chaos falls under the reign of one man who has given himself the title, the *Sovereign of Shadow*. He is not to be taken lightly. There are many who follow his radical and merciless philosophies."

"The… Sovereign of *Shadow*?" Chandice voiced.

"Yes," Medric explained, void of any visible emotion. "He leads a movement called the *Dominion of Shadow*, striving to bring all of Agadin under his rule and fanaticism. To refuse him is, if you are lucky, death. The number of his victims is nearly endless."

His eyes rested on Kaldon as he continued. It was as though the Knight's gaze penetrated deep into his very core.

The Knight said, "There is a time for everything: A time to sit, and a time to rise. Now is a time to rise; to stand. We are at war, and every one of us must decide on which side we will fight."

As mad as it sounded, Kaldon sensed the truth in his words. While living on the streets of Rundle, he'd grown adept at reading people. As much as he wished it weren't so, Medric was speaking truth.

With his eyes still on Kaldon, the Knight became silent, allowing his words to sink in. Kaldon shifted uncomfortably in his chair, wondering if anyone else noticed the Knight's attention directly on him.

Kaldon heard a shrill yet familiar sound. His attention turned from Medric, trying to narrow-in his hearing enough to make out what the sound was. It sounded like the shriek of something human, but at the same time, not. The scream became clearer as he focused, and then he knew exactly what the sound was.

The tavern door burst open with a loud jerk. Everyone jumped from the sudden jolt. Betty let out a scream. Two men, local farmers, stumbled into the tavern, wrestling with the source of the shrieking.

Its scream was deafening.

The creature was like nothing Kaldon had ever imagined existed. It was about four feet tall, covered in dark brown fur with arms and legs writhing chaotically. Protruding from its back, its bat-like wings appeared broken. The creature's tail was reptilian, wildly thrashing about, attempting to hit the two men trying to hold it. The beast's beady eyes darted about in panic as it snapped its extended jaw; its elongated claws were just out of reach from gashing the farmers. There was no doubt in Kaldon's mind that it was the creature he had seen flying over Rune Forest the night prior. It was a Kreel.

Claude peered over at him with a look in his eyes that Kaldon had never seen before. Claude was terrified, just as the lot of them were.

Chapter Five

The Message

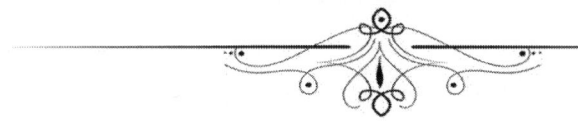

"**H**old it down!" one of the men shouted, trying to wrestle it onto a table as the Kreel ferociously contorted and writhed. Another man jumped to his feet to help.

Kaldon clenched the wooden chair he sat upon. Looking over at Medric, he was surprised to see that the Knight was watching the men, unfazed. He seemed impatient, bored even. The Kreel was nothing new to him.

"Ont!" Medric shouted.

One of the other three Knights immediately stood. "Yes, First Knight!" he responded militantly.

Ont was built of solid muscle with a shaven head. He was a larger man, much larger than Medric.

"Deal with this," Medric commanded, waving his hand. Ont smirked, walking over to the men.

"Let go," Ont said in a deep tone.

The three looked at the large Knight with blank stares. Struggling to speak due to the strain of the circumstance, the most confident of the men spoke. "Sir, no disrespect, but you don't even have your sword drawn."

Ont quipped with a slight grin. "If I needed my sword, it would be in my hand. Now, let it go."

Reluctantly, the three men let go of the Kreel, which instantly jumped away from the table, its tail lashing. Suddenly unbound, the creature lunged towards one of the guests. Before its foot even left the ground, Ont had the Kreel's neck gripped in his mighty fist. The Kreel pawed at Ont with its gangly, yet dangerous talons. Lifting the creature from the ground, Ont's muscles tensed.

Holding it at a distance, moisture began shimmering on Ont's forehead as he walked toward the tavern's exit. Once outside the tavern, the door slammed, muffling the screams. Not a single person in the tavern made a sound. Visibly shaken, each strained to listen as the cries of the Kreel slowly ceased.

One of the three men, still breathing heavily and trying to regain his strength, spoke up. "I was on an evening stroll in the downtown core with my daughter when that fiend leapt out at her. I was able to deflect it. I was lucky that Bruce and Dale were nearby to help me seize the beast."

Bruce, the other farmer, inclined his head in agreement, not saying a word. The man was clearly in shock.

"Great Divinity, I've never seen such a dreadful thing," Chandice whispered, as though speaking to herself.

Medric laughed to himself, but not because he thought the situation was comical. He laughed because he knew the Mountains of D'aal had coddled these people, leaving them unaware of the dangers and the world existing beyond the barrier. Even though his laugh was quiet, it still caught the attention of the entire room.

Medric's tone was foreboding. "The Kreel you just saw was but a child. Still highly dangerous, but a child nonetheless. You better hope you never run into a fully grown Kreel."

Kaldon looked over to Claude, whose eyes were transfixed on Medric. In fact, everyone was. He was sure nothing such as this had ever happened in Rundle – surely not in their lifetimes.

"How big do they grow?" one of the guests bellowed out.

"The largest I encountered was ten feet tall," Medric responded.

Gasps filled the tense air.

The Knight continued, "Kreel are not intelligent; they are threatening because of their strength. The Kreel tonight was young and had not come into its maturity. If it had, tonight would have turned out very differently. Mature Kreel are nearly solid muscle and have the strength of a dozen strong men."

The mayor stood to his feet with a question. "Knight Medric, what should we do if we come across a fully grown Kreel?"

"I have seen Knights of Agadin killed by Kreel," Medric said definitively. "I haven't heard of a single Knight besting one fully grown. You cannot beat them in battle; they are too strong. You cannot outrun them; they are too fast. Your best bets are to outsmart them or hide."

Before more questions could arise, Chandice stood, addressing the group. "The Knights leave tomorrow in the morning. Knight Brenton has agreed that once they get back to where they came from, he will send men to Southeast Agadin who will help the smaller cities prepare for war."

At her word, the final Knight of the three, Brenton, rose and bowed toward the guests. Brenton stood proud. He looked to be about Medric's age, in spite of the fact that he wasn't yet greying.

With his side-swept brown hair, he looked rather reserved. Kaldon doubted a Knight could carry such a quality. Each Knight seemed to carry an aura of danger.

Chandice continued, "Knight Brenton will send warriors he has personally trained. They will organize and equip us. Brenton is quite studied in Dolan Thain's teachings, majoring in strategy of war and combat. He is committed to lending those who can teach us to defend ourselves against the Kreel and the Sovereign of Shadow's warriors."

Ont walked back into the tavern, wiping his hands on his clothes. It didn't take much to imagine what had happened to the Kreel. His entrance didn't faze the guests; most were already stunned. What was commonly a vocal and opinionated group was distinctly silent. Even at the news of Brenton sending men to train them, the guests sat in quiet shock. They were not warriors; what did they know of war?

Medric could see the looks of defeat on their faces. Slicing through the silence, he said, "I think we'd best call it a night. I know many of you have much to consider based on the things you have heard and seen this night."

In subdued agreement, one after another, the guests stood up and began to leave. Claude held a weeping Betty watching his guests file out of the tavern. Even though he was rough in personality, Claude had a heart to make people feel safe. There was conflict on his face. He wanted to say the right words, yet there were no words to say. Many of these folks had just discovered that they were up against the unimaginable, that they would potentially die in an unavoidable war against a merciless tyrant.

Kaldon knew Claude and the rest of the staff would want to talk through what occurred that evening, but he needed to figure this out for himself. What did this mean for him? Kaldon knew how to fight, but he was no warrior.

He stood up and began to head out the door with all the other guests. He knew the others likely wouldn't understand him taking time by himself, but he didn't care. He needed to think, and where better to do that than his secret place?

In the dark alley, Kaldon sat against the wooden dumpster that concealed the hidden manhole, the door to his secret place. He had long ago quit going into sewers. Not only was it an awkward squeeze now that he had grown, but it no longer fit who he was. Sitting in a damp sewer was no longer a comfort to him.

He thought about the Kreel and the book he found in his father's office. Things were not only changing for Rundle, or even Agadin—things were changing for him. He knew he had a part to play in all of this, but he didn't know what it was. The emblem he wore around his neck was etched in his mind, the same symbol upon the book resting in his pocket.

The First Paragon. The title ran through Kaldon's mind.

The alley dimmed darker than usual. Looking up, he saw exactly what he didn't want to come across. Four men walked down the alley towards him. He'd encountered them a handful of times when he lived on the streets, they were a part of one of Rundle's gangs. He stood.

"Hey, isn't that Kal the sewer rat?" one of the men balked.

"Yeah, I remember him. He denied us when we tried to recruit him," another said.

They quickly surrounded him. The leader looked Kaldon straight in the eyes, wagging a knife in his face. "You denied us? I'm surprised we didn't kill you right there."

Breathing steadily, Kaldon's hand now clenched around his sword's hilt, ready to draw at any second. He'd taken out several men at once before and wasn't concerned. He'd fought his share of gang members in the past and was quite sure he had more ability with a blade than most did in all of Rundle.

Kaldon unflinchingly looked at the leader and quietly stood his ground. He wouldn't fight unless he needed to, but if he did, these four would leave crawling.

Without warning, one of the men dropped to the ground with a scream. The remaining three who stood, turned in panic. Kaldon watched in confusion as the scene unfolded before him. He saw steel raised. He heard grunts and the sounds of rushed movement. In the black of night, a warrior in onyx clad was dodging every knife-swing coming at him. Once Kaldon could discern the cloak from the shadows, he realized it was Medric.

The remaining three launched at the Knight, trying to take him out. Suddenly, a kick to the face took down one man. The final two men, with knives in hand, swung furiously. Kaldon wondered if he should help, though Medric didn't seem to need it. The Knight easily dodged every swing, not even using a weapon. When the leader stepped in for a stab, Medric grabbed his arm and broke the man's grip on the knife. The steel hitting the street rang through the alley. The leader yelped. A swift strike to the jaw left him unconscious.

For the fourth man, all it took was a look from Medric, and he was running to escape the Knight.

"You come to think in dangerous places, Kal Wendal," Medric said, now facing him.

Kaldon was taken aback by the fact that the Knight knew his name.

"Yes, I know who you are. I've watched you," Medric said, showing no hint of being fatigued from the fight.

"I've noticed," Kaldon replied, as though to tell the man he wasn't as subtle as he thought he was.

"Did you?" Medric challenged. "It didn't seem so at the city hall this morning."

Kaldon frowned. He hated being bested. He was nearly certain the Knight hadn't seen him. "Thanks for dealing with those men, but I didn't need the help."

Medric laughed to himself. "I'm aware of that. Those men were amateurs. I can tell by the look of you that the sword hanging on your hip isn't for decoration."

"Then why did you come here? Why were you watching me?" Kaldon asked, unmoving.

Medric paused for a moment, then answered. "I came to Southeast Agadin for several reasons. The first was to honour our Warrior General, Dolan Thain. The second was that we needed to warn the mayors of the surrounding cities that war would inevitably reach them. Finally, there was an important mandate I had when coming here. I didn't come on my own accord."

Medric continued, "Ont, Brenton, and I were sent by a very powerful man. A *Seer* sent us. Seers know mysteries that are not common to regular men. They can see the future—they can read people's souls. The Seer told me to look for a man in the Warrior General's hometown who wears the pendant you have hanging around your neck."

Kaldon looked down at the pendant. He had heard of Seers before, but only in the stories his mother told him. He didn't know if he believed such people existed.

"Why should I believe you? How can I know whether or not to trust your words?" Kaldon prodded.

"The Seer told me to share a message with you," Medric said. "It is a short message and doesn't mean anything to me, but I wouldn't doubt if it does to you. The Seer told me to tell the one who wore that pendant this:

"You were created for more than the depths of the sewers. One day, you will soar among the stars. One day, you will be someone great."

The words pierced into the caverns of Kaldon's soul like the thrust of a sword. One of his most intimate moments was just laid bare before him. How could this Seer know the very words he spoke aloud as a child?

"The Seer mentioned one other thing," Medric went on. "He said I should make the offer for you to come along with Ont, Brenton and myself when we leave Rundle tomorrow."

Hardly able to find his words, Kaldon mustered out a question. "For what purpose would I come with you?"

Medric sternly looked into Kaldon's glazed eyes, saying, "For the purpose of being trained for greatness."

Chapter Six

Venturing Onward

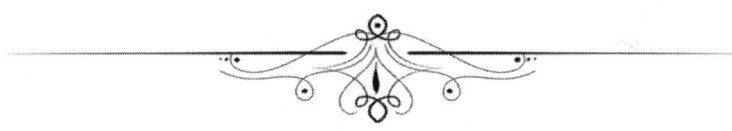

Kaldon sat across the table from his dear friends Claude and Betty. Both sat with a hot tea to warm them in the freshness of the morning. He had woken them early to talk with them. They were both visibly shaken from the incident with the Kreel the night before. Although not many hours had passed, news had likely spread across the city concerning what happened at the Templar's Well.

While Claude and Betty were usually jostling with their words, this morning they were not. There was somberness in this meeting between the three. They knew there was a serious reason for him to have called on them before the light of dawn.

"Well, Kal," Claude began. "Why are we up this early?"

"I'm leaving Rundle," Kaldon said straightforwardly.

Betty looked up at her husband, waiting to see his response. Claude shifted in his chair, not showing much emotion.

"You're leaving Rundle?" Claude said.

In silence, the three sat until Claude's eyes met Kaldon's. "Tell me why."

Now Kaldon was the one shifting in his chair. When he found his thoughts, he spoke. "I need to leave because this is all I've ever known. I am leaving because I fear that if I don't, I will never truly discover who I am, or who I could become."

Watching his two friends, the words of the Seer wrung through his mind. *"You were created for more than the depths of the sewers. One day, you will soar among the stars. One day, you will be someone great."* He knew Rundle was a tether to him, binding him to his past.

"Where will you go?" Betty asked gently.

Kaldon looked around at the wooden walls of the tavern, taking it all in. It was a place of safety to him, a refuge. He no longer desired safety; he no longer craved security. In recent months he had grown restless and it had evolved to feelings of purposelessness. He had outgrown his surroundings. He could now either remain suffocated and stunted by what once comforted him, or find out how wide his wings would expand.

"I will go to the Mountains of D'aal for now," Kaldon responded. "Medric came to me last night after the incident with the Kreel. He told me of a training facility in the mountains called the *Peak of Lore*. He said it is where people are trained for war, where Knights of Agadin are born into their callings. I don't know if I will become a Knight, I only know I need to go."

Claude's eyes widened at the mention of the training of Knights. He quickly regained his composure. "Let me tell you something I've learned over the years, Kal. Often, as we grow up, people place expectations on us. They try to trap us in those expectations. If we allow ourselves to be caged by what others expect, those expectations become our limitations. We need to intentionally step away from those assumptions, or we risk never discovering who we truly are. I understand your decision."

Kaldon felt as though Claude had put into words what he felt. He needed to step out of others' expectations of him. "You're right. That is exactly why I need to leave Rundle."

"I can't say I didn't expect this," Claude confessed. "With what you have gone through, and have overcome already in your young life, I've always known there is something significant about you. You need to discover what that is."

After a moment, Claude continued. "You know how I know there is something significant about you?"

Kaldon looked up at him, awaiting an answer.

Claude said, "It's because in the whole time I have known you, even with everything you have gone through, I have never seen you compromise your integrity. You always stand for what is right, even when the cost is great. No matter what life brings, you never cower or make excuses. I've always respected you for it. I am proud of you. It is no small thing to walk away from all you have ever known."

"Thank you, Claude," Kaldon said, letting the words sink in.

Not knowing how to receive or react to such a direct compliment, he changed the subject. "It's a lengthy trip to the Peak of Lore. The journey will take weeks. We leave immediately."

Kaldon had spent much of the night packing and repacking his belongings. He didn't have much to bring: a few changes of clothes, hardened bread, and a water-skin to last him until they came across a river stream. His pendant, sword, and newly-found book would travel with him.

"You know what I find convenient, though, Kal?" Claude grinned, "That you are taking off now when the tavern is a complete mess from last night. Who will I get who can wield a mop the way you can?"

Kaldon couldn't help but smile.

Standing up to leave, he turned to Claude, "Oh ya, I forgot to tell you, Claude. Do you remember Tom, the guard from city hall?"

"Of course, I do. He's a regular," Claude replied. "What of him?"

"I promised him three nights of free drink and a meal on the house."

Claude laughed heartily. "Did you now?! Well, the second you're back in Rundle, you are working that off—plus interest!"

Even through the pain of saying goodbye, Kaldon laughed. "I give you my word, my friend."

Kaldon bid his two friends farewell, seeing their eyes glistening as they pushed back the tears.

Walking out of the tavern, he closed the door to the Templar's Well. He sensed that in doing so, a door was being closed in his life. A season had come to a finish.

The road was calling him, beckoning him to venture onward into adventure and purpose.

Engulfed by the thick, towering trees of Rune Forest, Kaldon felt small. Marching through the dense forest, the wind stung their cheeks with autumn's chill bite. The trees were bright yellow, heralding the promise of winter's arrival. Many roads led out from Rundle; however, they didn't take them. Medric determined it would be wiser to make their own trail. Thieves wouldn't be an issue to the four, but they chose to avoid unnecessary hindrances. They also knew that if there were Kreel about, the creatures would likely have their eyes on main roads, looking to make a meal of travellers. Medric said it would be much harder to trace their tracks if they took an unexpected route.

Medric was the lead and Ont second, Brenton flanked the rear of the single file with Kaldon stationed third. Three days had passed since they left Rundle, and most of that time they had trudged on in silence. Kaldon wasn't sure how to act around men such as these. They were practically legend. Even though he was shielded between Knights of Agadin, he was unnerved knowing that behind any group of trees or boulder could be a Kreel.

Kaldon wasn't comfortable initiating conversation with people he didn't know. He preferred to remain quiet, observing. Still, he had questions that needed answers. He also needed something to take his mind off of the potential threat.

"So," he ventured. "Who is this Seer who sent you to Southeast Agadin?"

Medric looked back over his shoulder at Kaldon to answer his question. "The Seer's name is Locrian. He comes to the Peak of Lore frequently, helping ensure the training facility is running properly. Last I heard, he was on a mission. Knowing the Seer, it is likely a dangerous one."

"The Seer comes and goes from the Peak of Lore? You mean, he doesn't run the facility?" Kaldon questioned.

"Great Divinity, no!" Ont blurted out. "I don't want to even try and imagine what would happen if that man were in charge."

Kaldon couldn't help but notice the extreme contrast between Medric and Ont. Medric was social and intentional. His words and ideas were well thought out, whereas Ont was abrupt. Brenton, for the most part, stayed silent. Kaldon hadn't heard him say much of anything nearly their whole trip so far.

Medric continued, "Seers are not often gifted to build. They are more-so gifted to guide those who build through what they see in visions and such. They often function as advisors."

Kaldon ducked under an upcoming branch as he thought about what Medric was saying. "Do Seers counsel kings and queens?"

"Yes. They also counsel others who lead and build," Medric said. "There are only a handful of legitimate Seers alive, you know. There are many who have gifts of prediction. The gifted can discern and perceive things here and there; however, a Seer is another thing entirely. Seers see time from a perspective that others cannot. We live lives that are linear, as in, we can remember the past, experience the present, and anticipate the future. Seers do not have a linear perspective of time. They have the bird's-eye view of history's timeline. In many ways, what they see in the future can be just as real to them as the present day. This makes a Seer's word instructive, yet also dangerous. A Seer's weapon is his or her tongue. Kingdoms can be risen up and torn down by their very word."

That was a lot for Kaldon to wrap his head around. "I can't imagine what it would be like to be around a man such as this *Locrian,*" he said.

"You don't know the half of it," Medric said. "Locrian is a unique man. Most are not recognized as an authentic Seer until they reach their late fifties in age. It takes nearly a lifetime of training to shape a Seer. The standard is high, and the training is vast and intense. Locrian is only in his early thirties. He teaches and instructs Seers twice his age. He comprehends things about visions and the flow of time that most Seers approaching the end of their lives are only beginning to scratch the surface of understanding. He is a Seer, yes, but he is also a prodigy of sorts. With Dolan Thain gone, Locrian is now arguably the smartest man in all of Agadin."

Kaldon nodded. "Why would Locrian send you all the way to Southeast Agadin to bring me to be trained?"

Ont looked Kaldon up and down. "Beats me. No offence, but you don't look all that special to me."

Kaldon looked away, hardening himself to the jab. Medric and Brenton stayed silent.

Kaldon chose not to care what Ont thought of him, so he continued prodding with questions to better understand the world he was venturing into. "If Seers counsel kings and queens, is the Peak of Lore run by a monarchy?"

Expecting Medric to answer, he was surprised when Ont was the one to speak up. "The Peak of Lore is led by a man greater than a king. Kings cower before his blade. The man who governs the Peak of Lore is a *Paladin*."

Kaldon was realizing how sheltered he'd been his whole life. Seers? Paladins? These men casually threw around terms he didn't know the meaning of.

His curiosity forced him to say it, knowing it would remove any question of his ignorance. "Paladin?"

Ont's hand came up to his forehead. "This *boy* doesn't even know what a Paladin is!"

Kaldon looked towards Brenton, hoping the Knight would offer insight, but his look was met by a silent stare.

"Those behind the Mountains of D'aal have been coddled for quite some time, Ont. It isn't his fault," Medric said. "The time for cradling is over. The Sovereign of Shadow has already risen to greater power."

Seeing that Medric wasn't going to answer Kaldon's question, Ont rose to the challenge. "Many think Knights are the most formidable warriors. Yes, we are well trained, but we are by no means the most skilled of warriors. There are many Knights throughout Agadin. Knights travel in threes throughout the land on mission. Some Knights even help direct armies and train common warriors for war. From the best of the Knights, there are few chosen to become *Blades*. The most skilled of the Blades are chosen to become *Bishops*. The very best of the Bishops are chosen to be trained as a Paladin. Paladins are the best of the best. Any weapon you could imagine, they have mastered; every style of fighting, they've perfected. They are masters of battle and war. They cannot be bested. The man who leads the Peak of Lore is a Paladin."

Kaldon was struggling to digest the knowledge that the legendary Knights of Agadin were almost the bottom rank in the system of warriors, just above common warriors.

Ont continued, "The stories that circulate about the Paladin who governs the Peak of Lore are essentially endless. My favourite is the story of how he once killed a thousand warriors single-handedly in battle. *One* battle."

Kaldon's mouth gaped in astonishment.

"Ont, you know that isn't possible, don't you?" Medric asked in correction. "No man could kill a thousand men singlehandedly."

"I have it on good word that he did. He isn't called a Paladin for no reason," Ont rebuffed, as they marched deeper into the abyss of trees.

"Have any of you ever met this… *Paladin*?" Kaldon asked, trying to pull out as much information as he could.

"Never," Medric confirmed. "Such men aren't accessible, even to Knights or Blades. This is true, especially for Tolek, the Paladin who runs the Peak of Lore. Like Seers, Paladins are extremely rare. I have heard there are very few Paladins alive in all of Agadin. For all I know, Tolek could be the only one."

Kaldon reached his hand into his pocket, running his fingers over the symbol inscription on his father's book, *The First Paragon*.

"You both know much about Seers and Paladins. Tell me, what is a Paragon?" Kaldon asked as his fingers traced the symbol.

Ont squinted his face in thought. "I have travelled much of Agadin and have heard my fair share of titles, but I have never in all of my life heard of a Paragon. You, Medric?"

Medric kept his eyes forward to the uncharted forest. "Never."

As Kaldon's fingers pressed into the symbol on the book, the mystery tugged at him. Reaching the top of a hill in Rune Forest, through an array of dead leaves, he could see the shadow of the Mountains of D'aal in the distance. The colossal, darkened-purple stones stood proudly. Somewhere in them was the Peak of Lore, the place he would be trained and where he hoped answers would be found.

There was a vast world before him, one he didn't know; a land filled with Seers, Paladins, Blades, and war. Worst of all, the Sovereign of Shadow—a man he feared to learn of, yet knew it was only a matter of time before he did.

Chapter Seven
The Life of a Seer

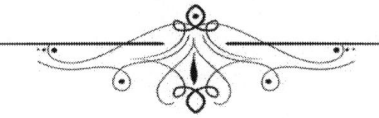

Flinching from the pain of the cold, stony floor against his calloused hands, Locrian had never been crouched in one position for so long. His knees began to sting. He ached. Hiding under a wooden table, he was protected by the cloth hanging over the sides, which blinded his enemies from seeing him. The chatter of guards and various warriors was all around him. The occasional fight broke out, followed by sounds of thrashing and brawls. He knew about fifty men were gathered in the dining hall. Locrian had already passed countless guards while breaking his way into the heart of Gallaway Morgue. He had never encountered this many guards at once during his mission.

"You are a fool, Locrian," the Seer whispered to himself. "You may be somewhat courageous, but you are a fool nonetheless."

His mind began taunting him. Here was the mighty Seer who had unlocked the mystery of time, now hiding under a table. Hiding, not only under a table, but in a very uncomfortable position for nearly an hour and three quarters. He almost laughed aloud. He forced a shift in perspective, reminding himself that this was for good reason. Gallaway Morgue was arguably the most guarded prison in Northern Agadin and one of the bases for those captured by the Dominion of Shadow. If circumstances weren't so dire, he would never have attempted such a ridiculous feat. It was said that not only could no one break out of the prison, but historically, no one had ever left. They called it *the Morgue* for a reason, he mused. The place was allegedly impenetrable, not only in how it was built, but also because of how protected it was. Skilled warriors and guards stood at attention behind every corner. Prison cells were not only plentiful, but rumour said each cellblock had its own torturer. Based on what Locrian had witnessed, these rumours were true. He hadn't only broken into the prison, but he was planning to break someone out.

Breaking into Gallaway Morgue would seem like insanity, but Locrian was no novice. Patiently waiting for the right moment to charge into the depths of the prison, he pulled out the blueprint he'd created. His pale-blue eyes squinted, scanning the ratted paper. Wiping the perspiration from his bald head, he studied the blueprint. He had meticulously observed the *River of Time* for months now, so he was to properly execute his plan.

Most Seers spent a lifetime striving to cultivate an intimate connection to the River of Time. Locrian was the exception. At a young age, he was able to comprehend his link to the wondrous place, learning to access it at will. Whenever he desired, he would concentrate, and he had access to the River of Time. His mind would flood with visions. The visions invited him to step out of the temporal to see through the eyes of eternity.

Recent months saw Locrian sitting in his private quarters awaiting the right visions to navigate the Morgue. As the visions unfolded in his mind, he not only wrote down what he saw, but he also wrote the time frame of what he saw. Studiously preparing this way for months enabled him to write the time-blueprint for a successful rescue. He had spent countless hours creating it, down to the very second. Based on the visions, he knew the movements of every guard in the prison, every room, hall, and cell. Most importantly, Locrian knew the timing—when there was a window to slip by without being noticed. The intricate task needed to be executed with utmost patience and precision. In short, the time-blueprint was a masterpiece. Never had a Seer, to his knowledge, constructed a blueprint of future time frames based on visions.

Crouching underneath the table, he waited for the specific moment his blueprint said would approach within minutes.

A loud crash erupted a few tables down from where he was hiding. Men scrambled about, shouting and fussing.

Locrian rolled his eyes. "Brutes," he mouthed to himself.

Sneaking past fifty trained guards and warriors seemed impossible; however, he had time on his side. He knew a common misconception about Seers was that they were masters of time. Seers were *not* time's masters, nor could they manipulate time. A Seer's gift was to be intimate with time. One must know its intricacies and partner with it. He understood time in the same way a Paladin understands the sword. Time was a weapon. A tool. A friend.

Counting down the minutes before he needed to move, he recalled the training he endured as a child. He thought of his mentor, Alden.

As much as Locrian disliked his mentor, he was now thankful for the endless years Alden forced him to sit, focused, to pattern his mind to the sound of a metronome. The tool musicians and minstrels used to keep their instruments in sync with proper tempo was the very thing that tuned his mind to the rhythm of time. He sat at his wooden desk for hours listening to the perfectly measured tocks. The ticking of seconds still wrung, resounding in his soul as an eternal reminder of who he was created to be: a Seer.

Whenever Locrian would complain about listening to the metronome, Alden would remind him, "All of eternity is made up of singular seconds; therefore, a Seer needs to understand time. A Seer needs to know seconds, in and out. You cannot build for the future until you master what you have been given in the present."

This is what guided Locrian to see the River of Time in visions. This lesson gave him the skill to construct his blueprint.

Alden, now mature in age, had greatly distanced himself from him. He had surpassed his mentor in many ways. Alden had a fragile ego, and it was widely known that Locrian was more than exceptional. The student outgrew the teacher.

Suddenly, a man's voice arose amidst the ensemble of guards. The guards slowly quieted, granting others the ability to hear what was being said. "Guards of Gallaway Morgue, it is time for us to offer our voices to the one we serve."

Locrian knew this was his moment.

The leader bellowed, "Everyone, stand and close your eyes. It is time for us to give our gratitude to the Sovereign of Shadow."

Locrian shifted uncomfortably on hearing the man's title.

Counting down to the exact second, Locrian crawled out from under the table. Based on his blueprint, he knew the prayer to the Sovereign of Shadow would last for exactly four minutes and twelve seconds. He didn't worry about the leader or any of the guards opening their eyes; the rules of their master were strict. To open one's eyes while giving gratitude to the Sovereign meant the death penalty. No exceptions. If the rule was questioned, authorities quoted their Sovereign directly: *"To open your eyes during such a divine moment is more than disrespect. It is treason, punishable by death."* Locrian knew it was all absolutely ludicrous.

He stood, stretching stiff arms and legs as he looked upon the oversized dining room. Fifty men stood with their eyes clamped shut as the leader muttered gratitude to a man who had no regard for human life. A man whose dark obsession with self-enthronement drove him to proclaim himself a divine being, demanding to be worshipped as such. Locrian despised every moment of the enslaved gratitude. What shook him the most was the look on the faces of the men. He assumed such hardened men would despise this practice, yet it was obvious they did not. They seemed sincere. Each man exuded passion during the gratitude; some even had tears slowly dripping down their stony faces. He should have been moving on, but was frozen, taken aback by the scene of men enthralled by the rule and the insanity of the Sovereign of Shadow.

As tears streamed down their deceived faces, anger tumbled and toiled within Locrian like a raging fire. He knew it would burn in him until the insane teachings of the Sovereign of Shadow ceased to exist.

Disgusted, he turned his back to the guards, rushing down one of the cryptic halls of the Morgue. The deeper he delved into the dungeon, the more suffocated he felt by the walls enclosing him.

Coming to a hall he needed to cross, he pressed against a wall with his smooth, bald head resting on the cold rock. He could feel its coolness on his heated skin, his head damp like a fever. He heard the three guards on the other side of the wall.

The guards shuffled, weapons clanging from their belts. The Seer hugged the wall, shifting awkwardly as his newly acquired bow and arrows dug into his back. Other than the metal staff he brought on missions, Locrian strongly disliked carrying weapons. From his point of view, a skilled Seer shouldn't need a physical weapon. Time should be the weapon. However, this time, the bow and arrows were necessary. He had gone out of his way significantly to obtain them. The bow was a part of his plan. He had already made his way through much of the labyrinth. He was close to his destination, so close to finding Anneya's cell.

Screams of anguish echoing down the halls, he didn't want to imagine what caused the sounds. The art of torture was honed in the Morgue, where Anneya had been a prisoner for over half a year.

Although his plan was perfectly timed, sneaking around was exhausting physically. Hyper-awareness taxed his mind. He had a constant internal clock counting down to the very second since his arrival at the prison. The only way to keep on time with his blueprint was to count the seconds. One misstep in counting could ruin everything. He could hardly believe he had been here for nearly twelve hours already—twelve hours of rushing around, waiting, hiding, freezing-still, and counting seconds.

It was time for him to move. He counted down the seconds.

Three.

The exact second when two of the guards would be facing in a direction where they would not see him as he passed by.

Two.

The third guard would close his eyes for exactly thirteen seconds, drifting into a light sleep.

One.

Spinning around the corner of the wall, just as he foresaw in visions, the two guards were facing away, and the third had his eyes shut. Locrian scurried silently past the first two guards. That was the easy part. The hard part would be unhooking the key for Anneya's prison cell from the third guard's belt before his eyes snapped open. He knew three seconds had already passed, leaving him with only ten seconds before the guard awoke from his momentary slumber.

He saw the key dangling from the guard's belt. The guard's chest ascended and descended in a restful posture. Gripping the key, Locrian pulled gently, trying to unhook it.

Nothing.

Seven seconds left.

His hands began to shake. He trembled, fearing his quivering would wake the guard prematurely. If the guard awoke, he knew his own screams would soon join those he heard in the prison cells.

Locrian, you fool, he thought to himself.

Two seconds.

With the final attempt and a gentle pull, the key slid from the guard's buckle. Key in hand, he ran nimbly to take shelter behind another stone wall. Huffing in exhaustion and his heart beating wildly, he leaned against the stone wall once again in relief. Trying to catch his breath, he mused that although he foresaw every moment taking place in the Morgue through his visions, one mistake could alter what he saw. Trip once and a guard could see him, ruining months of work and most likely ending his life. That was the challenge in building plans around what you saw in the River of Time. The river was not definitive; it was fluid. It could be altered, disrupting its flow if you weren't careful.

Pulling out the blueprints again, he saw that he had forty-five seconds to rest until his next move. He exhaled slowly as his finger traced over the blueprint from the hundreds of guards he'd already avoided to where he was now. Now was the trickiest part—rescuing Anneya. On the surface, it would seem navigating the guards was the biggest challenge. It wasn't. The hardest challenge would be convincing a prisoner of Gallaway Morgue to leave. One would think a prisoner would jump at the chance to escape, but torture twisted people's perceptions. It crushed their hope, shattering their will to persevere—to live.

As he briefly rested, his mind flooded with images of Anneya as a small girl. Her feet would pitter-patter on the marble floor as she ran, playing through the halls in the Peak of Lore. The poor girl was raised in horrific circumstances. Abandoned as an infant, she was adopted by a man who became her father. Due to abuse in her home, the Peak of Lore took her in, dedicated to training her as one of their own. She wore the scars proving her abuse. The most memorable of them was a white thick mark descending from the outside corner of her left eye and down her cheek. The scar brought sorrow to her young face. It was a constant reminder of what she endured as a child. The Peak of Lore played a role in redeeming her childhood. Her teachers, advisors, and peers became her family.

The other reason Locrian remembered her so well was because of the unique calling over her young life. He didn't know her personally. He hadn't needed to. As a Seer, he saw people beyond their present reality. He could read their destiny like a scroll written over their lives.

Anneya was no longer a little girl; she was a grown woman. More than a woman. Anneya was first trained as a Knight of Agadin. Excelling more quickly than most, she mastered the way of the Knight. That led to her being one of the few Knights chosen to become a Blade. This is why Locrian needed the bow he retrieved. Those trained as Blades are given a weapon at the beginning of their training. They are taught not only to fight with their weapon; they are taught to become one with it. This is one of the elements separating a Knight and a Blade. Knights are admirable fighters, but a Blade is another thing entirely. A Knight can wield a weapon. A Blade *is* the weapon. This bow was given to her when she began her training. To a Blade, their weapon is an extension of who they are. This bow had been a part of Anneya since her teen years, and he was counting on her responding to that.

Although Locrian saw the magnitude of her purpose, her calling was not definitive. It was potential. He'd seen those with weighty callings over their lives come and go. He had seen them fail, even die. It was as though their destiny and potential were stolen by the wind, erasing the imprint they could have left. He vowed this would not happen to Anneya. She was too profound a key in their battle against the Dominion of Shadow.

Locrian wasn't rested enough to move on, but there was no choice. Just as his blueprint said, the dungeon door was around the corner. The black door looked like a dungeon door would. The iron block seemed impenetrable. Taking the set of keys from his pocket, he approached the door.

The key penetrated the keyhole, resulting in a click. He slipped in, slowly shutting the door behind him. He was stunned by how dark the cell actually was. Only a faint light trickled in through a small window too high up the wall to see through. The light hovered through the dank air, resting on the cemented floor.

Ragged and cold, Anneya laid on the floor.

She looked up at Locrian, dried blood caking her face. He saw the distinctive teardrop scar carved into her cheek; the one she bore since childhood. He shuddered to imagine the horrors likely done to this woman.

"Great Divinity..." he whispered. He rushed over to Anneya, placing a hand on her shoulder, ever so softly. He wanted to speak, but seeing her broken upon the grimy floor robbed him of words. Looking up at him with hollow eyes, it was as though she didn't even see him.

Locrian thought the stone walls of the cell felt like being in a stone-cold womb. Not a womb birthing life—this womb was a grave where death encountered people long before they met their end.

Opening cracked lips, Anneya tried to speak. "Please..." she whimpered.

Locrian leaned in closer. "Please what, my dear?"

Anneya forced the words out. "Please... Kill me." Tears streaked down her bloodied face.

"Oh no, my dear," he smiled gently at her with empathy in his tone. "Your time is not done quite yet. I have seen your destiny. I have read the scroll over your life and you have quite the mark to leave as of yet."

The woman spilled over in tears, silently weeping on the Seer's shoulder. It occurred to him this was likely the first time in many months here where the physical touch she experienced wasn't violent.

He placed a gentle hand on her matted, golden hair. "Your spirit may be broken right now, but this is not the time to lie. It is time to stand. It is time to remember who you are."

He slowly eased his hold on the woman and rose to stand over her. Coming here, he'd known the biggest obstacle to her escape would be her lack of willingness to fight for her own life. She needed to hope again. As the Seer stood over the shattered woman, he spoke. Locrian did not speak the way a regular man would. He spoke as a Seer. With a mighty decree, he spoke with trained certainty. A Seer not only wields time as a weapon. A true Seer also wields words. They used the word of truth to pierce into the deepest caverns of a soul.

"Anneya Padme, Blade of Agadin, you were not created to cower. You were born to shape history. You were fashioned to impact eternity. Rise and take your bow. Remember who you are!"

His words cut through the air into the core of her heart. She flinched at the impact. A Seer's words, when wielded properly, are comparable to an earthquake in a person's core. They can summon a strength one may never have conceived of that was even there. They can awaken what had lain dormant for a lifetime.

Locrian then pulled forth the bow strapped to his back. The silver handle glimmered in the moon's light, matching the glow now visible in Anneya's bewildered eyes. Her eyes were no longer empty; they were transfixed, ignited. He watched her begin to transition from a posture of defeat to one of courage. He knew very well that his words did more than spark hope in her, for hope was not resting—it was dead. His words resurrected her hope. He gave life where, mere moments ago, there was none.

Her eyes began sparkling as Locrian placed her bow in her hands. The bow of her youth was a tangible reminder of who she was. Leaving the burdens of the hardened ground, she rose. The once broken spirit now stood whole.

For the first time in the history of Gallaway Morgue, death did not win. In the deepest of dungeons, in the darkest of caverns, hope was born anew.

Chapter Eight

Fleeing the Morgue

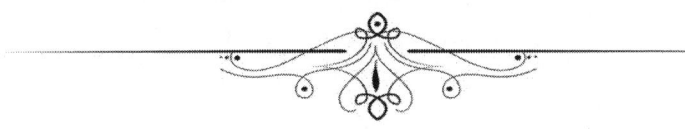

"Would you hurry *up*?!" Anneya hissed under her breath.

Locrian rubbed his face in frustration. As meticulous as his entrance plan was, so was the exit strategy. Each step was intricately calculated to the very second. Now, he was finding it next to impossible to stick to his blueprint with Anneya along. The woman was impatient. Blades often were. He had lost count of how many times they should have been waiting to move, yet she would charge onward, disregarding caution. Mind you, he had also lost count of how many guards she left slain behind her.

"Great Divinity! You are going to get yourself imprisoned all over again, and me along with you," Locrian blurted out.

"You are certainly right. If *you* don't hurry up, we will both be captured," she quarrelled.

He rolled his eyes. Stubborn Blade. Blades understood natural law. In many ways, they didn't have the ability or patience to understand things such as visions or time.

Working their way out of the core of the Morgue, they still had quite a way to go. Based on the blueprint, there were roughly three hundred guards to kill or evade. Anneya had no problem taking down a guard or two, but even she couldn't take down an entire prison worth. To successfully pass them all required essentially three hundred separate scenarios needing to be executed perfectly. On top of that, they were pressed for time.

As the two left the Blade's former cell, their first move was to capture a female guard, knock her out, and lock her in the cell. With the Blade's skill in combat, that went smoother than Locrian thought it would. It would likely be quite a while until anyone noticed her gone, still, if they didn't leave the prison soon, it would only be a matter of time before they were found out.

From around the corner, he heard keys clinking about. "Anneya, there are guards around the corner. Grab their keys," the Seer said.

"I'm on it," she said unflinchingly.

Instead of pulling out her bow, Anneya grabbed two arrows. She had been doing this through most of their escape. Her arrows were constructed of a light, yet solid metal, allowing them to double as individual weapons.

She darted around the corner. Locrian didn't need to watch her to make sure she was safe. The guards wouldn't be a challenge to a Blade. Instantly, four gasps were followed by four thuds. *That was quick*, he thought.

"Done," she said casually, coming around the corner with four keys swinging from her finger.

Gallaway Morgue was laid out so that those imprisoned for treason against the Sovereign of Shadow were in the deepest recesses of the dungeon, where Anneya was. Where they were now, mid-depth, housed the murderers. Closer to the fringe of the prison were the more common criminals.

Locrian peered down the left hall. "Anneya, when we free these four murderers, you're sure they'll run down the left hallway?"

"Oh, *believe* me, they won't go right," she assured him.

"How do you know?" he prodded.

Her silken face went blank. "To the right are the torture chambers for this division of the Morgue."

He shuddered. "Well... that's a fine reason not to go right then, isn't it?"

She looked away, her silence answering the question for her.

They each took two keys and headed for the iron-cell doors. The murderers in these cells had been imprisoned there for years. Locrian was counting on it. He needed men who had lost their minds, men who would make a scene.

Opening the first and second doors, they were met by squinting eyes peering into the door's light. Each man's hair and beard had grown to an unreasonable length, revealing how long they had been captive. Locrian nodded in approval.

"Let them run," Locrian said quietly to Anneya.

As soon as each of the men realized the two weren't guards, they sprang to their feet and ran. Exiting their cells, the murderers ran down the left wing of the hall, just as Anneya said they would.

"Smart girl," Locrian said to her.

She responded with a smirk.

The men ran down the hall, shouting and hollering. Locrian smiled at the brilliant distraction. As he began opening the third door, the murderer inside pushed it wide open and bolted down the left hall, following the others. Locrian knew it wouldn't be long before guards took notice. He hoped the guards would follow the noise to the left side of this division, forcing them to cluster into one group. This would give him and Anneya the chance to quickly pass through unguarded halls.

"Just one more prisoner," Anneya said as she began turning the metal key in the fourth and final door.

The lock clicked, and the door burst open. The murderer growled and leapt out, knocking Anneya to the ground. The ragged man pounced on her, reaching for her throat. She pushed on his chest, preventing him from strangling her. Rotting teeth snapped at her face. Grime dripped from the man's unruly beard and hair.

"Locrian!" she gasped, struggling.

Locrian rushed over to quiet the growls that not only threatened her life, but could also betray their whereabouts. With a crack, he struck the man's head with his staff. The murderer went limp, unconscious.

She kicked the man off her. "I hope only three men will be enough," she said, catching her breath.

The Seer grabbed her hand to help her up. He hoped what happened would level her overconfidence, showing her the severity of their situation.

Shouts from the prisoners bellowed through the halls, followed by the sound of guards' boots clomping upon the prison floors in a hurry.

"The guards are locating to the prisoners," Locrian said. "We need to leave. Now."

The Seer and Blade quickened, weaving through the corridors. Halls were now vacant, giving them a clear escape. The plan had worked better than expected. Locrian was surprised at how many guards left their posts after the three escaped prisoners. Judging by how loud the three were, the guards may have thought there were nearly twenty men.

Corridor after corridor they dashed. Soon they were standing at the mouth of the Morgue. This door seemed to be the only way in or out of the prison. They stood before the exit, seven guards standing in the way of their freedom, their backs turned to the two.

Locrian was still counting seconds. His internal metronome was still ticking and tocking. He knew in a few moments they could sneak past the guards without being seen.

"We are so close," he whispered. "We need to wait for the right moment to sneak by. Wait for my cue. I will tell you exactly when we can move."

As Anneya listened, she saw beyond the guards. Morning light crept in through the door of death that was Gallaway Morgue. Even where she stood, she could feel its warmth on her face. She could feel the touch of freedom.

Anneya spoke out loud, intentionally summoning the attention of the guards. "To be honest, Locrian, I have completely lost my patience with waiting."

The guards turned to the sound of her voice. The Blade ran head-on at them, no weapon in hand. Locrian watched as the Blade leapt into the air. Moving with deadly accuracy, she kicked and jabbed, striking whatever pressure points she could find. She was trained to assess quickly and eliminate any threat. She was the weapon.

Within seconds, all seven guards laid at her feet unmoving. Locrian froze, awestruck by what he witnessed. The woman had potential indeed.

Knowing he and Anneya were hardly out of plain sight, Locrian tucked his arm under hers, leading her behind trees surrounding the prison. Behind a thick wall of bush and greenery, two horses awaited them.

"Just where I left you girls," he said, patting the brown steeds.

As Anneya was protected and hidden under the shield of greenery, sobriety hit her. She was free. She squinted at the sun's morning gaze shining directly upon her for the first time in six months. Falling to her knees, she laughed, running her fingers through the grass. Dirt clammed underneath her fingernails as the breeze tickled her golden hair. It was ecstasy.

Locrian watched her eyes shift to what laid beside the horses.

"No..." she whispered in disbelief.

Upon the ground was armour—but not just any armour; the armour of a Blade. Quickly rising to her feet, she didn't delay in strapping the armour around her. Locrian knew they didn't have time to waste, but was taken in by the moment nonetheless. The armour of a Blade was a fearsome thing to behold. The silver covering stuck close to her. The blood-red metal shoulders extended out like razor-sharp spikes. They were the mark of a Blade.

Before she could fully take in the moment, Locrian grabbed the tuff of her armour. "Celebrate later," he said, looking back to the dreadful prison. "We need to distance ourselves from this horrid place."

She let out a sigh. Mounting the majestic steed, they raced into the light of morning. Locrian watched the woman ride free, away from Gallaway Morgue. No longer chained, the sun bathed her face. She beamed at the embrace of freedom.

After several hours, they stopped to let the horses regain strength. As they sat on a fallen tree, he caught the Blade looking back towards the Morgue.

"Anneya... No one is coming," he comforted her. "My visions showed me that the guards are a great distance away."

"Locrian…" she said, looking downward to avoid making eye contact.

The Blade fidgeted her hands together awkwardly. He realized that such a trained warrior wouldn't be accustomed to owing her life to another.

He placed his hands on the woman's shoulders. "There is no need to give thanks, my dear. It was an honour to rescue you."

She smiled in gratitude.

Perhaps, inside, there is still part of the young girl I once saw at the Peak of Lore, he thought to himself. The spark was still there. She leaned over and tightly hugged the Seer for a moment before moving away.

"Anneya, you cannot return to the Peak of Lore just yet. I have a mission you need to embark upon."

"Name it. I will do anything you ask," she said.

"I had a vision," the Seer pronounced. "There is someone needing your help, just as you did mine."

He reached under his robe, pulling out a pendant hanging from his neck. It looked like a compass, but wasn't. It was a bronze-circular symbol with five points coming from its centre, piercing through an outer sphere.

Locrian continued, "Ride to the Mountains of D'aal and find the one wearing this pendant. He will need your help. Do you recognize this symbol?"

The Blade looked at the symbol in wonder. "This symbol is not known to many, but one of my trainers at the Peak of Lore taught me about it. It's called a *Legacy*—worn by those who are destined to be *Protectors of Agadin*. Only the most formidable are called to wear them, only those who are chosen."

He nodded, confirming her words.

"You are one of these Protectors, Locrian?" she asked.

He looked off distantly to the Mountains of D'aal. "I am. It is both a privilege and a tremendous burden."

Anneya was taken aback by his answer. "Is the one who needs my help also a Protector of Agadin?" she questioned.

"He has the potential to be. He has potential, just as the rest of us do," Locrian said. "You best be going, Anneya. More than I can say depends on this mission."

She climbed the steed, now rested. "Truly, thank you for rescuing me."

He nodded. He felt good about the rescue, but there was much more behind the mission than just him saving one Blade. It was for the sake of Agadin and for what would be accomplished through this particular Blade.

She rode off towards the destiny awaiting her.

Pulling out his time-blueprint, he looked again at the complicated sketches and patterns. His masterpiece. Locrian knew this blueprint was something Seers and Philosophers would likely study for years to understand the complex mechanics. He also knew that the story of him breaking a Blade out of Gallaway Morgue would likely be told for generations. The story would echo throughout history.

"Simply another day in the life of the Seer," he chuckled to himself, taking the saddle.

Chapter Nine

Silent Knight

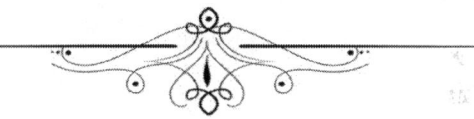

Kaldon stepped in, deflecting the blow with his short sword as Brenton swung his blade. Brenton brought his knee into Kaldon's ribs. Hard. Kaldon doubled over trying to regain composure.

In the thick Rune Forest, Kaldon's training had already begun. Terrain from the Mountains of D'aal was beginning to meet with the forest. Sets of trees marked a natural arena. Fallen tree trunks laid as obstacles preventing easy footing. Ont was off scouting the forest, Medric sat on a log at the sidelines, observing the fight.

Kaldon lunged at Brenton, swinging his sword down at the Knight. The Knight effortlessly sidestepped. Brenton was much quicker than others he had fought in the past. Without delay, Kaldon brought an elbow around, striking the Knight in his abdomen. Upon impact, he was surprised to feel a twinge of pain course through his elbow. The Knight's stomach was solid muscle. It was like striking a wall made of stone. Brenton took the blow without even a grunt. He didn't step back, nor falter. The Knight was already driving in towards him once again.

Road of a Paragon

"Good recovery, Kal!" Medric shouted from the log.

As they sparred, Kaldon thought of the war taking place in Agadin. He thought of what would happen if the Dominion of Shadow made it over the Mountains of D'aal. Rundle would be overtaken. His home city would likely be destroyed. His thoughts dwelt on the man who was a mystery to him: the Sovereign of Shadow.

His thoughts were abruptly ended as he sidestepped over a fallen tree. Swinging at Brenton again, the blow didn't faze the Knight. The Knight was already plotting his next move. In his mind, Kaldon envisioned Brenton coming in for impact with his blade against his right shoulder. Trusting his instincts, he moved to dodge the attack. Just as he imagined, Brenton came in for his shoulder. Kaldon avoided the hit.

Kaldon smirked. He could beat most by skill alone; however, Brenton was a fully trained Knight. He needed to depend on more than skill. He needed his intuition.

Ever since he was young, Kaldon had exceptional intuition. This was one of the reasons he was so good with a sword. He began noticing it when defending himself on the streets of Rundle. At times, in the quickness of a battle, he felt as though everything would slow down. In that stillness, the moment was his to take. He was never quite able to understand it. It was as though he could anticipate an action or attack before it took place. It was as if he could see seconds into the future. This skill had saved his life on more than one occasion. He wished he could control it, but he couldn't. It came and went with no certainty.

Brenton came at him again with several attacks. As images passed through Kaldon's mind, he responded accordingly, blocking each attempt. Metal clanged, resounding through the dense forest. As long as he responded to what he saw in his mind, he figured he actually stood a chance against the Knight.

He stepped in to strike Brenton's right side. The Knight deflected the blow. As Kaldon's sword bounced off Brenton's, his mind went blank. He hated how he couldn't control the timing of when he could use his intuition. Brenton moved quickly. Panic rushed through Kaldon. Without his intuition, he couldn't foresee Brenton's actions. Unexpectedly, the Knight slammed his foot into the centre of Kaldon's chest. He flew back, landing on twigs and leaves, winded. He laid on the ground panting.

"I win," Brenton said, seriousness in his tone.

Kaldon was surprised at how hard Brenton actually kicked him. His chest throbbed. The rest of his body was already aching from the fight.

"Kal, not bad for your first fight against a Knight of Agadin," Medric said. "You were much better than I thought you would be. You've got skill with a blade. What you lack is technique."

Brenton slid his iron sword into its sheath and leaned against one of the oak trees without saying a word.

Kaldon felt his chest already beginning to bruise. Medric walked over and helped him to his feet.

Medric spoke quietly to him, so as not to let Brenton hear. "I can tell you don't like him, Kal, but he is one of the most qualified Knights I know. He is trusted to train others in battle," he said, vouching for the Knight. "You may have thought you were holding yourself well against Brenton, but he was taking it easy on you."

Kaldon remained quiet.

Medric shouted to the silent Knight. "Brenton, do you have any tips for the lad?"

Brenton eyed Kaldon. "I do, actually."

Kaldon was surprised to hear him speak. He hadn't heard him say more than a few sentences since leaving Rundle.

Brenton spoke directly to his pupil. "Kal, you fight well, but I could tell by how you move that you were just reacting to my actions. Fighting is about more than being reactive; it is about strategy. It isn't just about knowing how to swing a sword with confidence; it is about knowing your enemy. As we fought, for every move you made, I had my next four moves planned. Like Medric said, you don't lack skill. However, learning technique will take you beyond being decent with a blade. It will make you excellent."

Kaldon could only nod at the sound advice, not willing to test his voice as the air slowly returned to his lungs.

The sun began melting into the horizon. Nightfall was coming. Medric spoke up. "We have a bit further to travel today. We will then take turns on watch tonight in case Kreel are about. Ont will follow our trail to catch up with us once he is finished scouting."

Brenton inclined his head in agreement. Kaldon wanted to rest after the fight, but they needed to travel onward. As he sparred with Brenton, the war they were in became more real to him. He could no longer evade the truth of what was happening in Agadin.

"I need to know about the Sovereign of Shadow," Kaldon stated plainly.

Medric paused before responding. "I suppose it is time you knew more about what we are facing."

Medric began packing to continue their journey. "The Sovereign of Shadow's name is Tymas Droll. He reigns from *Gorath,* far away from here."

Kaldon remembered learning about Gorath in school, before he was forced to drop out. While the Southeast of Agadin, close to the Mountains of D'aal, were often colder in temperature,

Gorath was supposedly much warmer. Like dried lands, it was a place of sweltering heat. Apparently Gorath was quite formidable in size.

Medric continued, "As you already know, the Sovereign's empire is called the Dominion of Shadow. Tymas' name is now feared throughout Agadin, anywhere North of the Mountains of D'aal. For years, Gorath kept to itself, as did the Sovereign. Now we know they were preparing for domination all along. The Sovereign's Dominion first began overtaking smaller towns, expanding as they did. He now has an army so large that a few major cities have been completely overrun. The terror he has inflicted is so vast that kings tremble at the mention of his name, and children suffer night terrors. This is about far more than simply overtaking the lands; this is about owning the people outright. He wants to enslave us by corrupting the minds of those throughout Agadin with his philosophies."

"Insanity..." Kaldon murmured.

Medric kept going as if he didn't hear. "The Sovereign believes he is divinely chosen to enlighten Agadin in the way of the Shadow. He forces the passive to submit to his rule. Those who are brave enough to stand against him are eliminated. He believes he is moving Agadin forward into a divine vision."

Unnerved, Kaldon shook his head. "How could anyone believe such a thing?"

Medric continued without answering. "The Kreel appeared not long after Droll and his Dominion came out of hiding, attacking the places they were warring with. Some believe it was a coincidence. I don't believe in coincidences. I am certain the Kreel serve him. In fact, I believe he spawned the creatures himself."

How was it possible for one man to have such power? Although hesitant to ask, he knew he needed to know. "Surely there are people willing to fight him. Are there any cities that have won against him?"

Medric seemed reluctant to share. "Many throughout Agadin have embraced the Shadow, Kal. Those who follow his teachings are everywhere. There are likely some in Southeast Agadin that no one knows of. The Sovereign has people who have embraced the Shadow hidden in cities, many in high places of influence."

"You are saying anyone could have embraced the Shadow?" Kaldon asked.

"Anyone," Medric said faintly. "Just as anyone can embrace good."

Forcing himself not to look at Brenton, Kaldon thought of how the man kept to himself and how hard he kicked him. Something didn't fit. Kaldon put his hand on his chest, still feeling it throb. He didn't trust the Knight.

Medric continued, "Many aligning with the Shadow have great influence. They are strategically hidden in cities to reverse and change the mindset of the people, bringing them under the rule of the Sovereign. They gather information and wait until the appointed time to send in a *Swarm*."

"A Swarm?" Kaldon hesitantly asked.

Medric sighed. "A Swarm is a large grouping of Kreel which destroys those who oppose the Dominion of Shadow."

Kaldon felt his blood beginning to boil. He had never heard of such heartless tactics of war. "How is it that Droll can control such beasts, let alone large groups of them?" he asked heatedly.

Brenton unexpectedly spoke up. "The Sovereign is able to control the Kreel because of the *Nahmen*."

At the mention of the Nahmen, there was a momentary silence between the three. Medric looked on edge. It appeared the Knight didn't trust Brenton as much as he led on.

Brenton clearly didn't care if Medric felt uncomfortable, continuing. "After the Sovereign sends a Swarm of Kreel, a Nahmen always follows. They are dreadful creatures. Nahmen have humanlike qualities. They are the size of a grown man. However, their skin is grey in pigmentation. Every Nahmen has a Swarm of Kreel they oversee and have an unseen connection to. They control them."

Medric cut in. "The Nahmen control and instruct the Kreel through more than a connection to command. They see directly through the eyes of every Kreel they govern. The Kreels' eyes are windows for Nahmen to peer through. This way, the Sovereign has spies throughout all of Agadin. His eyes are everywhere. These are the things we are aware of regarding the Nahmen. The extent of their abilities is not yet known to us."

Kaldon was trying to wrap his head around all he had just heard. How had he been so ignorant of what was taking place in the world around him? No, it wasn't just him; it was everyone in the Southeast end of the Mountains of D'aal. The world was unfolding before him, and it was a scary world indeed.

Brenton interrupted his thoughts. "The most feared part of the Nahmen is that, since they are not human, they are void of emotion. They are ruthless, with no regard for or compassion for the living. They turn entire cities upside-down with their Kreel, sending them in to shred the defenceless and to tear through the most formidable of warriors. With their Kreel, the Nahmen enforce the bending of cultures in entire cities to the teachings of the Sovereign of Shadow. Tymas Droll believes no one has value or worth unless they have earned it through radical devotion to him. He raises only the strongest and most ruthless to positions of importance. The cities he overrules are backward because the culture contrasts anything that is morally right. These become places where there is no regard for life, no regard for people as individuals."

Kaldon's eyes wandered into the wooded land of Rune Forest. Even though he had not seen a Kreel in the forest, he knew they were about, hunting. He hoped he would not face one, but he knew it was likely inevitable. After all, the Sovereign of Shadow had eyes everywhere.

Chapter Ten

In the Shadows

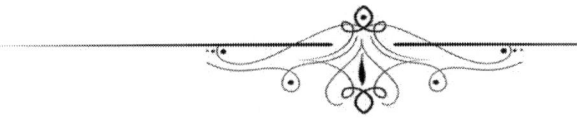

The first snowflakes of the season dusted the land, chilling the night sky. The others slept as Kaldon kept watch, his back against an imposing oak tree. It would be roughly an hour before he would wake Ont to relieve him. He was glad to sit and rest; his body ached from his fight with Brenton earlier that day.

Looking up through the trees, he could hardly believe they were at the foot of the legendary Mountains of D'aal. In the morning, he would venture through them. *If only Claude could see me now*, he thought.

He looked around before pulling out the leather-bound book he found in his father's memorial, *The First Paragon*. Running his fingers over the book's inscribed symbol, his other hand traced the outline of the same symbol hanging around his neck beneath his cloak. This was the first time he felt safe pulling the book out to examine it. He didn't feel comfortable sharing it with the Knights.

In the silence, he carefully skimmed the pages. As he skimmed, an occasional snowflake landed, kissing the bronzed pages. Page after page, he quietly perused the words written in Old Agadin. Though he could make out the occasional word, he found himself lost in a labyrinth of unknown symbols.

He shut the book, breathing heat into clasped hands to stay the sting of cold, sighing in frustration. There were answers hidden within the pages. He was certain of it.

Warm for the moment, he determinedly returned to the opening page of the book again. His eyes rested on the bold title. They widened when he saw something he'd overlooked before. There was a faint subtitle.

The first word of the subtitle was *Tahlim*. He silently mouthed the word, trying to interpret it. It was one of the simpler words of Old Agadin. After a few tries at fumbling through potential meanings, he concluded it meant "Story." It wasn't the word that shook him; it was the name that followed it: *Dawntan Forlorn*.

Kaldon remembered the stories his mother once shared with him. He always thought they were more fairytale than truth. He knew better now. Questions rose within him. *How could one man actually dethrone evil? How could things have gotten so dark in Agadin that even the sun didn't shine?*

Now, four thousand years later, the Dominion of Shadow threatened to destroy them. Kaldon silently mouthed the title and subtitle aloud into the black of night. *"The First Paragon: A Story of Dawntan Forlorn."*

Chills crept up his frosted skin. He wondered if this was truly a record of the man's life. Was Dawntan, in fact, a Paragon? The *first* Paragon? Kaldon knew this book held answers to appease his curiosity, but there must be even more to it. His father's letter said the book held secrets. When he casually asked the Knights if they spoke Old Agadin, as he expected, none did. They told him it was a dead dialect and that no one wasted their time studying it. They further offered that the Philosophers who had a handle on the tongue were all dead, leaving scrolls written in the language abandoned. Kaldon listened without comment at that time, but knew better than to give up his search.

Kaldon was still staring at the legendary name when the sound of leaves crunching behind the trees ahead alerted him. Slowly sliding the book back into the pocket of his cloak, he listened keenly. The sound could have been a small animal, maybe a fallen tree branch. Maybe it was an enemy soldier. It could also be something far worse.

He suddenly realized that if the sound was from a threat, he was likely in plain sight of it. He moved deliberately, trying to avoid ruffling the leaves under him. Crouching low, he hid behind a large tree, peering towards the origin of the sound.

A low hum of hoarse breathing ascended into the night. Although the night was brisk, he felt the heat of anxiety rush through him. Trees began to shake, twigs snapped, and leaves rustled. Refusing to panic, his face flushed red.

Just then, the largest creature he had ever seen emerged from the darkness. The Kreel standing before him was well over nine feet tall, built of solid muscle from top to bottom. Dark brown fur worked as camouflage, and its claws hung like short swords. The reptilian tail brushed the wind with treacherous strokes, and enormous bat-like wings protruded from its back. Its long, sharp teeth were highlighted on the black canvas of the night.

The Kreel lifted its head into the night and let out a piercing shriek. The scream cut into Kaldon's courage, making him bleed fear.

Pull it together, he thought to himself. He knew panic would bring death.

Kaldon jumped as something grabbed his shoulder, pulling him further behind the oak tree. A hand gripped his mouth,

Road of a Paragon

preventing him from gasping. His tension lessened, realizing it was Brenton. The Knight loosened his hand from his face, gesturing for him not to make a sound.

Without speaking, Kaldon mouthed Medric and Ont's names, asking if they were safe. Brenton shrugged his shoulders.

They both pressed their backs against the trunk of the tree, trying to steady their breathing. The footsteps of the beast came closer. The breathing of the Kreel grew louder and seemed agitated. Sweat beaded Kaldon's face.

"Stay still," Brenton whispered.

With a thud, the Kreel forced its mighty hand against the tree they hid behind. The sniffing of the Kreel quickened and was followed by a growl. Brenton locked eyes with Kaldon. It knew they were there.

A sudden shout startled them. Now the Kreel was moving away from them. Kaldon cautiously peeked around the tree to see Ont standing before the Kreel, a sword in hand. His mouth dropped open, shocked at seeing the Knight facing the beast alone. Ont must have known they were discovered and was trying to draw attention away from them. The Kreel loomed over him.

A battle cry erupted from Ont's mouth as he ran, lunging at the Kreel. Kaldon knew he stood no chance of slaying such a creature alone, but all three of them might stand a chance. He stood, stepping out from behind the oak.

"Get down!" Brenton rasped, trying to stay as quiet as possible.

"No," Kaldon said defiantly. He knew once the Kreel was done with Ont, it would come for them. He needed to act.

As Ont slashed at the beast, the Kreel snarled, deflecting every swing with its mighty claws. Kaldon unsheathed his blade, charging towards the foul beast.

Seconds before he reached the Kreel, its brawny arm barreled toward Ont. He tried to block the strike, but the sheer strength of the Kreel's claws cut right through him, splitting his chest. The Knight let out an inhuman sound, and then, nothing.

Kaldon could see Ont's lifeless body splayed out on the forest floor. He could hardly believe what he had just seen. When he'd heard stories of heroes dying, it sounded glorious, magical, even. There was nothing glorious here. It was vile.

The Kreel turned, facing Kaldon. Looking into the silver eyes of the shadowed beast, he wondered if a Nahmen was behind them. Barred teeth dripped saliva, snapping like knives. He lifted his sword, pointing it at the Kreel.

Its claw came down at Kaldon like a falling tree. He skirted the swing. He saw several arrows whiz past his head at the Kreel. It stood unflinchingly as the arrows ricocheted off its chest. Before he could act, Brenton was at his side.

Brenton flew at the beast, furiously slashing at the left side of its body. Kaldon followed his lead, targeting the Kreel's right side. The Kreel deflected most blows, and what it didn't block seemed to bounce off its skin.

Slashing with all of his might, suddenly the moment went still. Quiet. It was as though he was in the moment, yet watching himself against the Kreel in slow motion. Exhaling in relief, he knew he'd tapped into his intuition.

In the lens of his mind, he saw a swing from the Kreel coming directly for his head. Instinctively, he ducked low. As he did, the Kreel's arm barely missed him. Kaldon took a mental note that listening to what he saw in his mind would determine life or death for him.

Suddenly, the Kreel bellowed a pained screech. He saw that Brenton had finally pierced its skin on the left thigh. The Knight's sword stuck out from the Kreel's colossal leg, slowing it slightly, but not nearly enough.

The reptilian tail of the beast spun, clipping Brenton in his side. The blow made the Knight falter. Its claw lashed at Brenton, slicing his arm open. He fell to his side. The wound was deep.

The Kreel advanced toward Kaldon, swinging its claws and tail. He tried his best to follow his intuition as he dodged, pivoted, and deflected. *Stay calm,* he told himself. He needed to think of something fast. The Kreel must have had a weak spot.

Kaldon gasped as the razor-sharp talons flew past his side. *Close. Too close,* he thought as the Kreel lifted both arms, stretching to full height. The Kreel moved in to strike him with full force. Kaldon saw an opportunity. He dove between the beast's pillared legs. Before the Kreel had time to turn around, Kaldon swung his sword with all of his might, cutting through the back of the beast's knees.

The Kreel thundered a shrill cry as its knees hit the ground. Kaldon heard the creature's struggling breaths. In defeat, it stretched forth its bat-like wings. The sheer girth of them was daunting. Brenton's sword was lodged, still jutting out from its leg. It used the force of its wings to hoist itself up from the bloodied ground. Wailing, the creature fled into the night sky.

Adrenaline pumping through his aching body, Kaldon fell to the ground, panting in exhaustion. Looking down, he saw his clothes had rips and tears. Thankfully, it was his clothes and not his skin.

Kaldon looked up to see Ont's lifeless form beside him, the fallen Knight of Agadin. To the other side of him sat Brenton, not slain, but severely wounded. Brenton was already tying fabric around his arm, a dressing for his gashed limb. In exhaustion, Kaldon rolled over with the side of his face planted in the dirt.

His sight began to blur. He thought of Dawntan Forlorn, a legendary hero who, before that day, he believed was a myth.

Now, he didn't know what he thought. Creatures such as Kreel and Nahmen, heroes such as Knights, were once a mystery. Now, mystery and myth were becoming reality.

His sight began fading to black. Unconsciousness invited him. Closing his eyes, Kaldon accepted the invitation.

Chapter Eleven

Emerging Darkness

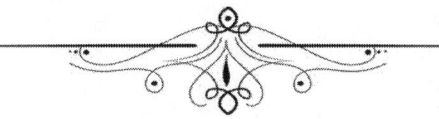

The trees of Rune Forest were left behind as Kaldon, Medric, and Brenton navigated the rocky terrain of the Mountains of D'aal. The immense mountains were regal. Snow covered them like a royal diadem, adorning them in white. Winter had arrived. Travelling through the powdered terrain, their mood was dark, being forced to leave behind their fallen brother, Ont.

Travelling through the mountains, Kaldon encountered heights he'd never fathomed existing. They had already threaded along numerous precarious places, looking down from narrow pathways on death-defying ledges. He questioned whether they would live to speak of more. When fear clawed at his stomach, he focused on the Peak of Lore and the answers he hoped to find there.

Exhaling, he watched his frozen breath float into the air. He remembered the cold nights of living on the streets in Rundle, huddling in his secret sewer, trying to keep warm. As cold as that was, it was nothing like the mountain chill. Every gust of wind felt like a cut, stinging his flesh. The Knights seemed unfazed by the cold. They simply trudged onward.

Since the clash with the Kreel, the days grew colder and harder. So did Brenton. The silent Knight was off scouting their trail for danger. Brenton had grown more distant than he already was. His wounded arm didn't help; it needed tending to. He often kept to himself, out of sight, scouting the trail. They hadn't seen him for hours, which was much longer than usual.

Passing a large crag of rock, Kaldon brushed his fingers over the stone, feeling its cold touch. The mountains were a wondrous place, mystical even. Why did he feel so uneasy in this frozen paradise?

A sudden spasm of anxiety coursed through him. The adrenaline rushing through him was a stark contrast to the winter stillness surrounding him. The anxiety had sporadically spiked within him since they entered the mountains.

He caught Medric watching him again. That hawk-like stare had followed him more frequently since the incident with the Kreel. He wondered if the Knight sensed he was on edge. Medric arrived at the scene soon after the Kreel retreated. Both Knights must have been wondering how he defeated the Kreel. Neither mentioned it. Their dark mood hadn't offered an opportunity for much talk. Kaldon could wait. He wasn't eager to try answering a question he couldn't fully grasp the answer to. He could still hardly believe he had lived through such an ordeal. It was surreal: the tears in his clothing, Brenton's arm, and the loss of Ont were proof of how real it was.

"I'm worried about Brenton," Kaldon said plainly to Medric, hoping to break the Knight's unnerving gaze. "His wound is likely infected. Worse, he looks pale."

Medric was unmoved by Kaldon's remark. "Yes, he looks sickly. He's dying."

"Dying?" Kaldon questioned.

Medric nodded. "Kreel claws aren't only dangerous because they can cut. Their body produces a poison that covers the talons. A Kreel gash is more often than not lethal."

He was taken aback by how matter-of-factly Medric spoke about Brenton's condition. He spoke as if Brenton were already dead, as though he didn't have a chance at surviving. Kaldon looked around, trying to see if he could spot the silent Knight. He could not.

After the attack, the Knights and Kaldon paused to honour Ont despite the risk. They burned his body in reverence for his life and service to Agadin. Then, they hastily forged on, knowing that remaining in the same location would put their lives at further risk. Since Brenton's sword was lost in the battle with the Kreel, he had adopted Ont's.

"Are there herbs that could dull the poison?" Kaldon asked.

Medric shook his head. "No. He needs to see a healer before the poison sets in deeper. There is a town of healers in these mountains, but it is much too far out of our way for us to travel there. Even if we did go, there is no guarantee they could heal him. He would likely be long dead before we reached them."

"There must be something we can do." Kaldon wasn't sure how he felt about Brenton, but the man followed him in the charge against the Kreel, and he wanted him to live.

"All we can do is wait to see if he will live or die," Medric stated.

They trudged onward. Although all three were in a darker mood than usual, Medric seemed more indifferent about Ont's death. Perhaps they were not overly close, or perhaps he was numb to men falling in battle. Kaldon, however, was not unscathed. As he scaled the rocky mount, he couldn't help but think about how still Ont's body laid. He had never seen a man killed before.

Lost in his thoughts, another jolt of anxiety rushed through him. A sense of warning swelled in him. Other than Brenton taking much longer than he usually would, Kaldon couldn't pinpoint what was amiss.

A loud sigh came from the Knight's lips. "Kal, I need to know. How did you best a fully grown Kreel?" Medric finally asked.

A little unnerved, he replied, "I told you I was decent with a sword." The truth was, he didn't fully understand it himself.

Medric stared straight ahead. "That was more than the ability to wield a sword well, Kal. I've seen you spar with Brenton. You are good, but not *that* good. You watched Ont, a fully trained Knight of Agadin, slain before your eyes by the beast you bested. Brenton may not have been killed that night, but he would have been had you not done what you did."

Kaldon knew it was true, but stayed silent. His anxiety was inexplicably growing. "I just did what needed to be done. I followed my intuition."

Medric looked at Kaldon. "Explain that to me. What do you mean by *intuition?*"

Kaldon rubbed his hands together, trying to warm them. "I don't know how to explain it really. I have always used my intuition. It is what helped me to survive my whole life. At times, it is almost as though I can see what happens in my mind before it happens in the natural world. It is like an instinct."

Medric listened.

"When I fought the Kreel, before it came in to strike, I saw flashes of its actions in my mind before they took place. That's how I knew how to respond."

Medric's brows were raised. "No… You understand *foresight?* That's impossible. You haven't had any training."

"Foresight?" Kaldon asked, creasing his forehead.

"It makes sense. That's the only way you could have outmaneuvered the Kreel," Medric murmured aloud in thought.

Kaldon noticed that the more he talked with Medric, the more his uneasiness increased. His uneasiness shifted from a feeling he felt to something like waves mounting inside of him.

"I didn't even kill the Kreel. I got lucky," Kaldon said, trying to sound casual, so as not to betray the anxiety he was feeling.

"Lucky?" Medric scoffed. "I have never heard of a Knight who could best an adult Kreel, let alone accomplish foresight the way you did. Every Knight I know of encountering an adult Kreel has died. Period."

He continued, "I have never met a Knight who could use foresight. Bishops begin learning about the ability in their training; however, I haven't heard of any who could see as clearly as you must have while defeating that Kreel. Foresight is essentially seeing the way a Seer sees visions, but not as elaborate. The lesson is then taking these visions and partnering with them in battle. Through it, you can see an attacker's actions before they happen, allowing you to adjust your moves accordingly. I wouldn't doubt that a Paladin could wield this ability. To say that this is rare would be an understatement. For one to be able to tap into foresight on instinct alone is unheard of."

Kaldon didn't know how to take in the information. He didn't even know if he believed what he could do was as profound as Medric said it was. What Medric said was rare, was common to him. It was a skill he learned in order to survive.

He clenched his fists in discomfort. He had hoped his sense of uneasiness would lift, yet it grew more amplified. He was having trouble thinking clearly due to its intensity.

Medric began to speak quietly. "Locrian was right. You truly are profound. Rare. I suppose this tells me how important you actually are—why I was sent on this mission."

He watched the Knight walking beside him. Something was different in his demeanour. Thoughts rushed at Kaldon. Thoughts like how Medric was unaccounted for during the fight with the Kreel; how casually he took Ont's death and Brenton's sickness.

"Kal, do you remember how I told you Locrian was a great man?"

Kaldon's nerves were blaring in alarm.

The Knight looked at him. "What if I told you there was a greater man of power I answer to?"

In a flash, Medric pulled a dagger from his black cloak and jumped at Kaldon, knocking him to the ground. He struggled on the icy snow with Medric instantly on him, trying to force the blade into his chest.

From on top of Kaldon, the Knight hissed. "The Sovereign of Shadow knows who you *are*, son of Dolan Thain!"

White-hot panic flooded Kaldon as he struggled against the Knight.

Through the blur of snow, Kaldon could see Brenton running towards them. With a blunt strike, the silent Knight kicked Medric's side, forcing him off him. In seconds, Brenton had Medric pinned on the ground.

Kaldon drew his sword and charged at Medric. Before he reached the Knight, Brenton let out a blood-curdling shout as Medric drilled his dagger into his already wounded arm. Brenton collapsed, going limp as his body hit the ground.

With Brenton unconscious, Kaldon was on his own against the Knight. Surprisingly, Medric was already on his feet. Kaldon swung at the Knight. With sword and dagger in hands, Medric deflected. Medric charged at him, swinging both sword and dagger with wrath. He had a look of madness across his face. The Knight was moving at such a quick speed that Kaldon was having trouble keeping up. He didn't know how long he could last. The Knight cut down at him with confounding force. As the Knight's sword hit Kaldon's, it forced him to his knees and sent his sword flying. He heard the metal blade clang against the stone of the mountain.

Kaldon looked up at Medric. A menacing smile spread across the Knight's face. Medric lifted his sword. Kaldon thought about Rundle, about the Templar's Well. He thought about how he would never see the Peak of Lore.

As the sword came raging towards Kaldon, he saw a flash of silver flutter through the air. He watched as an arrow arched past him, hitting Medric in the chest. The arrow penetrated the Knight's black armour, piercing his heart. The Knight fell where he once stood.

Kaldon heaved, trying to grasp the fact that he was still alive. Looking in the direction from where the arrow came, he saw a woman with a bow in hand. Her blond hair blew in the chilled wind. With her chest held high, her silver breastplate was pale in the shaded sun. He had never seen anything like her. What stood out to him the most was the armour mantling her shoulders. The metal extended out like blades, marked in crimson red. It was the same red that now streaked the once white snow, spoiling its purity.

Chapter Twelve

The Carrier

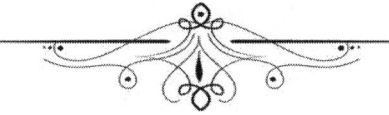

Medric's corpse laid crumpled on the snow. The traitor met the fate he deserved. Brenton was still unconscious, breathing in unsteady breaths. Kaldon, reeling from the chaos, saw the female warrior running towards Brenton.

"What is wrong with the Knight?" she demanded.

Kaldon rushed past Medric's lifeless body to Brenton. "He was cut by an adult Kreel. He is poisoned."

The woman placed her hand on Brenton's forehead. "His fever is rampant." She put her ear against the Knight's chest. "Great Divinity, he is dying."

Kaldon felt a stab of frustration. He hated feeling helpless and wished he knew how to help the Knight. He knew he'd misjudged him. Brenton saved his life, and now he was dying.

"Is there anything you can do to save him?" Kaldon pleaded.

The armoured warrior gave a faint smile. "Of course, there is. Everyone knows Blades are trained in the ability of healing," she said confidently. "I am no *Master Healer,* but I will try my best."

Staring at the woman, he remembered the Knights saying the most gifted of them were chosen to be trained as Blades. He was surprised she ranked as high as she did, being nearly his age. He became transfixed by the scar starting at her left eye and sloping down her face. It looked like a teardrop, adding an even more intimidating element to her.

The Blade laid one hand over Brenton's arm where his wound was. Her other hand hovered over his chest, moving it back and forth as though searching for something.

"I can feel the poison," she stated. "It's moved past the shoulder into his chest. If it reaches his heart, there will be nothing anyone can do to save him."

Kaldon watched the Blade at work. With her hands poised over Brenton, she closed her eyes. To his natural eye, it didn't look like anything was happening. However, in mere seconds, he felt the atmosphere around them thickening somehow. There was power coming through her hands. He suddenly felt lighter, airy, almost. A situation that had been tense and fear-filled only moments ago radiated with inexplicable peace.

She worked tirelessly as the process unfolded. With Brenton lying before him, he knew Medric laid behind him. He was reluctant to look back at the traitor he once thought was a friend. A Knight of Agadin attempting to murder him was all the proof he needed. Anyone he met could have embraced the Shadow. He could now only rely on those who had proven themselves. Brenton earned that trust and, after saving his life, so had the Blade.

"No… no… no…" the Blade whispered in a soothing tone as Brenton's breaths were becoming unsteady. The Blade didn't waver in her process of healing, and the Knight's breathing became consistent again.

Medric's words about foresight came into Kaldon's mind. He thought about the Kreel, about Ont, and yet, one thing was pressing to consume his mind above all else; the Sovereign of Shadow knew who he was.

The traitor's words screamed inside his mind: *"The Sovereign of Shadow knows who you are, son of Dolan Thain!"*

The son of Dolan Thain. Those words were a knife to his heart. The identity he hid his entire life was known to the most dangerous man alive. His stomach knotted.

Brenton moaned lightly. Looking over at the Knight, Kaldon's mouth fell open. The Blade sat over the Knight with sweat beading from her face in dedicated concentration. He watched as the wound on Brenton's arm began to slowly mend. Flesh pulled together like the tightening of fabric as the wound closed. All that was left was a distinct scar. Kaldon was dumbfounded.

Brenton jerked as his eyes snapped open. The Knight inhaled with force and fought to steady his breathing. As the woman removed her hands from his chest, the power Kaldon felt in the atmosphere dissipated in a split second.

Brenton staggered to sit up. "Where is Medric!" he gasped out in coughs, reaching for his sword.

The Blade quickly pressed her hand against the Knight, pushing him back down. "I killed him," she replied, her hazel eyes never leaving the Knight. "You must lie down. Your state is still fragile. You were minutes from death, but I was able to pull you back."

Brenton coughed as he laid back down, giving in to her request.

The Blade continued, "I felt the Kreel's poison in you. I was able to remove some of it; however, it burrowed far too deep into your chest to get it all. You should be strong enough to last until we reach the Peak of Lore. There are healers there who are far more gifted than I am. They can remove the rest."

Brenton nodded, clearly not happy to still have poison in him, but thankful to be alive.

Kaldon spoke up. "Thank you for saving my life and for saving Brenton. What is your name?"

The Blade looked at him with her shoulders back. "I am Anneya Padme, Blade of Agadin."

She looked at Brenton, bowing her head. "It was my honour to protect one who carries a Legacy."

A curious look crept over Brenton's face. "A Legacy? What Legacy?"

"The Seer, Locrian, told me I would find a *Carrier* in the Mountains of D'aal and that I was to save his life. You must be him," she said matter-of-factly.

Brenton laughed, sitting up, clearly sick of lying still already. "There are only a handful of individuals in the world who carry a Legacy. I have never even seen one myself. I wouldn't even know a Legacy if I saw one. Do you honestly think a Knight of Agadin would be a Carrier? Never in history has a Knight of Agadin carried a Legacy. I am no Paladin."

Anneya looked away, confused. Slowly, she looked over to Kaldon. "Then it must be you. You are the Carrier."

Brenton interjected. "Kal? Kal isn't a Carrier either. He's from Rundle, a small city past Rune Forest."

"I don't believe it. Show me what is around your neck," the Blade demanded.

Kaldon pulled the necklace out from his forest green cloak. The bronze compass-like pendant with five points twirled in the wind as it dangled from its metal chain.

Anneya kneeled before Kaldon. "I lay my life down to serve you, Protector of Agadin."

Kaldon stood stunned as the Blade of Agadin bowed before him. Brenton paled more than he already was at the sight of the Legacy. Kaldon knew Brenton had known about the pendant— all of the Knights did. That was how they knew how to find him in Rundle. However, the symbol apparently held more significance than he had known.

Brenton shook his head, breaking his stun. "Blade, you don't need to bow before Kal. He is just an ordinary man."

Brenton then looked at Kaldon, still shaking his head. "Kal, I had no clue that pendant you wore was a Legacy. I don't know where you would have gotten such an artifact."

Kaldon kept quiet.

The Blade rose. "Knight, you say he is just an ordinary man? However, he carries the ancient symbol." Anneya looked to Kaldon. "There are only a few titles that qualify someone as a candidate to carry a Legacy. Tell me, are you a Paladin? A Philosopher?" Her eyes widened in bewilderment. "Are you a *Roek*?!"

Kaldon's mind was racing. "I am none of those things," he said plainly. "I'm simply myself."

The Blade peered through pensive eyes. "Alright, you don't have to tell me if you don't want to yet. Humility is a trait I can rarely relate to. If you are a Paladin, then I might be lucky enough to finally meet someone who could actually teach me a thing or two with a weapon."

Kaldon could tell Brenton was annoyed by the arrogance of her remark.

The Blade continued, "I will go with you back to the Peak of Lore. It isn't too far, yet. You boys will likely need me around if you want to stay alive."

As Brenton turned away, Kaldon could swear he saw the Knight roll his eyes.

After hours of travel, dusk draped itself over the Mountains of D'aal. Medric's body was left where it fell, letting the animals make use of it.

Rock and trees surrounded them. Brenton sat on a stone near their modest fire. They kept the fire small so as not to draw unwanted attention. The rocks they sat on were warmed by the flames, so the three could have respite from the cold. Kaldon could see sickness still lingering in Brenton, though it laid dormant. He hoped Anneya was right that he was strong enough to make it back to the Peak of Lore.

With Anneya off looking for scraps of wood for the fire, he had the chance to say what was weighing on him. "Brenton, I need to apologize. I misjudged you. I haven't trusted you since Rundle. Yet, you were the one who saved my life."

Brenton sternly regarded him before speaking, "Do you know why you trusted Medric above me?"

He didn't expect Brenton's response to come in a question. He took time to gather his thoughts before responding. "I suppose because Medric was friendly. You weren't."

"Flattery is a common tool for manipulation, Kal. Remember that," Brenton said, stretching out his newly healed arm. There was still strain on his face. "I accept your apology. However, there is a prominent lesson for you to learn through all of this."

"What is that?" Kaldon asked.

"Never mistake charisma for character," Brenton stated. "The reason I took this mission was that Medric was coming. He had a smooth tongue, and I never trusted him. I've had my eye on him for several months. When Locrian gave word that three Knights should travel deep into Southeast Agadin, one of the Knights appointed was mysteriously killed. No one knew who committed the crime. Shortly after, Medric volunteered to take the slain Knight's place, heightening my suspicion of him. I convinced another Knight to drop out of the mission and took his place to watch Medric. Thank Divinity, I did."

"I won't argue with that," Kaldon said, shaking his head.

"Why didn't Medric kill me back in Rundle? He had the opportunity. He was the one who shared Locrian's message with me. He could have killed me then," Kaldon mused.

"Ont and I would have known. We were all aware of the message Locrian had for you." Brenton began quoting the word. *"You were created for more than the depths of the sewers. One day, you will soar among the stars. One day, you will be someone great."*

Brenton continued, "He probably expected us to be killed by the Kreel. He would never have expected the Kreel to be beaten. It is also possible that Medric played a role in the Kreel knowing our whereabouts.

Kaldon had never thought of that. It made sense given his proclamation of allegiance to the Sovereign of Shadow.

"You know, Kal, I believe the message Locrian spoke about you. I wouldn't have believed a Kreel could be defeated if I hadn't seen it myself."

Kaldon watched the fire as it licked the still, crisp air.

Brenton continued, "Now I know Lorcian's words were true. Medric confirmed it."

Kaldon looked up to Brenton. "You heard what Medric said?"

Brenton smiled a contemplative smile. "Oh yes, I heard everything. I heard about the gift of foresight you carry. It truly is remarkable. It is remarkable for anyone to see the way you see. That you've had no training is unfathomable. I have spent much of my life studying Dolan Thain's teachings. I never thought I would be sitting across flames from his son."

Kaldon showed no expression as he gazed into the ruby fire, his secret no longer hidden.

"Is that where you got the Legacy? From your father?" Brenton asked.

"It was my father's, yes. It was given to me by my mother when I was a child. I never met Dolan Thain. He left my mother shortly after I was conceived."

Brenton could see the young man's internal turmoil. "Don't worry, Kal, your secret is safe with me. I give you my word that I won't share it with anyone. However, I'm not the one you need to worry about. The Sovereign of Shadow knows who you are."

Kaldon looked up. "Thank you, Brenton. I've hidden my father's identity ever since I turned ten years old. That the Sovereign knows about me is far from comforting. How would he know—or why would he care who I am? I am no one."

"I am no Seer, but I believe there is a role for you to play in what is occurring in Agadin. Locrian obviously thinks so, and apparently so does the Sovereign of Shadow. Just as Medric embraced the Shadow, there are others who have as well. A Knight pledged to the Shadow is known as a *Dark Knight*. The Sovereign has many who have embraced his ways. I wouldn't be surprised if the Sovereign has *Dark Seers* serving him: those who use the gifts of a Seer to advance his Dominion. If he does have such men and women serving him, this could be how he knows who you are."

Before Kaldon could respond, Anneya fumbled into the campsite carrying scraps of wood to feed the fire. Dropping kindling into the flames, the Blade took a seat on one of the heated stones.

"So, what are you two talking about?" she questioned.

"Dark Seers," Brenton said in a cryptic tone.

"Ah, keeping to a lighter topic, I see," she teased.

As Brenton let out a laugh, Kaldon didn't. Instead, his hand moved to the pendant. The Legacy. It felt heavier now, knowing it had far greater significance than simply a connection to his father.

As the Knight and Blade continued their banter back and forth, he started tapping his heel, impatience leaking out of him. His questions needed answers. Mystery provoked him.

Kaldon cut into their conversation. "Anneya, tell me everything you know about the Legacy I carry."

Chapter Thirteen

The Great War

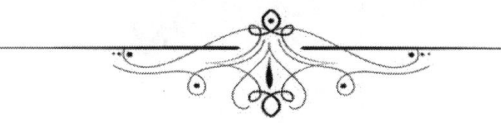

"You know *nothing* about the Legacy you carry?" Anneya asked, disbelief written all over her face.

"Not a thing," he responded, shaking his head.

"So... you *aren't* a Paladin?" she frowned.

Kaldon shook his head again. "Like I said, I simply am who I am."

Brenton was checking the acorns on the fire to see if they were fully cooked. The three were concealed, encircled by trees, protected from sight.

"Okay, then how did you come to own it?" she questioned.

Not knowing how to answer without revealing who he was, Kaldon hesitated. Brenton cut in protectively. "It doesn't matter where he got it. The point is he has it, and we need to understand what it is."

Kaldon smiled at seeing Brenton's spirit returning.

"Don't worry, I'll tell you. No need to get testy with me, *Knight*," the Blade quipped with a grin.

Handing them their dinner, Brenton leaned back, crossing his arms.

Anneya hungrily popped an acorn in her mouth and grimaced. "Ech, this is bland! Where did you learn to cook?"

"I am a Knight, not a chef," Brenton said sardonically.

Kaldon smirked, chewing quietly. Their quips reminded him of how Claude and Betty would banter. It reminded him of home. Except between Brenton and Anneya, it wasn't flirtatious. They were military. Warriors. They likely understood each other in a way that others didn't, creating an ease between them.

"True enough," she said, chewing her dinner.

"My wife is the better cook," he said with a grin.

"You're married?" Kaldon never considered a Knight to have a personal life.

"I am. Her name is Flor. We have three daughters." Fatherly pride beamed from the Knight.

Kaldon was beginning to see that Brenton was not only a Knight, but a man of honour.

"Will I meet them?" Kaldon asked.

"Oh yes," Brenton said, still beaming. "They are at the Peak of Lore awaiting my return. Knowing those little rascals, they probably won't leave you alone."

Kaldon and Anneya laughed. The flames danced, and they ate in comfortable silence, each to their own thoughts. Kaldon pulled out the Legacy, holding it outward in front of him. All three gazed at the ancient symbol as the fire's light shone upon it.

Anneya leaned over to touch the pendant, her fingers gliding over the ancient metal. "Kal, in order for you to understand the Legacy you carry, you need to know about *the Great War*. Being from Rundle, I doubt you would be schooled in it."

"You're right, I never learned of the Great War. How long ago was it?" he asked.

Shaking her head, she went on. "You don't understand. The war is happening now and always has been. Everyone at the Peak of Lore knows of it. There are many in Agadin who do, and many who, like yourself, do not. Some have never been taught of it; some have chosen to deny its existence. The Great War is the battle between light and the darkness threatening it."

"The war between light and darkness…" Kaldon murmured aloud.

"Yes. The war between the *Kingdom of Light* and the *Dominion of Shadow*, to be exact. It is called the *Great War* because it has gone on since the dawn of time."

"The Dominion of Shadow?" Kaldon asked. "The Sovereign's empire?"

"Yes, the Sovereign and his army have much to do with the Great War, currently. Don't misunderstand, the Dominion of Shadow isn't a specific group of people. It isn't an army, nor is it simply the dogmata of the Sovereign. It isn't an *it*. It is a place."

"A place? I have never heard of such a place in Agadin," Kaldon queried, eating his poorly cooked dinner.

"Exactly. Neither the Kingdom of Light nor the Dominion of Shadow are in Agadin, at least not in the way you mean." As she explained, Brenton listened knowingly.

"Let me explain it like this," Anneya elaborated. "Remember when I was healing Brenton? Did you feel anything while it was taking place?"

"Yes, I've never felt anything like it before. It was like a distinct sense of peace, amplified," Kaldon said, stumbling to put words to the experience.

She nodded knowingly. "Well, what you were feeling wasn't simply power. You were feeling a *place* invading this realm. You were feeling the Kingdom of Light. It is a kingdom not of Agadin. What you were feeling and experiencing is eternity."

Kaldon blinked, bewildered. "You were bringing the place of eternity, the Kingdom of Light, into Brenton?"

"That's a simple way to put it, yes. The Kingdom of Light is where *Divinity* dwells—he who created all things. The creator of all things…" The reverence in her voice was evident as Kaldon remembered stories his mother had told him about Divinity: the one who breathed everything into existence.

She continued, "When Divinity created mankind, he fashioned us with a link to the Kingdom of Light. Our inherent link is how we can call it forth. When you saw Brenton healed and felt power, you were feeling the essence of the Kingdom of Light. You were feeling the *culture* of a place where chaos and pain don't exist. This is why you felt such peace. The force of the Kingdom of Light is so powerful that it healed Brenton's sickness and pain. The realm of eternity was invading our own. That kingdom was, in essence, being established in Agadin."

Seeing his confusion, she comforted him. "It must be difficult to wrap your head around. Those of us from the Peak of Lore have the concept ingrained into us from childhood. You will come to understand in time."

Anneya waved her hand to the snow-covered mountains surrounding them. "Look around, these mountains look like paradise. Yet, they pale in comparison to the Kingdom of Light, to what eternity is. If the Mountains of D'aal were a drop of water, the Kingdom of Light is an ocean. If these mountains were a flicker of flame, the Kingdom is the sun. There is no sickness or disease there. There is no anxiety, sorrow, or depression. It is an abode of perfection—flawless."

Marveling at the thought of such a wondrous place, Kaldon was silent. Even Brenton looked impressed as the Blade described the Kingdom of Light.

"So, what of the Legacy then?" Brenton cut in.

"I will get there, Knight." Sounding annoyed, she looked at Brenton. "Before Kal can understand the Legacy, he needs to understand the Dominion of Shadow as well."

She continued, "Just as the Kingdom of Light is a place, so is the Dominion of Shadow. They are exact opposites. Where the Kingdom of Light is an ecosystem of perfection and peace, the Dominion of Shadow is one of destruction and mayhem. This is what the Sovereign wants to bring to Agadin. He wants it to mirror the Dominion of Shadow. The Dominion is where the Kreel and Nahmen were summoned from by the Sovereign. They are not creatures natural to this realm, which is why we have only seen them in recent years. They were summoned from the spiritual land of death and decay."

"How did he summon Kreel and Nahmen from the Dominion of Shadow?" Kaldon asked, astonished.

"No one knows," Anneya shrugged her shoulders. "We didn't know such a thing was possible. The Sovereign has powers we don't yet understand."

Kaldon sat back in disbelief. "How do people access the Kingdom of Light and the Dominion of Shadow?"

"There are many ways to access the Kingdom of Light, such as healing, as you witnessed. We still do not know all of the ways to access the Kingdom. Seers and those with gifts of foresight can access the Kingdom as well. They do so by seeing into the River of Time through eternity's perspective; as they do, they are seeing into the Kingdom of Light. As far as how people access the Dominion, only those who have embraced the Shadow know."

Kaldon leaned back. He had a hard time wrapping his head around Agadin, let alone eternity. This would take time to sink in.

Brenton chimed in. "Many of us from the Peak of Lore have dedicated our lives to seeing the Kingdom of Light established here in Agadin, bringing peace to the land. We believe this was Divinity's original plan, for us to call forth this perfection. Sadly, fiends like the Sovereign and the fools who follow him want the exact opposite. The Sovereign wants to dominate people and become the grand ruler. He aims to make Agadin a land of death and darkness. There are others who believe this Great War is simply folklore. They believe the events taking place around them have no greater meaning. We know better. There is a war taking place, and this war is more than the armies battling; it is a spiritual battle. It is a war between Light and Shadow: between good and evil."

Anneya looked at Kaldon's Legacy. "I have never met anyone who carries a Legacy, other than Locrian." She looked into Kaldon's emerald eyes. "You may be called as a *bringer of the Light*."

Kaldon sat wide-eyed and still. Silence lingered for a time, until Brenton spoke. "Anneya, can you speak to us about the Legacy now?"

She nodded, shifting on her heated stone. "It is said that Divinity appointed some as Protectors of Agadin. He called a select few to wage warfare for the Kingdom of Light in a history-altering way. The Legacy is worn by these Protectors. It is a symbol confirming they are truly chosen."

The Blade pointed to the Legacy hanging from Kaldon's neck. "The inner circle is symbolic of the Kingdom of Light," Anneya explained. "The five radiating points coming out symbolize five different types of Protectors who Divinity has called and chosen."

Brenton's brows were raised. "Divinity has appointed *five*? I could likely guess a few, but five?"

"Yes, five," she confirmed. "One of the points symbolizes a Paladin; those who have mastered the physical body. The second is for the Seers, those who partner with time. The third is for those who stretch beyond the limits of the mind, *Philosophers*. Those three are best known to most; however, there are two more Protectors, those who have died out long ago."

"What are they?" Kaldon asked in anticipation.

In the cold of night, Anneya leaned closer to the fire. "The final two Protectors are the *Shan-Rafa* and the *Roek*."

"I have never heard of such titles," Brenton said in thought.

"Few have," she said, warming her hands by the flames.

"Tell me about them," Kaldon persisted, putting aside his empty plate.

"The Shan-Rafa are expert healers," Anneya said.

"Like how you healed Brenton?" Kaldon questioned.

"Great Divinity, no," she laughed lightly. "A true Shan-Rafa hasn't been proven for nearly two thousand years. The Shan-Rafa were so gifted in healing that it is said they could call life back to the dead."

"They could raise the dead?" Kaldon asked, leaning closer.

"Legend says so, yes. A Shan-Rafa couldn't only call the Kingdom of Light to impact Agadin, but they could also call a spirit back into its body, giving it life again. They were also so proficient in healing that they were known to be practically indestructible."

"How is that possible?" Brenton voiced.

Anneya elaborated. "A true Shan-Rafa could heal so quickly that if a sword cut through, they could heal themselves as quickly as they were cut. Many Shan-Rafas were gifted fighters as well. In many ways, considering their ability to heal themselves so quickly, they could be a fair match against even a Paladin."

Brenton was taken aback. To believe one could or would want to stand against a Paladin was incomprehensible to him.

"And the Roek?" Kaldon asked.

"Like the Shan-Rafa, the Roek died off thousands of years ago. A Roek can do what is called *Commanding Creation*. It is said that Divinity gave mankind authority over creation. A Roek can command the elements of Agadin. They were often masters of commanding one element, with a basic knowledge of the other three. A Roek would dedicate their entire life to knowing every facet of that element. While a Paladin may wield a sword as their weapon, a Roek would wield fire, water, wind, or earth."

Kaldon thought back to the stories his mother told him, the ones he thought were fairy tales. "Can someone learn to be one of these five Protectors?" he asked.

"No," Anneya answered. "This is why there hasn't been a true Shan-Rafa or Roek for thousands of years. You are either born as one of the five Protectors or you are not. That said, you can be born with the calling, yet completely miss it if you do not train accordingly. A Protector may be born, but they also need to be shaped."

She continued, "Appointing these five Protectors was Divinity's plan to keep Agadin balanced, so that the Kingdom of Light would reign throughout Agadin. Now, with two of the five missing, there are distinct weak spots, giving an opening to the Dominion of Shadow. The land is not balanced. Divinity is looking for those who will bring balance again."

Brenton cut in. "That makes sense. On top of that, this means those embracing the Shadow have perverted Divinity's original intention with these Protectors. Now there are Dark Seers, Dark Philosophers, Nahmen, Kreel, and who knows what else."

"That is true," Anneya confirmed.

At that, Brenton stood. "Thank you for sharing with us, Blade. I have never heard the Kingdom of Light explained in such a way, and I need to let your teaching on the Legacy sink in. This is enough for one Knight to sit on for an evening."

Anneya nodded. "Very well, Knight Brenton."

He disappeared into his personal tent.

Kaldon and Anneya sat alone before the thinning fire. The cold was beginning to blanket them, and night was rolling over the skies. As badly as Kaldon wanted to go to bed after such an ordeal of a day, he knew he couldn't. There was still one question that needed an answer. It had nothing to do with the Great War, the Sovereign of Shadow, or the Legacy. The question was about the Blade, the lone warrior who saved his and Brenton's lives. Kaldon knew the warrior was hiding something from them.

Chapter Fourteen

Heat Amidst the Cold

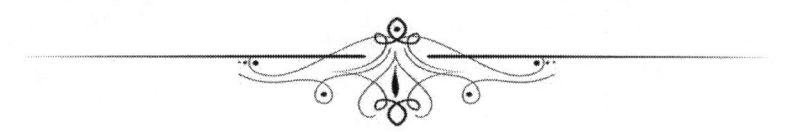

The fire settled, burning more modestly than before. Kaldon felt the heat from the stone beneath him beginning to cool. He felt more uncomfortable being alone with Anneya than he would have preferred. Not only was he not used to being around people of such importance, but he hadn't grown up around many women.

He pushed through his timidity. "Thank you for sharing with me. I didn't grow up learning such things."

"I'm glad I could help you understand what is happening in Agadin," the Blade said, staring into the fire.

"Agadin is more of a grim place than I ever would have imagined," he said, processing aloud.

She sighed. "Tragically, most people choose not to believe it even when they are told."

Since meeting the Blade, something seemed out of place to him. He trusted her. She saved his life, yet there was a question burning in him.

"Anneya, where did you come from?" Kaldon asked.

The Blade broke eye contact with the flames. "I already told you, I am from the Peak of Lore. Before that, from a small town near the Lore, before those at the training facility took me in."

"I know you are from the Peak of Lore, but that's not where you came from before coming here," he pointed out. He saw by how the Blade carried herself that she was self-assured. He also sensed she was tired, bearing more of a deep weariness than a physical drain.

He continued, "The Knight's told me that after Locrian gave word for them to head for the cities in Southeast Agadin, that he himself was leaving on a mission—a dangerous mission. If he told you to come to the Mountains of D'aal, it must have been while he was on this mission."

Looking away, her hazel eyes swelled with tears, which then tumbled down her flushed cheeks. Her tears matched her white scar.

"I'm sorry," he said. "Did I say something I shouldn't have?" He was unnerved seeing how quickly her tough exterior dissolved.

"No… no, you didn't," she said quietly. "It's true that he was on a dangerous mission. It was a rescue mission."

"You were helping him rescue someone?" Kaldon asked.

"It was me he was rescuing," she said, her voice barely above a whisper. The flickering fire waned to heated embers before she began again. "Locrian broke me out of one of the most guarded prisons in all of Agadin, Gallaway Morgue. I was imprisoned for fighting against the Dominion of Shadow," Anneya said solemnly as she gently cried. Kaldon could tell the Blade wasn't comfortable letting people see her in a state of vulnerability.

"How long were you there for?" he gently asked.

"For just over six months... It is worse than prison. The torture..." Anneya burst out sobbing, burying her face in her hands.

"I'm so sorry," Kaldon said, placing a hand gently on her shoulder to comfort her. "You are safe now." The words felt awkward coming from his mouth, considering she was a Blade, a more than formidable warrior. Still, he felt she needed to hear it.

"Thank you," Anneya laughed gently, wiping away her tears. "It feels good to talk about it. You are the first I have shared with."

Kaldon smiled. "Can I ask you something else?"

Anneya nodded and sniffled.

"Did you get your scar from Gallaway Morgue?"

She paused before answering, knowing he was referring to her teardrop scar. "No, this was from my childhood. My adopted father had a staggering temper."

"I'm sorry..." he said. "Can you heal it, like you healed Brenton?"

"No," she answered, shaking her head. "Healers say scars cannot be healed. They say scars remain to remind us of what we've overcome."

"I like that," he said, nodding.

"I do too. This scar is also a reminder of how I was a victim. Those memories I don't need reminding of," she confessed.

He looked up at her. "In that case, if I knew how to, I would heal it for you."

She smiled. "Some believe that Shan-Rafa could heal scars. Are you a Shan-Rafa, Kal?"

"I don't think so, but you never know. I do carry a Legacy after all," he teased, trying to lift her spirits.

She covered her mouth, stifling a laugh. He was happy to see her face light up.

Before either of them had the chance to speak, a loud and sudden *thud* disrupted the stillness surrounding them. The impact quaked the terrain, causing the stones to tremble.

Instantly alert, they looked around. *Was it another Kreel?* Kaldon wondered, questions firing in his mind. *Could he best another one? Could even a Blade win against a Kreel?*

Through an array of pine trees where the sound came from, a faint glow glimmered. Without a word, Kaldon stood, pushing past his caution. It may have been a Kreel; however, his instincts told him it was not. As the light shone between snow-covered trunks and branches, the allure of mystery pulled at him.

Anneya put a hand on his arm. "Kal, don't. I may be a Blade, but what if it's something too dangerous?"

Considering how skilled a fighter she was, her level of caution seemed uncharacteristic. She was well aware that creatures existed in Agadin that she could not match.

"Come with me," he said, his gaze stuck to the light.

She looked uncertain.

"It can't be a Kreel, look at the light." Kaldon pointed toward the shining gleam. "Kreel are more discreet. Anneya, I can't explain it, but I think we need to leave now and see what the source of that light is. Should we wake Brenton?"

She shook her head. "No, his rest is crucial right now. It will help him to fight off the poison."

Kaldon watched the light glimmer, transfixed by its glow.

Anneya sighed. "Alright, you take the lead then."

"Done," Kaldon responded.

As they approached the pine trees, she watched him to see if he would turn back. He did not. He needed to see what the light was coming from. As they advanced, the air began to thicken. Heat began manifesting upon their cold skin.

He brushed past the branches of pine with Anneya following. Nearing closer to the source, he turned back. Placing his finger over his lips, he cautioned her to be silent. The deeper the two wove into the cluster of trees, the more the heat began to swell. Kaldon could not remember the last time he felt so warm. The surrounding heat deadened winter's bite.

Past the initial barrier of trees, they now stood with a barren patch of mountain rock before them, surrounded by a circle of pine trees. In the middle of the rock stood a magnificent creature, emanating heat.

Kaldon squinted in curiosity, and Anneya blinked away tears. Before them was no ordinary bird. It stood the height of a man and a half, with a rounded face and piercing golden eyes like metal medallions of great worth. Its sizeable feathers were magnified by the intricate patterns adorning them. Its mighty talons gripped the cleft of rock beneath it. It was cloaked from head to toe in fiery flames. Reds, yellows, and oranges rolled over the graceful creature as it watched Kaldon and Anneya. It was a bird of fire.

Anneya laughed out loud in disbelief. "Look, Kal," she said, pointing, trying to remain as quiet as possible so as not to frighten the bird.

Kaldon was too stunned to respond. With glistening eyes, he recalled the fire he had seen in the sky as a young boy. He remembered peering through the sewer hole, watching the flames soaring through the skies of Agadin. The fire captivated him deeply then, just as it now did. He knew in his heart these were the same flames that gave him strength as a young boy.

As fire danced upon its intricate feathers, the bird stood still. Strangely, the fire didn't make the bird look menacing. It was truly a creature of majesty, illuminated by divine fire.

"I never knew such beauty existed." The words escaped Kaldon's mouth as he stood in awe.

Anneya moved her hands from covering her mouth. "In Agadin, there aren't only creatures that bring death, such as Kreel. There are those that inspire hope."

She continued, "You have no idea how rare these birds are. This is an ancient bird. When I was a young girl, I heard of an older man at the Peak of Lore who claimed to have glimpsed one of these from a distance. Most people didn't believe him. Other than him, I have never heard of anyone who has seen one. It is said that these are birds sent by Divinity from the Kingdom of Light. They are birds from eternity. It is believed their purpose is to watch over those who Divinity has chosen to protect Agadin."

Kaldon mustered words past his astonishment. "What are they called?"

Anneya let silence briefly linger as she looked at the majestic creature. She allowed herself to take in the moment as the heat from the bird stroked her delicate skin.

A smile stretched upon her warmed face as she said, "This legendary bird is called an *Owyl of Light*."

Chapter Fifteen

Order Within Chaos

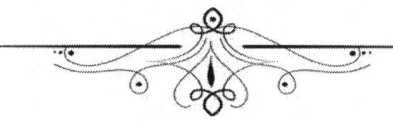

"Finally, it is finished." Tymas Droll sighed, gently placing his feathered pen on the wooden desk.

The book had taken a long time to write. It wasn't something he could rush through, for this was no ordinary book. This would establish the rules for the Dominion of Shadow in Agadin. It was the law his people would live by. Those in Gorath, the Sovereign's hometown, already understood the directives. Now it was time for all of Agadin to live by them as well.

As Sovereign of Shadow, Tymas knew ruling people was more than giving speeches. You needed to be an administrator. People need more than a face identifying a movement. They need order and to be told what to believe. Momentum could happen by sheer force, but order took thought and intentionality. Closing the book, he read the title, *The Law of Shadow.*

A smile spread across his smooth face. He knew in that moment, more than ever, he truly was chosen to lead the Dominion of Shadow in Agadin.

Leaning back in his chair, he thought back to how the Law of Shadow came to him. Furion had begun to visit him as a child. She would come to him in the world of dreams while he slept. Then, twelve years ago, she came with a new purpose. In a dream, she came with instructions for him to pen the Law of Shadow. Many times, during years that followed, she educated him in the ways of the Shadow and told him what to write. There was likely none in all of Agadin who understood the Dominion as he did; the spiritual land of death and power. Comprehending such a place was a lost art.

Just as the Kingdom of Light was governed by Divinity, the Dominion of Shadow was governed by the *Entity* known as Furion. That it was she, herself, who chose Tymas filled him with pride. He now understood her quite intimately. He was her pupil. He had been personally taught by the supreme ruler of the Dominion of Shadow. He let out a subtle laugh at the very thought.

Standing, he stretched the stiffness from his muscles. His beige robe was adorned in sandy trim with markings written on it. The script was Old Agadin. He was quite savvy in the tongue, since he'd spent nearly his entire life studying it. Furion directed him to learn the language in order to feast upon the knowledge of men and women living centuries and millenniums before him. He could read ancient books written by Dark Seers and Philosophers of old. He could consume the mysteries they revealed.

Walking around his princely office, the weight of his curls bouncing with each step made him smile. His hair had always been a crown to him. He thought it regal. Once a golden yellow, it was now streaked with silvers and whites. A changing crown, he mused. Fitting for what was to come. He lifted his hand to stroke his smooth chin. Never one for facial hair, he was fastidious about removing even the slightest of stubble. In his mid-forties, a deceiving look of purity glowed on his face. It was childlike, almost.

His office consisted of many rooms, all connected by arched corridors shaped by fine craftsmanship. Walking through his workspace, his eyes took note of sections of books and maps sprawled out in varying corners. He knew his office didn't look orderly. It was messy—chaotic, even. Somehow, within the chaos was a system only he understood. It was the system of domination Furion taught him. He knew why every book was placed where it was, as well as why each was opened to its particular pages. It had taken him years to accumulate all of these books. He was a student of history, possessing books thousands of years old written by Philosophers.

He knew that at any point in history, when kings or queens made decisions and uttered commands, there were always Philosophers observing and deciphering their actions. Within these books were philosophies revealing why some kingdoms rose and others fell. These books held the keys to why some rulers succeeded and others failed. The history in these books gave him wisdom unknown by ordinary men.

He ran his fingers over maps hanging on his walls. These were maps of all of Agadin; blueprints of different regions and cities, names of generals, kings and queens, and the names of people he would one day rule. He slowly made his way to the window, looking out upon the rough terrain of Gorath.

From the high tower, his eyes settled on a worker chipping away at rock in the distance. Tymas' tower stood high above the vast city his dominion reigned from. The city itself was impressive, boasting significant works of architecture. That worker, looking the size of an insect from his vantage point, was one of *his* people. One of *his* children. This was one of the many. Tymas considered them privileged to live under his reign. Now that his law was complete, this man would have guidance in a greater way of life, Tymas thought.

The day was crisp and clear, his eyes wandering to distant lands. Although too far away to perceive, he looked in the direction of the Mountains of D'aal. Tymas shook his head in frustration as he thought of his Dark Knight, Medric. He had never liked the Knight; however, his skills in manipulation and deceit were valuable. He now knew he had overestimated Medric's ability. One of his Dark Seers foresaw Medric's failure to kill the son of Dolan Thain in a vision. His Dark Seers told the Sovereign about the young man—about his potential. The son of Dolan Thain had no clue what he could one day become. Apparently, he was called as a rare type of Protector of Agadin. That meant that he could become an obstacle to the Sovereign. Kal Wendal needed to be eliminated.

Medric's impotence meant he would need to deal with the annoyance himself.

His eyes roamed the expanse before him as a sly grin crept across his soft face. He would extend his reign to D'aal and beyond to the Southeast region of Agadin. He needed more people to rule. Tymas knew they would resist him at first, just as they all did. He would gain control of them. They would be made to realize they needed him. He was, after all, the Sovereign of Shadow.

His methods would look chaotic. Chaos brought about fear, which was a most expedient tool in overcoming resistance. Ruthlessness was a necessary quality to gain control, he thought. True, his Kreel were hardly pleasant creatures, and his Nahmen could be considered worse. The system leading to his absolute reign would be birthed from chaos and by these creatures exacting it. Furion had trained him well. Many cities throughout Agadin had already fallen under his hand and will. While many saw him as merciless, he knew them ignorant.

Tymas thought of how he didn't only need to rule the Mountains of D'aal. There was something hidden within the mountains that he needed to acquire, something much more valuable than a city or followers. Tymas thought back to years prior when Furion came to him in a specific dream. Furion spoke to him about how he needed to find ancient artifacts from throughout Agadin.

He needed to collect bones.

Tymas remembered the first of many bones he found several years ago, just outside Gorath within a forest's cave. At first glance, Tymas was taken aback by its sheer size. It had taken nearly sixty men to carry the bone back to his tower. At first glance, he could hardly imagine what type of beast such a bone could belong to. Such a beast could make the bravest of men tremble. A creature of this size would intimidate even the Kreel into submission. From throughout Agadin, he had already accumulated all of the bones as Furion instructed, all except one. It had taken him years to do so, and many lives had been lost in this pursuit. Some were his men, others were not. Tymas knew these lost lives were a small price to pay. Attaining these artifacts was essential to his plan. The bone, resting somewhere within the Mountains of D'aal, was the last he needed.

In due time, the Sovereign thought. Tymas' train of thought was abruptly cut short by a knock at his door.

"Come in," Tymas Droll said with an inviting voice.

"Sovereign, you are taking in the scenery of Agadin, I see," Geran said while standing at the door.

Geran's intimidating form nearly blocked the entire doorway. The man was made up of solid muscle, like a mountain in the flesh. Dark armour covered him from top to bottom—armour as dark as shadow. Geran had a shaved head and a neatly cropped beard. The man was the Sovereign of Shadow's right-hand man; Tymas' oldest friend. While Tymas led the Dominion with strategy, Geran furthered the Dominion through physical brutality. Geran led and commanded the Dominion of Shadow's army. He was the General of the movement.

Tymas looked up at the General with excitement in his eyes. "Geran, my friend, my law is complete."

Geran's voice erupted in a gruff laugh. "It is finally finished?!"

Tymas adamantly nodded his head.

"We mustn't waste time then," Geran said. "I have one hundred trained scribes ready to duplicate what you have written. Can you imagine what will happen once your law is distributed? Once this is in place, we can begin utilizing the army to a much greater measure. Agadin will be in your hand, Sovereign."

Tymas was well prepared for the distribution of the law. He had spent the last three years training hand-chosen men and women under his dark doctrines and philosophies. Furion taught the Sovereign; the Sovereign taught his teachers. These teachers were stationed in the cities he had already occupied, readied to teach those who lived there. Ruling people wasn't only about gaining land or making kings bow before you. In order to make your reign last with longevity, you needed to bend people's minds to your way of thinking. In this way, Tymas would duplicate his vision within every heart under his Dominion. He could feel his heartbeat quickening even at the thought of it.

"Yes, get the scribes to work immediately," Tymas said pensively. "I would like the law to be carried to our overseers of cities within the next several days."

"The scribes will be commanded within the hour, Sovereign," Geran replied militantly.

"You know Geran, I have been thinking," Tymas said, turning back the window. "It is not enough to simply distribute my law and have our teachers instruct the people; we also need some form of testing. After all, as their ruler, I am, in essence, their father. They should not only know my law, they should respect and fear it."

Geran's eyebrows raised. "Yes, Sovereign. What testing did you have in mind?"

"As my word and teachings are law, then my people should not only read it, they must memorize it, word for word. My law is not open to interpretation. I should think three months would be enough time for my people to have this book memorized, don't you, Geran?"

"You are very gracious, Sovereign, you are very kind to give them so much time. What of those who fail to have your law memorized by the time of their testing?"

Tymas turned back to face his friend. "They will need to be made examples of, won't they? It is only fair. After all, not being willing to memorize my law would be to reject my teachings. We can't have that form of treason about. Don't you agree, Geran?"

"You are very right, Sovereign," Geran said with finality. "My soldiers stationed in each city are more than capable of following through with punishment."

"Yes, they are, old friend. You have trained them well. Swift public deaths should suffice. Leave the bodies where they fall. This will teach my people the importance of my teachings."

"Your willingness to take time to teach those you lead is moving, Sovereign," Geran said sincerely.

"Oh, I must take time, Geran. Furion once taught me a prominent lesson: leading is not only about showing the way, but about revealing the consequences of veering off course. This is why my job as Sovereign of Shadow is not only to guide my people, but to discipline them."

Chapter Sixteen

The Peak of Lore

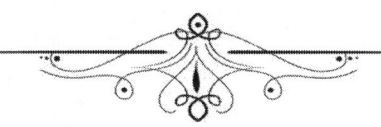

Mounds of rocky stone enveloped them. Kaldon could hardly believe they were in the presence of the Peak of Lore. From a distance, it was so well disguised that it looked like simply another mountain standing amongst its stony peers. Yet, the stern slate exterior was just a ruse. Anneya and Brenton told him that the inside of the mountain would be another thing entirely. There were good reasons for the camouflage. It was not only for the security of those living there, but also it was the place where Knights were trained and Blades were forged.

It wasn't until they came closer that Kaldon saw the difference between the Peak of Lore and the other mountains. His eyes widened. His breath quickened as he took it in.

A walkway of huge flat stones led up to a grand entrance magnificently encased by symbols engraved deeply into the mountain stone. Its mouth stood four times taller than that of a fully grown man. Towering trees stood erect like watchmen on each side of the door, masking its location. Windows and doors were carved into the mountain, presumably indicating the dwellings of its occupants. Down one side was a waterfall frozen in mid-fall. Below was a frozen pond, shimmering like a snow-dusted diamond. From Kaldon's view, looking over a cliff, all he could see was an ocean of mountains surrounding the legendary hidden castle.

Walking towards the door, high-pitched giggles suddenly erupted from the entrance. In a burst, three young girls tumbled out running at full speed towards them. Their enthusiasm was palpable. Kaldon figured them to all be less than eight years of age.

"Papa! Papa!" the girls squealed as brown curls bounced with each leap.

Kaldon looked at Brenton. A Knight as tough as they came had tears filling his weary eyes. The two older looking girls bolted into Brenton's arms. He grunted at the impact, letting out a hard laugh.

"My girls!" he shouted, kissing each on the forehead. The smallest of the three, looking little more than two years old, came fumbling up behind her sisters. Brenton picked her up in a bear hug. The young girl laughed and writhed as he kissed her face.

"Girls, it is so good to see you," Brenton said, lost in their excited laughs.

The Knight pointed to Kaldon and Anneya. "I have some friends I would like you to meet."

"Girls, this is Kal and Anneya—good friends of your Papa." Kaldon noticed immediately that the two oldest girls kept their distance from Anneya. Her crimson shoulder blades were a symbol of who she was. These small girls clearly knew what they meant. In contrast, with Kaldon, the two eldest watched him bashfully, giggling and whispering to each other.

Brenton leaned in. "Seems the girls might have a bit of a crush on you, Kal."

Kaldon laughed, waving to the two blushing girls.

"Kal and Anneya..." Brenton placed his hand on his oldest daughter's head. "This is Hayley, she is seven." Moving his hand to his second oldest, he said, "This is Haddy, born to us four years ago." Still in his arms, he held out his youngest daughter. "And this is Honey, who just passed two." Honey smiled and let out a squeal, causing everyone to spill over in laughter.

"Girls, where's your mother?" Brenton asked in anticipation. Hayley and Haddy pointed back to the entrance of the Peak of Lore. The billowing brown curls left no question as to who the woman standing there was. In a light and simple, yet elegant dress, Flor was watching them. Her arms were folded, a yearning smile lit up her face.

Without a word, Brenton handed Honey to Anneya and ran to his wife. Sweeping her into his arms, his kiss wasn't discreet in showing his passion for his wife. Hayley and Haddy covered their mouths, giggling at the sight of their father and mother in an embrace. Kaldon was overjoyed, knowing that Brenton deserved the happiness he clearly found in his family.

As the couple reacquainted themselves, Kaldon looked back at Anneya, who had Honey held out at a distance. He furrowed his brow. "Why are you holding her like that?"

"How else am I supposed to hold her? I've never held a toddler until now," she said, extending her arms out.

"She won't break. Hold her closer to your chest," Kaldon laughed. Anneya regarded the wide eyes looking back at her. Honey wiggled excitedly, her big brown eyes beaming with a drooling smile.

"Alight, you can come a bit closer." Anneya smiled back, cautiously pulling Honey in for a hug. "You have just accomplished quite the feat, little one. You are so cute that you have softened the heart of a Blade." Honey squealed out a laugh. Anneya and Kaldon laughed with her.

As Brenton and Flor finished greeting one another, they walked toward the others, their arms tightly around one another. "Thank you for keeping Brenton company," Flor said softly. Gratitude was evident in her tone.

A startled look came over her face. "Brenton? Where are Ont and Medric?"

The three were silent, looks passing amongst them. Brenton spoke up. "Flor, Ont was felled by a Kreel. As for Medric, we were right: he had embraced the Shadow."

Flor covered her mouth in shock, knowing it could have easily been her husband who hadn't returned. "Thank Divinity, you've come back to us."

"Anneya killed him. She saved our lives," Brenton said, looking at the Blade.

Flor gave Anneya a nod, followed by a grateful smile.

The Blade spoke up. "We left the traitor's body where it lay. He will neither be mourned nor remembered, except as a cautionary tale." The grim and authoritative tone of the Blade stood in contrast to her body swaying the child she was still holding.

"We are just glad you're home, my love," Flor said reaching up to touch his hair, brushing it to the side. At that, Brenton's face began to hollow.

"Brenton?" Flor voiced in concern.

Slouching with a sudden grunt, the Knight staggered to his knees and began to pale. Hayley and Haddy rushed around their father in concern.

"Papa?!" Hayley began to panic.

Brenton slid to the ground, rasping coughs coming from him.

"Great Divinity, get him to a healer. The poison needs out of him," Kaldon barked as he hoisted Brenton back up to his feet.

"Poison?!" Flor shouted in shock.

"We'll explain later." Anneya abruptly handed Honey to Flor. She and Kaldon grabbed Brenton under the arms, quickly ushering him through the entrance while Flor briskly followed with the children in tow.

Passing under the stone arch of the entrance door, Kaldon was awestruck. While the outside consisted of only stern stone, the inside was another thing entirely. It was a breathtaking masterpiece. The grand room boasted pillars standing hundreds of feet high. Every inch of where his eyes met, the walls were seemingly engraved by master sculptors. Grand staircases led up to higher places within the mountain. The colossal castle must have risen thousands of feet upwards in height. A multitude of people scurried about. Kaldon could hear the buzzing hum of men, women, and children going about their day while others sat at tables conversing.

At the sight of a wounded Knight, people scurried from every direction to help while others bolted deeper into the mountain to find healers.

Before long, they were in a smaller side-room with a bed to lay the Knight down on. The room was quaint and clean. By way of the markings of excellence, it was just as impressive as the great hall. Brenton laid with staggered breaths scratching out of him. Flor kissed his hand before taking the girls outside to comfort them. It pained her to leave her husband's side.

Anneya leaned over, whispering to Kaldon. "Master Healers come to these rooms to do more significant healings. They are the highest-ranking healers in Agadin, below Shan-Rafas."

At the moment, Kaldon wasn't interested in being schooled in healing; he just didn't want Brenton's family to be without a husband and father. He wanted the man to live.

Suddenly, the door was jerked open by a petite woman further along in years. She had an aura of intensity surrounding her. She stepped in without a word, a flowing robe of maroons and midnight blues adding to her mystery. She approached the Knight.

"Kal, brace yourself," Anneya whispered.

Kaldon scratched his itching beard, realizing for the first time how long it had grown since Rundle. "For what?"

"How Master Healers heal is far more intense than someone with a simple gift of healing like myself. They channel more of the Kingdom of Light for healing than others do. It can be quite overwhelming for some. She will need to release the exact amount of eternity into Brenton. Too little, and the poison will remain. Too much, and the shock of experiencing the force of eternity so abruptly may stop his heart. It could kill him," she said with certainty.

"I haven't trained my entire life to work around loud mouths," the older woman snapped. "This is serious. If you can't quiet yourselves, leave."

They immediately went silent. Kaldon mused to himself. Knowing Anneya, the silence would likely be short lived.

The old woman pulled out a weathered hand from beneath her robe. The hand began to glow a sun-like gold. Kaldon was transfixed by it, knowing he was seeing a glimpse of the Kingdom of Light. The woman ran her hand over Brenton, much like how Anneya did to heal him on their way to the Peak of Lore. However, while Anneya fumbled to find the poison, the Master Healer moved with refined certainty.

Leaning towards Kaldon, Anneya broke her silence as he'd known she would. She whispered faintly so the woman would not hear. "She is about to release the Kingdom of Light into Brenton."

Kaldon was excited to feel that tangible peace once again. With a sudden jolt, Brenton's body illuminated as the force of eternity was released into him, dethroning the poison from its reign.

Stepping back from the sheer power flooding the room, Kaldon felt the same peace as when Anneya brought healing to Brenton; however, this was wildly amplified. Eternity spilled out into the small-side room. Light lit up the atmosphere.

The sensation consumed Kaldon, pulling him in. He quickly found himself on hands and knees, overcome by illuminated glory. The weight of the sensation pushed him down, face flat upon the stone floor. Everything disappeared around him; everything but the sensation of the Kingdom of Light.

Closing his eyes, consumed, he soaked in ecstatic bliss.

Kaldon's eyes slowly opened. He jerked, groggily taking in what was going on around him. Comforters draped over him as he shifted in the large bed. The first thing he saw was Hayley and Haddy watching him. The two girls covered their mouths, snickering as he cluelessly looked around, not knowing how he ended up in another room entirely.

Brenton stepped in. "You girls leave Kal alone. Let him wake up."

"Awe, but Papa, we want to play with him," Haddy piped up, her tiny fists popping up on her hips.

"Yeah, well, you can see him later," Brenton said, ushering them out of the room.

"What is going on here? How did I end up in this bed?" Kaldon said almost in a panic.

Brenton smiled. "While the Master Healer was removing the poison from me, you came under the power of the Kingdom of Light."

"I've felt the Kingdom before when Anneya healed you," Kaldon protested.

"True." Brenton nodded. "However, Anneya doesn't know, as a Master Healer does, how to channel as much of eternity into this realm. You haven't grown up experiencing the Kingdom of Light. You need to acclimatize to it."

"Apparently," Kaldon said, rubbing his head while trying to wake up. "Are you free of the poison?"

Brenton pounded his chest with a fist. "Completely. The Master Healer did well."

"I'm very glad to hear that. I'm sure Flor is as well," Kaldon said, rubbing his head relieved. "Did Anneya pass out as well?"

Brenton laughed. "Oh no, Anneya is a Blade. The higher rank you achieve, the more you are trained and tested to adapt to the Kingdom of Light. Anneya is quite accustomed to feeling the force of eternity."

Brenton tried to hide his smirk, continuing. "You, my friend, are a light-weight. I've never seen someone taken out like that before. Even my daughters hold up better than you did."

Grinning, Kaldon slowly tried to stand. "How long was I out for? It feels like I was in a deep sleep for hours."

"Hours?" You have been out cold for nearly two days." Brenton laughed. "Like I said, you're a light-weight."

"Two days!" Kaldon said in shock.

Looking around for the first time, Kaldon suddenly became aware of his whereabouts. The bed he slept in looked like a bed made for royalty. A leather chair sat in the corner, before a wall adorned with books. The room was heated by a built-in fireplace that blazed brightly. The room reminded him of his father's private library back in Rundle.

"This is your room, where you will be staying," the Knight said. "Since the days are filled with rigorous study and training, we like our students to be comfortable when they retire for the evening. When you aren't training, you are free to roam the castle as you wish."

Kaldon was glad to hear he could do as he pleased while he was at the Peak of Lore. Running his hand over the comforter upon his bed, he knew it was a rich fabric. The bed in his room likely cost more than the house he grew up in as a child. He was used to the streets, not finer things. It would take him time to adjust to such a place.

Brenton cleared his throat, drawing Kaldon's attention again. "Since you spent two days sleeping, it gave me time to talk with my overseers. I know it's important for you to keep your foresight ability hidden for now. If any Knight or Blade were to train you, they would discover it very quickly. This is why I've convinced my overseers to let me personally train you."

"You will train me?" Kaldon asked, intrigued.

"I will train you, yes," Brenton said with determination in his eyes. "However, you need to understand something. I will not only train you, I will also break you. I will refine and shape you. I will take you from being capable, to being excellent. I will make you a weapon."

The Knight unflinchingly looked at Kaldon with seriousness in his demeanour. "Grab your sword, Kal. The breaking begins today."

Chapter Seventeen
Pursuit of Mystery

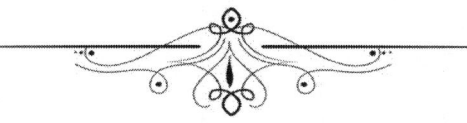

Brenton charged fiercely. As two wooden swords flew at him, Kaldon didn't realize they were a distraction until the Knight's knee whirled into his ribs. Kaldon absorbed the blow, bending from the hit.

The two sparred, drifting over the wooden floor. Individual training rooms were spread throughout the Peak of Lore. For weeks on end, this room had been Kaldon's training space. Brenton did not lie when he said he would break him. The training was rigorous.

Before he could regain composure from the strike, Brenton was coming at him from a different angle. Kaldon had never seen so many maneuvers. Brenton certainly did not lack technique. They would spar in the small, empty room, lesson after lesson, hour after hour. Each lesson concluded with Brenton besting him. The Knight seemed impenetrable. That alone drove Kaldon to keep going, driving him harder to find the Knight's vulnerability as a fighter.

This lesson was different. At the beginning of it, Brenton said he had one rule Kaldon needed to follow. The Knight could mercilessly throw attacks at him, but Kaldon was not to attack back; he could only block and dodge. Kaldon knew what that meant. There was no way he could block every blow. He knew pain was coming.

With a glint in his eyes, Brenton fiercely swung the wooden sword sideways. Ducking, Kaldon stepped back at the same time to prevent being hit. Noticing he was inching back towards a wall, Kaldon forced his way to the room's centre again. He knew being cornered in a fight often threw people into a mentality of survival, preventing them from thinking clearly. His body grew tired. His attention began to waver. The Knight had been coming at him relentlessly for nearly three hours.

He asked why he must endure being endlessly pummeled. Brenton responded with, "Your defence as a fighter is your foundation. You must become impenetrable. Once your foundation is set, you can build on it by learning proper attack."

Although the logic made sense, he knew there was another reason for this lesson. Brenton was trying to activate his foresight.

The Knight finally let his wooden weapons drop with a sigh. "Well, Kal, you're probably more exhausted than I am. Let's call it a day."

Kaldon sighed in relief. Not only was he tired, but he was also extremely sore.

"How did I do?" he asked between panting breaths.

"You did very well with this lesson. You blocked way more of my attacks than I thought you would." Brenton sheathed his wooden swords while attempting to steady his breathing. "Did your foresight spark at all?" he asked.

Kaldon stretched his aching body. "No." He shrugged his shoulders. "There was a moment, about an hour into the lesson, when I saw a vision of one of your attacks. It helped me deflect the blow. Other than that, my mind was blank."

Brenton nodded. "I was hoping this exercise would give us some clarity as to what summons your ability. I am determined to help you unlock this."

Kaldon realized he was clenching his fist. He and Brenton had been at it for weeks, trying to discover what sparked his foresight. It felt limiting to him not knowing how to control part of himself.

"How has training been going with the Master Healers? Have you been learning to stand under the atmosphere of the Kingdom of Light?" Brenton asked.

"I'm gradually improving. I don't black out as easily as when I first arrived," he grinned.

Brenton chuckled. "I'm glad to hear that. I put in a request for them to put more time into you. Believe me, you needed it."

Kaldon agreed. He thought back to the classes. He would stand in a room while a Master Healer bridged the Kingdom of Light, bringing it into the atmosphere around him. The healer was testing to see how long he could stay standing. He still blacked out from time to time; however, he was slowly adapting to the potency of eternity.

Brenton's tired demeanour quickly turned to dread. "Great Divinity, Kal, you can't be wearing that thing out in the open!"

Not knowing what he was referring to, Kaldon followed Brenton's line of sight. Looking down, he saw his Legacy tossed down over his travelling clothes.

"It must have slipped out while we were sparring," he said, tucking the pendant back under the shield of his shirt.

"Kal, if people knew you carried a Legacy, it would stir far too many questions. Higher-ups in the facility would likely think you stole it. You have no idea what problems that symbol could create. It *must* be kept hidden."

"You know very well that kind of attention is the last thing I want," he retorted, tucking the pendant back under his clothing.

His brow still furrowed, the Knight threw him a cold towel. "Speaking of not wanting attention, what do you have planned for the night?" Brenton asked.

"To be alone with my thoughts," Kaldon said, wiping his face down.

"That's what I thought you would say," Brenton said as his jaw tightened. "I know you have had a few meals with me and my family, but you seem to keep to yourself a lot. Have you made any friends here? I know many of the students go to the pub or social gatherings after classes. Have you thought of going out?"

"No, I haven't," Kaldon said. "I have never been one for social settings. I feel more comfortable having just a few friends."

Brenton shrugged. "You are a lot more like your father than you may think. I heard the General liked to keep to himself. Have you at least been connecting with Anneya since you have arrived?"

Kaldon twisted his mouth. "Since she escaped Gallaway Morgue, it's like the woman is famous here. I can't seem to pin her down."

"Have you tried?" Brenton pressed.

"Not really," Kaldon confessed. He wanted to see Anneya again, but didn't know how to find her in the large castle.

"Fair enough," Brenton stated, not wanting to push any further. "I need to be on my way. I will meet you here tomorrow. Don't spend too much time on your own. Got it?"

"Got it."

Leaving the room, Kaldon walked through the halls of the Peak of Lore. They still weren't very familiar to him. Blazing torches adorned the walls. Since he preferred to know his surroundings, he spent his leisure time exploring a generous portion of the mountainous castle. The facility seemed endless. Whenever he thought he'd reached the end of a wing, he came upon more rooms, halls, and people.

When he first heard of the Peak of Lore, he imagined it would consist only of fighters. He learned quickly that it wasn't only designed for training upcoming Knights or Blades. Those who wanted to be trained in an intellectual capacity and those who wanted to be schooled as healers were welcomed as well. The castle was filled with all sorts of students.

Roaming the halls, his eyes lingered on the stone walls. Many walls were endowed with quotes from revered Philosophers who had lived throughout history. The markings were meant to inspire students in the facility. His father's writings were written on many of these walls. As students brushed past Kaldon, he halted, running his fingers over one of the texts engraved into the stone wall.

"Mystery is a gift. While some fear it, others perceive it as an invitation. Mystery inspires us to yearn for more. It beckons us onward to venture into the undiscovered and unknown."

- Dolan Thain

Kaldon stared at the inscribed words of his father, knowingly. He reached into his cloak, feeling the ancient book, *The First Paragon*. He felt the Legacy engraved on its cover. Curiosity pulled at him. He felt his mandate at the Peak of Lore wasn't just to learn to fight with excellence or to access his foresight. If there was someone at the training facility who knew Old Agadin, he needed to find them and learn the dialect. He needed to learn the book's secrets. He figured there must be someone in the castle who understood the ancient tongue.

Watching a group of students hunched over an assortment of books at one of the study tables, he felt a pang of frustration. His training included numerous classes he didn't expect to be taking. This meant adapting to a strict schedule. He had one class on the history of Agadin and another on the basics of healing. At first, he was intrigued with the class on healing, hoping to learn more about the Kingdom of Light. His excitement quickly dissipated when he discovered the basics involved having knowledge of using herbs as a form of medicine. There were other classes he felt were useless to him, such as mathematics and sciences. He valued such things, but didn't feel they benefitted him. Much of what he was learning in classroom settings simply didn't interest him—hence his frustration.

Similar to previous nights, as he grew weary of searching endless hallways, he found himself in the library. He figured there was no better place to find information on the lost dialect. The library was initially intimidating to him. The entrance itself must have been one hundred times the size of his father's private library back in Rundle. Every wall was lined with books. There were also many branches leading to other sections in the library, each with rooms of a comparable size. He wondered if there was more knowledge in this library than in all of Agadin.

Sitting at a wooden library desk, fumbling through an ensemble of books, a part of him wished Anneya were there to help him. Her knowledge from growing up in the Peak of Lore might give him some insight. He browsed from title to title, trying to find something concerning Old Agadin. Time passed as the library slowly began thinning of people.

His eyes grew tired, failing him after so much reading. Closing the book, he noticed a young man sitting nearby at one of the desks. Kaldon recognized him from his history class. His name was Mikiel. His messy mop of amber hair stood out in stark contrast to his pale white skin. What captivated him wasn't Mikiel himself; it was what he was doing. With two notebooks laid on the desk before him, he wrote in both at the exact same time, using his right and left hands simultaneously.

Two pens furiously scratching the soft paper, Kaldon leaned forward to see that the young man was writing two completely separate things at once.

Curiosity got the better of him. "Mikiel, how are you doing that?" he asked.

Putting both pens down on his notebook and looking up with a mischievous grin, he said, "Before I answer that, you need to at least tell me your name."

Kaldon forgot that Mikiel didn't know who he was. Nearly everyone knew Mikiel. He was quickly becoming famous for his pranks targeting different professors in the training facility. Kaldon wasn't fond of pranks, but the student seemed good-hearted enough. His mother was a professor and Kaldon's teacher on the basics of healing. Her knowledge of herbs was impressive.

"My name is Kal."

"Well, Kal, what you saw me doing is called *Fractioning the Mind*. Many attempt the skill, but few can master it like you just saw," he said, his eyes gleaming with cockiness.

Kaldon smirked at the young man's overconfidence, waiting for him to elaborate.

Mikiel continued, "I learned the mechanics of this skill in an old book a while back. It's an ability that Philosophers of old once used. I fraction my mind, so I can think of two things at once. This way, I get twice as much accomplished as I normally would. Some ancient Philosophers could fraction their minds up to seven times, meditating on seven things all at once."

Kaldon's head hurt at the very thought of trying to think of seven things at once.

"So, you are training to be a Philosopher then?" Kaldon asked.

"Maybe. Maybe not," Mikiel said with a sarcastic smirk.

Kaldon shook his head, laughing. "You seem like someone who is keen on keeping a lot of secrets."

"Well, how about you? Let's see how open you are," Mikiel said. "What is it that you are so adamantly looking for in a library such as this? Philosophers don't tear through as many books as you have been."

"I'm looking for information on the dialect of Old Agadin," Kaldon said straightforwardly.

Mikiel whistled. "Ah, another student of the Lore with an impossible self-imposed task ahead of them. Why would you want to learn a forgotten language?"

Kaldon looked at Mikiel pointedly. "We all have our secrets, don't we?"

Mikiel laughed. "I like you, Kal. You know, your task might not be completely impossible."

Kaldon's curiosity peaked.

"I've heard that Tolek, the Paladin, is a very learned man. He would likely know the tongue," Mikiel said, fiddling with a pen in hand.

Kaldon knew the young man was trying to get a rise out of him. Everyone knew the Paladin was inaccessible. In recent weeks, Kaldon heard rumours and mutterings about Tolek, the head authority of the Peak of Lore. The Paladin was a legend. As talked about as he was, he hadn't even met anyone who had ever seen Tolek, let alone met him personally.

"We both know the Paladin isn't accessible. Do you have an actual solution for me?" Kaldon asked, already growing tired of Mikiel's games.

"There may be another option," Mikiel said, his smile evaporating from his face. "Have you heard of the Philosopher, Fen? If there is anyone other than Tolek in the Lore who would know anything about Old Agadin, it's her."

"Where can I find her?" Kaldon queried.

"You are closer than you would think. She is always in *the Depths,*" Mikiel responded.

"The Depths?" Kaldon asked.

"Yes. There are three levels to this library," Mikiel said, waving his hand to the surroundings. "Just as there are various ranks for fighters, such as Knights, Blades, Bishops, and Paladins, there are also different tiers for thinkers. This floor of the library is for the first tier of thinkers. It's for all the students of the Lore, as well as *Scribes.* The floor below this one is reserved for *Scholars,* the second rank. There are specific books on that level that contain information that only Scholars can understand. Below that level are the Depths, a smaller library filled with books only for Philosophers. It's the final and greatest tier of thinkers. Only Philosophers are permitted in the Depths. That is where Fen spends her time. Since there are so few Philosophers alive, she usually has the Depths all to herself."

"Then I must go there," Kaldon said, looking down one of the corridors, deeper into the library.

"It isn't that easy. Like I said, this room we are in here is only the beginning of the library. The Depths is still a few hours downward into the mountain. Your real problem will be getting Fen to talk. The woman spends nearly all of her time in the Depths. Some say they haven't seen her amongst others in nearly a decade. The Philosopher has been isolating herself for years."

Kaldon stroked his bottom lip in thought. "I will find a way. If she knows anything about Old Agadin, then I need to hear what she knows."

Mikiel's mischievous grin crept upon his face again. "Good luck. In my opinion, all you are going to find are the ramblings of an insane woman."

Chapter Eighteen

A Stirring Restlessness

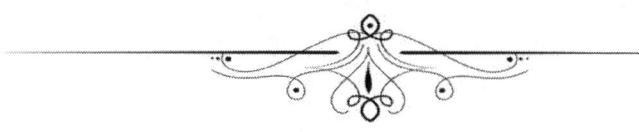

"Ocean blanketed the face of the earth. Waves sailed high, crashing and roaring throughout the sapphire landscape. With a shout, Divinity summoned earth and stone from the depths. Peaks of mountains pierced through watered floors. Mountains grew, taking their place. Forests and valleys took form. At Divinity's word, stars spun into being throughout the heavens, finding a place to rest and shine upon the world. Divinity sowed his emotion into his creation. Passion provoked Divinity to build. Wisdom guided his hand as he sculpted. Agadin would be a place capable of reflecting his very heart."

As the professor droned on about the creation of Agadin, Kaldon looked out a window carved through the mountain. Being so high up, clouds leisurely drifted by in the afternoon sky.

Stretching out his arms, he felt the stiffness in his muscles. The morning session with Brenton was rigorous, and the dull aching was already present. The Knight had again worked him tirelessly, but he'd expected that. What he hadn't expected was being stuck in classrooms nearly all day.

Still looking out the window, he was drawn to the silhouette of the mountains. They called to him, pulling on his longing for solitude. The Peak of Lore was full of people constantly moving in all directions; they were everywhere. Other than his private room, he was never alone. He avoided his room, other than to sleep. The opulence of it made him uneasy and clouded his thoughts.

It only took a few nights until he decided to find a more fitting place to be alone with his thoughts. When awake and not scouting the castle or in class, he ventured outside the walls of the facility. The rocky and untouched terrain fed his soul. His newfound secret place was the wilderness. Away from others, he relished the peace of exploring the forest and stony trails.

He was anxious for the insufferable class to end so he could go to the Depths. He needed to find the Philosopher, Fen. Mikiel described her as a vast well of knowledge walled-in by a sour personality. What key would unlock the vault of Fen? He felt an urgency to find her and his questions would not quiet.

"Mikiel!" Professor Sneel shouted. "Are you paying attention?"

Kaldon was startled back to attention. It seemed the only entertainment he had in class was when Mikiel would get bored and make a scene.

Mikiel stood from his chair and cleared his throat. "No, I was not paying attention at all, professor. I was distracted, you see. The sun has risen to the exact right height so as to cause a wondrous glow to shimmer from your balding head. It is truly remarkable."

Laughter erupted in the classroom. Mikiel took a bow, and then his seat, looking over at Kaldon with a smirk. Kaldon shook his head, astounded at how Mikiel had the ability to annoy and entertain him all at the same time.

Professor Sneel rubbed his eyes with a thumb and finger in frustration. "Mikiel, I would punish you, but I don't feel like spending yet another evening with you in detention."

The class laughed even harder. Mikiel's quarrels with professors were becoming legendary throughout the Peak of Lore. Some professors played along, finding it amusing, while others had no tolerance for it. Even so, time was brief before Mikiel rose to the challenge once again.

It wasn't long before history class came to a close. Before Kaldon could leave, Mikiel leaned over to him. "Did you go see the insane Philosopher yet?"

"I doubt she is insane. But no, I haven't seen her yet. I'm just about to head to the Depths now," Kaldon said.

"You're actually going?" he asked, leaning back, letting out a low whistle. "You know, there technically aren't guards who protect the Depths, but it's an unspoken rule that no one is allowed down there. I can't imagine the punishment you could face for going."

"I am going, consequences or not," Kaldon said definitively.

"Don't you have any other classes today?" Mikiel asked.

"My classes can wait. I can't stomach another lecture on mathematics or herbs today."

"My, aren't you the rebel—a quiet one, but a rebel nonetheless," Mikiel said with a smile. "I would come with you, but I'm not sure meeting her is worth getting punished for. Besides, I wouldn't want to miss the riveting after-class discussion."

With students clustering together in the classroom, Kaldon could already hear the discussion beginning. That was his cue to leave. "Thanks again for the information about Fen. I need to get going."

Mikiel nodded, turning to the group for the discussion. The Scribes were already arguing amongst themselves. Kaldon tried not to listen as they debated different theories of physics. Today, theories concerned the air velocity of where the Peak of Lore was placed in the Mountains of D'aal. The Scribes prattled in circles, dancing around ideas Kaldon knew would serve them no good in their actual lives. Their theories were occasionally interrupted by Mikiel's interjections. Kaldon was sure the young man's only reason for being there was to provoke the group for his own personal entertainment.

Starting his journey to the library through the halls, he grew annoyed just as he had in many of his classes. Based on his observations in recent weeks, many students viewed the facility as a crib, safely tucked within the walls. They were so consumed in their pursuit of knowledge that they were completely apathetic to the chaos occurring in Agadin. He knew better. The Peak of Lore seemed like a strong fortress of safety; however, he knew it wasn't out of the realm of possibility for it to become a tomb for its thousands of inhabitants. Nowhere was safe from the Dominion of Shadow. Medric taught him that.

There were some who saw the severity of their times. Brenton and Anneya had. Still, he was seeing that such awareness was scarce. Inhabitants and students alike seemed to be simply passing time. He didn't have time to waste; an urgency was growing within him. The Sovereign of Shadow knew who he was. Shadow was rising in Agadin. He wasn't content to wait for five years of schooling to end before being ready. He knew the Sovereign wouldn't wait. He needed to be ready immediately.

It didn't take him long to reach the library. Glancing over the first tier in the ocean of books, he saw one of the corridors leading down to the Depths. Hours of travelling downward were ahead of him, and he was anxious for what he would find there.

Suddenly, a loud laugh rose. He turned towards it. Squinting to focus in the dimmer light, he saw a group of women in one of the study nooks—Anneya was amongst them. The Blade threw her head back in a roaring laugh. The girls around her laughed with her. He couldn't hear why they were laughing, but found himself chuckling under his breath. It made him happy seeing her glow with joy. She seemed to have friends throughout the entire castle. He'd even overheard some of his male peers talk of wanting to court her. Apparently, she would have none of it. The Blade may be a social butterfly, but she was as stubborn as they came. He turned towards his descent when another loud noise stopped him.

"Kal!" Anneya shouted. "There you are. I haven't seen you in nearly three weeks!" The Blade's shout wasn't out of place in the room. It simply blended into the laughs and conversation taking place within the social library.

Springing to her feet, she bounded towards him. Since she wasn't out on mission, she didn't have her armour on. She wore simple clothes: a dark sweater and fabric pants. It was odd seeing her without her menacing crimson shoulder spikes.

"Where have you been?" she asked.

He was genuinely happy to see his friend again. "Anneya, it's great to see you. Brenton has been busy breaking me, and the professors have been busy boring me," he joked.

She laughed. "They will do that. What are you doing here?" she asked, seeing he was on his own.

"I spend a lot of time in the library," Kaldon said. "Books aren't common where I'm from, so I spend much of my time here reading."

Before he could elaborate on his real reason for being in the library, Anneya cut him off. "I grew up with all of these books. Sometimes I forget they are even around."

He smiled, admiring how candid she was. "Anneya, where have you been?"

"Oh, you know, here and there," she said, dodging him.

After an awkward silence, she looked away, shaking her head. "I'm sorry, I shouldn't be so vague with you." The Blade looked around to make sure there was no one listening to their conversation before continuing.

"I have been seeing the Master Healers several times a week. That's why you haven't seen me," Anneya said, running her hand through her golden hair.

He was happy to know she wasn't trying to avoid him. "Master Healers? Are you alright?" Kaldon asked quietly.

Her stare widened. "Oh yes, I'm fine physically. My time at Gallaway Morgue was difficult, both mentally and emotionally. They have been working intensely with me to heal my mind and emotions."

He was caught off guard by her answer. "I didn't know it was possible for someone to heal another's mind and emotions."

"Oh yes. It isn't as straightforward as healing the body, but the healers say I have come a long way already," she beamed.

"I'm just glad you are alright," Kaldon said, reassuring himself as he spoke. He had a soft spot for the Blade. He felt protective of her. She had saved his life. Together, they saw the legendary Owyl, the bird from eternity.

"Anneya, what are you doing right now?" he asked, twisting his brow.

"Well, I was going to go to the pub with a few friends. Why?" she asked.

"I have a project I am working on. I may need some help."

"Project? For one of your classes?" She wrinkled her face.

"Not quite. I need to learn a dead language," he stated.

"Ah, I see—an impossible project then," she teased.

He wasn't swayed by her remark. "I need to show you something. I have never shown this to anyone before." Shielding it from the others, he pulled the book out of his cloak.

Anneya's gaze went wide. "I have never seen a book so ancient. And the symbol on the cover…" Her tone hushed.

"I know," he nodded. "It's written in Old Agadin. I need to know what it says."

"Where did you find such a thing? And where do you plan on learning a dead dialect?" she asked cautiously.

Kaldon avoided her first question, hoping she wouldn't notice. "I am on my way to the Depths."

Anneya's face went pale. "The Depths? You aren't allowed down there. Brenton would be in a fit if he found out. Do you know who is down there?"

"I know very well," he said. "I am on my way now to convince Fen to teach me Old Agadin. I'm hoping she knows the language, but I don't know the way there."

She looked away in thought.

"I need you to guide me," he said straightforwardly.

She was taken aback by the request. "The moment I met you, I knew you wouldn't be content blending into the crowd here," she remarked.

"This is important, Anneya," Kaldon said in seriousness.

She nodded. "I have never been that deep into the mountain. Growing up here, I understand how the castle is shaped to some degree. I doubt you will find it on your own. If this is important to you, I will help you."

Chapter Nineteen
Walls that Hold Secrets

The second level of the library was in stark contrast to the upper floor. No Scribes or regular students were in sight. Still consisting of corridors and grand rooms, it was similar to the upper floor, yet on a compact scale. The library's first level was masterfully crafted to the greatest detail, but here, such details were not given as much attention. These Scholars, advanced in years, did not like distraction. They prized the content of books more than discussion. Mounds of books surrounded them on every table. Kaldon wondered if they knew how to fraction their minds like Mikiel did.

Slowly making their way through the corridors in search of a staircase leading to the Depths, he hadn't thought it would take them this long to reach this point. He'd lost count of how many times they'd taken a wrong turn and needed to backtrack. He was glad to have Anneya with him to navigate.

Every so often, the two were met by the disapproving eyes of Scholars lost in their studies. No one told them to leave. Kaldon was thankful no guards were about. Having Anneya with him helped. Although she wasn't wearing the armour of a Blade, all likely knew she was a Blade of Agadin and the fugitive from Gallaway Morgue. She was someone who they would not want to get on the bad side of.

Anneya whispered so as not to disturb the focus of the Scholars. "Did you hear the news about Brenton?"

Kaldon's forehead creased. "He didn't mention any news to me."

She shook her head. "Of course he didn't. He didn't tell me either. Flor told me when I was visiting Honey."

Kaldon let out a short laugh. It was surprising how far his faint laugh carried in this section of the library. At the sound, numerous agitated Scholars looked up at him. He lowered his voice apologetically.

"You and Honey are becoming close friends, are you?" he whispered.

"Oh yes," Anneya said, looking forward. "She has quite the temper. Flor said I have the right touch to calm her."

He warmed at the thought of the Blade soothing a young one. "So, what about Brenton?"

She glanced over at him as they walked. "Brenton shared with those in authority at the Lore what took place on the trip here from Rundle. How he had gone on the mission because he suspected Medric had embraced the Shadow. He also told them about the Kreel attack and Ont's death."

Kaldon tried to hide his concern. He hoped Brenton was discreet about the details surrounding all of those events. "So, does this mean that the authorities here know everything?"

"It means that Brenton is being promoted for his heroism," Anneya said. "It was quite the selfless task he took on himself to go on that mission to thwart Medric's plans. He is being promoted from a Knight to a Blade."

Kaldon was overjoyed at hearing such news. "When is this happening?" he asked, as they reached a place in the library that was far more secluded. Not a Scholar was in sight.

"In a few days, there will even be a ceremony for him. I've heard rumours that the head authority of the Peak of Lore will be coming to honour him. Tolek, showing his face in public is unheard of. I've never seen a Paladin."

Kaldon wondered what it would be like to meet a man like Tolek. Being a Paladin, he was likely one of the greatest warriors alive. He wondered if such a man would understand his ability with foresight.

The two continued scouting the isolated section of the library. As they travelled deeper, bookshelves still adorned the walls; however, here, books did not fill them. It seemed to be a part of the library that was forgotten. As they delved deeper into the study halls, murmurs crept into the silence. Knowing how uncommon it was to even hear a whisper on the second floor of the library, Kaldon and Anneya looked to one another. They crept closer, following the murmurs. As they ventured through the halls, the voices ascended in volume.

"We are dawning a new era," one voice said, faintly echoing through the forgotten halls.

The pair neared a corner in the library, hearing the voice come from the other side. Discreetly looking around the corner, they saw that the corridor led to a room so deep within the second floor that it was hidden from view. In the shadows, five stood in the room, two women and three men. All wore the armour of Blades.

With concern sketched into her expression, Anneya brought her finger to her lips for silence. A library wasn't for Blades; the instinct for caution rose up in them both. One of the men spoke.

"I've heard the Sovereign believes the Dominion of Shadow is drawing closer to Agadin than ever before."

A female Blade piped up. "General Geran is apparently waiting for his command to send his army to the Peak of Lore. This is an army not only of warriors, but of Nahmen and Kreel. The Kreel have already secured numerous cities for us. It is only a matter of time before the Peak of Lore falls to the Sovereign. The General is savage. I would be surprised if he left any alive." The five laughed at such a dark thought.

Anneya's face paled in sudden comprehension. Before them stood five Dark Blades. Traitors, like Medric, were hidden amongst the warriors and families in the Peak of Lore.

In a deep tone, another Dark Blade said, "Once the army is on its way, the Lore will fall, and Shadow will be further established in Agadin. There is nothing Tolek can do to prevent it. I heard the Sovereign of Shadow himself will be coming."

Anneya leaned against the wooden wall. The Peak of Lore was her home. Kaldon hated that there were those who had embraced the Shadow hiding amongst them. With his hand resting on the hilt of his sword, he wanted to attack the Blades. He had taken out several men at once before, but he knew that even with Anneya there, they wouldn't stand a chance against five Blades at once.

Seeing the Dark Blades still lost in conversation, Kaldon nudged Anneya's shoulder, motioning that they should leave before they were spotted. She nodded in agreement. The two pulled their attention from the secret meeting back to the room they were standing in. Turning to leave, Kaldon felt his boot kick something resting on the floor. He watched a book slide several feet on the ground upon impact.

"No, no, no," he whispered as bronzed pages ruffled.

"Quiet! Someone is there," a gruff voice said from across the room.

Anneya looked at Kaldon with terror in her eyes as rings of steel echoed throughout the caved library. The Dark Blades had drawn their swords.

"Run," she whispered with dread in her voice.

They bolted through corridors and halls. Behind them, they could hear boots clomping upon the library floor. They knew that if they were caught, they would never see the surface of the Peak of Lore again.

Seeing Scholars again, Kaldon and Anneya were out from the isolated part of the library, back into one of the well-utilized study rooms. From behind, they could hear shouts echoing from the servants of the Sovereign of Shadow pursuing them. Metals clanged.

One of the Scholars rose to his feet, slamming his hand on the desk. "*What* is the meaning of this?!"

They dashed past the Scholar without answering, knowing the Dark Blades would soon be following behind with weapons in hand.

Darting around another corner, they ran headlong into a hallway arching both right and left. "Go left!" Anneya shouted to Kaldon, loud enough for the pursuing Dark Blades to hear.

Approaching the fork, she grabbed Kaldon's sleeve, pulling him to the right instead.

"Hopefully they bought it," Anneya said, short of breath.

They ran down the curved hall which grew drearier with each step they took. The walls and floor looked more worn than in other places and less tended to. They heard the shouts and clangs behind them beginning to fade away. Although they were lost in the library, they were safe momentarily.

Reaching the end of their journey through the second floor of the library, Kaldon and Anneya stopped. Before them was a cold opening of darkness. While the walls of the second floor were still somewhat decorative, looking down these stairs was like looking into the mouth of a cave. The only decor was dirt lingering on the cold stone walls. They had found the entrance to the Depths. They had found the entrance to a place where only the greatest thinkers in Agadin were permitted to tread. Kaldon wasn't a renowned thinker. He wasn't even a Knight, yet he was about to enter a private library intended only for Philosophers. Not only did they need to mine out the mysteries hidden in his book, but there was a truth raging in his mind: Shadow was rising. An army would inevitably come to the Peak of Lore. The Sovereign was hunting him. They had no choice but to go deeper still.

Chapter Twenty

The Depths

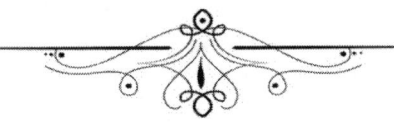

The Dark Blades were left behind; stone walls and a musty, charcoaled ceiling encased them. The cave-like atmosphere of the Depths set a cryptic and sombre tone. Dark and uninviting, the Depths were a stark and dank contrast to the rest of the castle. In the other levels of the library, bookshelves were crafted from rich woods. Here, books rested on shelves of chiselled stone. Since books were surprisingly scarce, only the rarest of books were kept in the deep library for the Philosophers.

Walking through underground hallways, Kaldon and Anneya were surprised to see that there were not only spaces for study, but also rooms for sleeping. They even stumbled across a quaint kitchen. It seemed as though it was set up for Philosophers to stay in the Depths for days or even weeks at a time. However, since entering this part of the Depths, they had not seen a single person—it seemed completely vacant.

Weaving deeper into the cavern, they heard faint mutterings cutting through the stillness. The muttering grew louder as they came to a central room. Stepping into the room, what they saw was an odd sight to behold.

There, in the middle of the room, sat a woman seemingly in her fifties. Even though tables surrounded her, she sat on the musty floor with nearly sixty books strewn about her in a circle. Her spindly body matched her frizzy-wild black hair, which was distinctly marked by bolts of silver. She looked as though she hadn't run a comb through it in months, if ever. Immediately, Kaldon knew this was Fen.

Nearly ten of the books in front of her were notebooks. She alternated from furiously writing to engrossing herself in the numerous texts around her. The Philosopher had a pen in each hand, writing two things at once with focused attention. Obviously, she knew how to fraction her mind. Dozens of books were opened to specific pages as she leaned towards them. She was not only writing numerous notes at once, but also studying a multitude of books simultaneously. Kaldon was awestruck at the impossibility of what he was witnessing.

"Excuse me," he said, clearing his throat. "Are you Fen?"

Even though Kaldon and Anneya were in plain sight, the Philosopher's eyes darted from book to book as she scribbled memos in her many notebooks.

Anneya grew impatient, speaking louder. "Excuse me!"

The Philosopher paused, looking up with eyes penetrating right through them. Kaldon knew he was looking into the eyes of a genius.

Fen spoke with an abrupt tone and scratchy voice. "Based on the fact that neither of you belongs here, it is none of your business who I am, now is it?" she said sternly, going back to her writing.

Kaldon felt Anneya's frustration sparking. The Blade opened her mouth to demand that the woman speak to them. He placed a hand on her shoulder to calm her.

"Let me do the talking for now," he whispered to Anneya. "She is a recluse. She isn't going to respond well to brashness."

"Fine," Anneya said, gritting her teeth in reluctance.

Taking a step closer to the Philosopher, he spoke. "What are you working on, Fen?" he asked gently.

Scratching on two notebooks at once, she answered. "I am studying and writing books."

Kaldon noticed she did not stop writing while talking to him. "You are writing books? More than one?" he asked.

"Yes," Fen stated. "I am writing seven at the moment."

"You can write seven books at once." It wasn't a question; it was a statement of near disbelief.

The Philosopher looked at Kaldon, annoyed. "Of course, I can write seven books at once. I am one of the greatest thinkers alive. Now, stop patronizing me and tell me what you want so that I can be left alone with my work."

After their descent into the Depths, Kaldon and Anneya were weary. Both were still on edge from their brush with the Dark Blades. They were already reaching the end of their patience. Kaldon could swear Anneya was about ready to pounce at the woman.

"Fine." He pulled his book out of his cloak.

"I need help interpreting this book. It is written in Old Agadin. I know it is a lost dialect, but I was told that if anyone could help me, you could." He placed the ancient book on the floor next to the Philosopher.

Fen paused in her studies. "Well, would you look at this." She lifted the book from the cold floor. "This book is quite old. It may even be fitting for the Depths."

"Can you help?" Kaldon pressed.

Fen placed the book back upon the pebbled floor. "I would love to study such a piece of literature. However, Old Agadin has been lost to me. I can't decipher it."

He was growing impatient. "Can't? Or won't?"

"Well, well, look who is getting pushy," she said, getting agitated as well.

Anneya took a step forward with displeasure.

The Philosopher let out a weak cackle. "What, are you going to try and force me to help you, Blade? I could likely understand some of the book; however, it would take far too much of my time to interpret. So no, I won't help you." Fen looked back at her books and notes, picking up her pens.

"This isn't just for my sake, Fen, it is for yours as well," Kaldon protested. "Shadow is rising in Agadin. Tymas Droll, the Sovereign of Shadow, has plans to send an army to the Peak of Lore. The Great War is raging, and there are keys in this book that can prevent the Dominion of Shadow from reigning in Agadin."

Fen stayed silent as her pens scratched upon paper.

"Come on, Kal," Anneya said. "Let's go back. This woman isn't going to help us."

Anneya was right. As things were, Fen would not help them. However, he had one last strategy. He hoped he wouldn't need to, but he only knew of one thing that might budge the hardened Philosopher.

Kaldon reached into his shirt, feeling the pendant his mother gave him. His pendant. It was the Legacy once belonging to his father. He ran his fingers over the five points, symbolizing the five Protectors of Agadin: Paladin, Seer, Philosopher, Roek, Shan-Rafa.

"Kal, no!" Anneya objected.

Ignoring Anneya's plea, he pulled out the pendant that hung around his neck. In the dark of the cave-like room, the pendant didn't look like anything significant. Yet, the symbol could not be mistaken.

"You carry a Legacy, do you?" the Philosopher said, surprised. "And who did you steal that from?"

Anneya was frozen. The Blade was running potential consequences through her mind of what could happen now that someone knew Kaldon carried a Legacy.

Fen stood up, getting heated. "Now, let me tell you something. That symbol you are holding is sacred. This is a symbol worn only by Protectors of Agadin." Speaking, Fen reached into her robe, pulling out a Legacy of her own.

Holding her Legacy before him, the Philosopher was nearly writhing in rage. "You have forced my hand. The Depths are sacred. These are reserved for ones such as myself, yet you barge in here demanding my loyalty simply because you are a gifted thief! I will make sure you both are banished from the Peak of Lore for this stunt. Tolek won't tolerate behaviour like this!"

Anneya was in a fighter's stance and ready to defend herself, not knowing if the Philosopher was going to get violent. Her face carried dread at how quickly the interaction was escalating, especially at the mention of banishment. Kaldon's face was hard—stern in boiling frustration.

His jaw tightened. "I know you aren't happy we are here. Believe me, we wouldn't have come if it weren't for good reason. You should know that I am no thief."

He didn't back down. As heated anger rose up in him, he weighed the potential consequences of his next words. He had to do it. There was no other way.

"This Legacy belonged to my father," Kaldon said.

"Your father?" Fen said sarcastically. "And who would that be?"

Quickly glancing at Anneya, he could read her confusion. He then spoke words that, until that moment, had never once touched his lips.

"I am the son of Dolan Thain."

Silence stilled the cavern. Not a breath was heard. With her hand covering her mouth, Anneya stood speechless. Fen's eyes were locked on Kaldon. The tense atmosphere dissipated into nothingness as the three stood in the hollow library.

The Philosopher slowly walked toward him. As her hands came up to his face, he flinched, not knowing her motives. Her hands cupped his face, and she looked into his emerald eyes.

"Yes," Fen spoke faintly. "I can see him in your eyes. I can see the genius that possessed him."

"You knew him?" The words escaped Kaldon's mouth. "You knew my father?"

Fen let her grip go, allowing her arms to drop. The Philosopher walked away at a contemplative pace. "I knew him, yes." She lifted her head up in a state of pride. "In fact, I was the one who trained him. I taught him how to unlock that brilliant mind. He had such a gift. I never thought I would be here in the Depths with his offspring."

He looked over to Anneya, who was still in shock at the revelation of his true identity. Tears brimmed in her hazel eyes. He had no words for her.

He turned back to Fen. "Will you help me, Fen?"

As the Philosopher lingered in her clear state of reflection, she slowly reached down and picked up the ancient book from the stone floor. The leather book looked fitting in her hands. Knowledge and wisdom were like an extension of who she was. The Legacy shone from the book's cover.

Carefully opening the book's cover, Fen peered at the writings on the first page. Passion glimmered in her eyes.

The Philosopher read aloud. *"The First Paragon: A Story of Dawntan Forlorn."* She looked to Kaldon with inquisitive eyes. "*Paragon* is a title I have not heard in a *very* long time."

Fen smiled a wide grin, saying, "This promises to be a riveting read."

Chapter Twenty-One
The World of Dreams

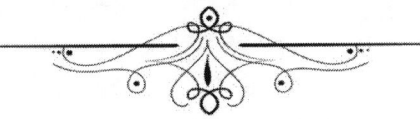

Rocking back and forth, Tymas sat in the wooden chair. Many of his dreams began this way, with him sitting in the shaded, familiar room. The room was simple, yet worn. The peeling walls were grimy, and other than the chair he sat on, the furniture was randomly placed. Two doors were in the room. One led back to the physical realm of Agadin; the other door led to the unknown. Tymas didn't dare open either. This was where Furion would come to instruct him. This room was in the world of his dreams.

The room had a window. Through a fragmented crack in the glass, wind howled in like a violent scream. The Sovereign of Shadow stood, walking to the window. He looked out and up at the sky. They still made him uneasy. He had been coming to meet with Furion in this place since he was a child, and still, the sight of them still made his stomach twist.

The skies were not as they were in Agadin. Blue indigo did not span the heavens. These skies here were chaotic and sinister looking. Dark purples and greys moved in threatening thrusts, and not a speck of light was in them. Light did not exist here. Tymas knew that behind the clouds were creatures he did not desire to see. As he watched, an occasional Kreel flew through the air, filling it with harrowing shrieks. This was where he had summoned the creatures from. He knew far worse beasts hid behind the veil of shadows. The land beneath the ominous sky was barren, with neither a tree nor a shrub in sight. It was like looking into endless nothingness, like an eternal well of void. The sight was unnerving. He didn't doubt that horrific creatures also roamed the barren landscape. He shuddered at the thought.

The first time he was first brought here in his dreams, he did not know where he was. Now he did. He was on the very brink of the Dominion of Shadow, the outskirts of the land of spiritual decay and home to Furion. The place terrified him, yet he was enthralled by the mystical land. He stepped back from the window. His stomach was in knots.

"Where *is* she?" he whispered to himself, looking down at the timepiece that was wrapped around his wrist. Tymas loved the little trinket. It wasn't long ago that a Philosopher had invented the timepiece. The Philosopher was now deceased, leaving behind a fascinating legacy—a tool to discern time.

Normally, the timepiece would tick and tock in a steady rhythmic pattern, counting hours, minutes, and seconds. This close to the Dominion of Shadow, the hands spun in a disorderly fashion, at times in opposite directions. They would spin in frenzied, accelerated circles. The sight made chills prick upon his skin.

Looking at the door leading back to reality, he longed for the comfort of the material realm again. Nevertheless, the disarray that lay beyond the window was the very place he sought to bring to Agadin.

Turning back to his chair, he jumped with a startle. A woman stood before him.

The woman looked human, yet not. Shadow draped over the Entity like a robe of black clouds. Below the smoke were onyx garments cascading to the floor. The face looked both menacing and emotionless at the same time. Her complexion was ivory white, with markings as black as ink starting from above her eyebrows, winding up her temple and forehead and disappearing underneath her ebony hair. The most unsettling feature of the woman was her eyes. Light eyes shone with a hazed blue. They looked deceptively appealing, yet there was nothing innocent about them. They were cold, uncaring. Void of compassion.

"Tymas," Furion hissed.

He was always taken aback by how softly she spoke, considering what he knew of her.

"It is time for you to move forward with our plans," the Entity directed. Send your army to the Peak of Lore. The time has come."

After all these years, he was still unnerved when speaking with her. She seemed petite, fragile even. He knew better than to view Furion as frail. She wasn't human. She was an Entity. One capable of powers he couldn't imagine.

"Yes, Master. I will command Geran to lead the army. He will be pleased," Tymas responded. "I have spies hidden in the Peak of Lore. Tolek and the others will not expect a thing."

Furion nodded her head. "Well done. The Paladin has stood in my way for far too long."

"Speaking of hindrances," Furion paused in thought. "What has taken place with the son of Dolan Thain, the one calling himself Kal Wendal? Has he been taken care of?"

Tymas thought about how the Entity never possessed all knowledge concerning what occurred in Agadin. She was not omnipresent. There were times when she knew of things that surprised him and other times seemed dependent on what he told her. Her sight was somehow blinded from the land of the living.

Tymas slowly shook his head in regret. "I'm afraid not. The Dark Knight I sent failed to execute the young man."

An unreadable look stretched across Furion's face. "It was wise to tell me the truth. I told you he wouldn't suffice. Medric has already confessed to me of failing in his mission."

"How could Medric have told you?" Tymas asked.

Furion held her hand in the direction of the ominous skies and the land of nothingness. "Medric's spirit resides here with me in the Dominion. Those who embrace the Shadow are mine for all eternity. The Dark Knight had to answer to me for his failure. I remind him of his incompetence often."

Tymas felt chills gliding over his body at such a dreadful thought.

Furion continued, "You are aware of what the Dark Seers saw in visions concerning the son of Dolan Thain. He needs to be killed before he discovers his potential."

"I will take care of it," Tymas said with certainty.

"You better," she said, her eyes digging into him.

With deceivingly graceful strides, Furion began pacing the small-worn room. "I did not summon you here today to simply advise you. I have a specific task."

"Anything, Master," he said distractedly, already thinking about storming the Peak of Lore. Geran would be thrilled to lead the army on such an important mission. The man had served Tymas for quite some time. He deserved a gift such as this.

"The time has come for a stronger link to be forged between Agadin and my Dominion," Furion said. "Are you *listening* to me, Tymas?"

His attention now hers, he gestured his head in agreement. "Yes. And, I couldn't agree more, Master Furion."

Furion smiled. "Now that you have completed writing the Law of Shadow, it is time. I want you to open the doors in this room."

He looked at her blankly. "Are you certain?"

Furion's hand slammed down on the nearby chair. "Do not question me!"

He took a step back. Seeing the Entity erupt in anger wasn't uncommon, but it still shook him.

Furion stopped pacing. "Be at ease, Tymas. You know ignorance upsets me."

She continued, "This room is a sacred room. It holds the potential to link Adagin and the Dominion of Shadow in a far more intimate way. As you know, I'm not truly here with you in this room. This is but a dream. My true form is in there," she said, pointing beyond the door to the spiritual land of death. "I can't open the doors. I am spirit, not flesh. I need someone from the material realm to act on my behalf. This is why I have chosen you and called you here."

Furion could see his hesitancy.

"Tymas," she coaxed. "I have been with you since you were a child. I have walked with you. I have groomed you. You are my chosen pupil. You have trained for these very purposes. It is time for the winds of the Dominion to blow into Agadin; time for the winds to draw more men and women to the ways of the Shadow. Open the doors, Tymas, and take your rightful place. Shape the link between worlds."

He let out a sigh. "As you wish," he said blankly.

Tymas' expression was vacant on the outside; inside, he was screaming with both delight and fear. He longed to experience the Dominion of Shadow in a greater measure, yet feared its uncertainty.

He slowly opened the first door to the material realm of Agadin. The easier of the two tasks was complete. He looked out into a world that was, in his opinion, waiting to be dominated by him.

He walked to the second door at the other side of the room. As he gripped the door handle, his heart began pounding. His stomach churned with anxiety and exhilaration. He knew some of what dwelled on the other side of this door: the skies of swirling shadow, the land-of-nothingness, and whatever creatures hid throughout the Dominion. He knew there would be creatures of Shadow. Furion dwelled there.

Turning the knob, he heard a click. As the door slowly creaked open, the Sovereign closed his eyes, both to his greatest delight and writhing fears.

With the Dominion of Shadow before him, he felt a caress of shadowed winds. The winds stroked his childlike face. It was like a kiss from death itself.

Through the shrill silence, all he could hear was a hiss escaping the powerful Entity. "Yesss…"

Tymas' eyes slowly opened. *What an intoxicating experience*, he thought to himself.

Returning to the confines of his office felt foreign after being in the world of dreams. Chills danced over his body, and the Sovereign revelled in what he'd just experienced. Based on what he read in history books, the Door of the Dominion had never before opened. Now it was open, and he was the one chosen to do it. He knew it would take much time for many of the effects of its opening to come into full effect. Other effects would take shape immediately. Tymas was glad to be out of Furion's presence, even though he would never give voice to such a thought. The Entity was unsettling to be around.

Looking up, he saw two of his Nahmen standing at the door to leave his office. Tymas usually kept a few of the Nahmen at hand in case they saw anything through the eyes of their scouting Kreel. Neither of the Nahmen was tall. In fact, they looked feeble in appearance, with few strands, if any, of hair at all. Their ash-grey robes stretched to the ground, matching their grey, lifeless faces. Simply the sight of such creatures cloaked the room in drabness. The creatures of Shadow were like vacant replicas of their creator, Furion. Tymas was still taken in by the fact that he had just experienced the Dominion of Shadow, their native land, in such an intimate way.

"Nahmen," the Sovereign said authoritatively.

Both Nahmen looked up and spoke in unison. "Yes, Sovereign of Shadow."

"The Door of the Dominion has been opened." Saying the words made his heart flutter in excitement.

Both of the Nahmen looked at Tymas with an expressionless gaze. Tymas wondered what it would be like to be void of emotion as the Nahmen were. He would think they would long for their home, the Dominion, to come to Agadin. They didn't. They simply existed and did as they were told. They were slaves to the way of the Shadow. However, the Door of the Dominion opening greatly benefited the Nahmen. It strengthened their bond to the Shadow, thus increasing their power. Up until this point, they were spies for the Sovereign and overseers to the Kreel, but now they were much more. He was eager to experiment with such abilities.

Instead of waiting for a reaction he knew wouldn't come, Tymas continued, "One of you is to alert Geran. Tell him to send word to ready soldiers stationed in overthrown cities near the

Mountains of D'aal. We will be leaving shortly for the Peak of Lore."

He caught himself smiling. Those from the Peak of Lore had been an annoyance to him and Geran for far too long. It would be good to be rid of them. With the help of the new abilities of the Nahmen, he and Geran would be able to make haste to catch up to the readying armies.

Immediately obeying, one of the Nahmen left the room in search of the leader of the Sovereign's army. The Sovereign's eyes then looked upon the remaining creature. Tymas Droll was tired after such an experience. He wanted to meditate on what just took place. He wanted to rest, but there was no time.

"Let's put to the test your new abilities," he said.

Tymas knew that the Nahmen's deeper connection to the Dominion meant they could live by its principles in a more prominent way. He read countless books on the Dominion and was mentored by Furion herself. He supposed he knew more about the Dominion of Shadow than anyone alive. He understood how the Nahmen's abilities would work. He had anticipated it for quite some time. Their connection to the Kreel was essential to their new unique gift. The Nahmen and Kreel were linked, and with the door of the Dominion now open, even more so.

Tymas looked down at his timepiece. The hands were in order, mechanically ticking as they should. With the Nahmen's new link to the Dominion, they didn't need to abide by natural law as they once did. They were free to venture as they pleased. Wherever a Kreel was, not only could they see through the beast's eyes as they once did, but now they could travel there themselves, in a split moment. Time and distance no longer caged them.

"Nahmen," the Sovereign decreed. "Where are the Kreel you oversee?"

The Nahmen spoke in an emotionless tone. "My Kreel are beyond the Mountains of D'aal in Southeast Agadin."

Tymas smiled. "Perfect. Transport me there, beyond the Mountains of D'aal. I have important tasks to accomplish."

The Nahmen's greyed mouth widened like the opening of a tomb. The hollow voice came forth. "As you wish, Sovereign of Shadow."

Chapter Twenty-Two
When Pages Speak

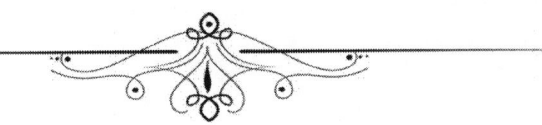

The pages of *The First Paragon* were illuminated by daylight shining through the entrance of the Peak of Lore. There were dozens of students studying and conversing in the foyer, yet Kaldon and Anneya were not swayed from their research. Both were arched over their translation of the book that laid upon the study table before them. They had spent countless hours in the Depths with Fen as she deciphered the ancient text. The Philosopher would write the interpretation in a blank book for them to study on their own. She spent hours upon hours scrutinizing the ancient words. Still, Fen wasn't close to finished. They only had the first nineteen pages complete, but they were nineteen pages brimming with revealing information.

They'd quickly learned the book was not only written *about* Dawntan Forlorn, it was written *by* him. It was a journal and an intimate record of one of his most daring ventures.

"Look at this, Kal. There's another reference to this *Marradus*," Anneya said, pointing to the name on the crisp page.

The pages told a fascinating tale about how the ruler of the underworld, Furion, had summoned a dreadful creature named Marradus from the Dominion of Shadow. Dawntan Forlorn vowed to protect Agadin from the otherworldly beast.

"What type of creature was it again?" Kaldon asked.

"A dragon," Anneya murmured in thought, her mind clearly focused on reading.

"Ah, yes." Kaldon had never heard of such a creature. Anneya relayed that dragons were once common in Agadin, but had been extinct for many lifetimes now. A dragon hadn't been seen since Marradus roamed the earth nearly four thousand years ago.

Anneya leaned forward, peering at the copy. "Look, here is a description of Marradus. Listen to this." Her fingers traced the words as she quietly began reading aloud.

"I had never seen a creature as vile as Marradus. I've encountered dragons; however, Marradus is not a creature from Agadin. Only Furion herself could summon such a monstrosity. It is undoubtedly a beast from the Dominion of Shadow. Entire towns have been demolished and kingdoms destroyed by its colossal claws. Thousands have been incinerated by the heat of its flames, and others have dropped dead from fear. No creature in history matches the enormity or strength of this beast. One of its teeth is the size of a grown man. A single swipe of its reptilian tail takes out hundreds of men. One gust of its breath can devour an entire town with its flames. The dragon's black scales are like vast shields stretching across the enormous reptile. It is truly terrifying seeing its wings stretched out as it soars at impossible heights. Seeing the beast sweep throughout clouded skies is a fearsome sight to behold. It does not glide with elegance. Its jagged twists are menacing, unsettling. Marradus is a demon dragon. It is death. Though the bravest of warriors cower before such a creature, I have no choice but to prevail. I must pursue Marradus. I must kill the demon dragon. If I do not, the land Agadin will be no more."

- Dawntan Forlorn
The First Paragon

"I never knew such a beast could exist." Kaldon rubbed his forehead with a finger and thumb. "A Kreel would look like an insect compared to such a creature."

"It sounds terrifying," Anneya agreed, closing the book.

As Kaldon dwelled on the image of Marradus, he looked over to Anneya, who was clearly doing the same. He was glad not to have been alive while such a creature inhabited Agadin. He mused that not even a fortress such as the Peak of Lore could stand against the winged serpent. He was eager to get the next set of transcribed pages from Fen. He wanted to know how the story unfolded.

"I need to ask you a question," Anneya spoke so softly that her voice was almost lost in the chatter of others.

Her questions were by no means scarce in recent days. She seemed to have just as many questions about him as she did about the book they deciphered. Kaldon expected as much. The Blade finally knew his true identity.

He looked up, inviting her to ask.

"If your father is Dol..." The Blade stopped herself. She looked around, making sure no one was paying attention to their conversation. "I mean, if your father is, *you know who*, where is your mother?"

He smiled a sad smile at the thought of his beloved mother. "She died when I was eleven years old."

"I thought as much," she said, empathizing. "How did she die?"

Kaldon hardened at the question. Not against Anneya, but to protect himself from the pain. "My mother suffered from addiction. She overdosed on scethane," he said plainly. Many in Rundle had lost their lives to the dangerous drug. He still grieved that his mother was one of them.

"I'm so sorry. Scethane is a terrible drug. I suppose it was after this that you began living on the streets?" she asked.

He nodded. The long journeys to and from the Depths gave them ample time to talk. He'd shared more about his life and upbringing with Anneya than anyone. She, in turn, shared much about her childhood. The Blade had faced more hardships than anyone deserved. She was abandoned as an infant, never having the opportunity to meet her parents, yet still she rose to the rank of Blade. He respected her for overcoming such obstacles in life.

His thoughts were disrupted at the sound of distant giggles. He knew what that meant. Looking behind him with a grin coming upon his face, he saw Hayley and Haddy walking towards them with Brenton and Flor. Honey was running in a fumbling gait at full speed towards Anneya. The laughter of the three girls eased his internal tension about discussing his mother.

"It's my little apprentice!" Anneya shouted when she saw Honey.

"Apprentice?" Kaldon asked.

"Oh yes, this little one has a temper. She could very well be a Blade one day," she said with a grin. "Excuse me."

Anneya stood and half-ran over to Honey, picking up the child and walking to the other two girls. She played with the girls, running and chasing them. Their enthusiasm fit in with the high-paced feel of the Peak of Lore's entrance. Brenton and Flor came and sat with Kaldon.

"How is the book coming?" Brenton asked with genuine curiosity.

"Slowly," Kaldon stated. "The beast that Dawntan wrote about sounds menacing. I can hardly believe something so terrible roamed Agadin."

Brenton and Flor knew all about Fen, the book, and the Depths. At first, Brenton was furious that Kaldon had broken protocol by going down to the Depths. Considering how little time Kaldon had been at the facility, he could have been exiled for the breach. Brenton quickly found himself won over by the mystery of the book.

"I'm still not sure what I'm looking for, but I know there is something significant hidden in those pages," Kaldon said.

Brenton looked to him with an inquisitive gaze. "I'm sure you will figure it out. Speaking of mysteries, I want to hear again about what you and Anneya saw and heard in the library."

Brenton was greatly dismayed by the revelation of the Dark Blades in the library and the words they spoke. After they had told him about what they saw, the Knight brought the information to his superiors in the facility. This resulted in a full investigation. Brenton was part of the committee assigned to find the Dark Blades. Warriors throughout the Peak of Lore were zealously trying to find the traitors. Everyone was asked to keep the information to themselves to avoid panic amongst the residents. Kaldon had already told the Knight nearly a dozen times what had happened.

Kaldon sighed, not wanting to go through the story again, yet knew there was no point in arguing with the stubborn Knight. He began, saying, "While Anneya and I were on our way to the Depths, we found ourselves at a secluded room on the second level of the library. There were five Dark Blades talking."

"And, what did you hear them say?" the Knight prodded.

"They said an army would eventually reach the Peak of Lore to dominate it," he replied. Such a thought still jarred his nerves. "After that, they began chasing us through the library."

Brenton had a thoughtful look on his face as he dissected every word that was said. "And, you didn't see where they went in the library?"

"No. We found the entrance to the Depths and went in to escape the Dark Blades and to find Fen."

Brenton nodded. "Very well then, but don't think this will be the last time I ask you to run through this story again. We need to find these traitors."

Kaldon knew that much. The Dark Blades needed to be stopped. Still, the five traitors weren't as much of a concern to him as the army that would inevitably reach them. He tried to distract himself from the dreadful thought as he watched Anneya playing with the girls.

Flor watched Kaldon as he stared at the four playing. "You know, Kal, it seems like you and Anneya are growing quite close."

Kaldon froze at the remark. "Yes, I suppose we have. What are you saying?"

Flor laughed lightly, seeing how quickly the young man grew uncomfortable. "Well, after the ceremony of Brenton's promotion, there is going to be a ball. Do you think you will ask her to dance?"

Kaldon's face flushed crimson.

"I'm not trying to embarrass you, Kal. I just wouldn't be surprised if she would be interested in having a dance with you."

Kaldon felt like shrinking; however, he forced himself to step out of his timidity. "Sorry to disappoint you, Flor, but Anneya and I aren't interested in each other that way. We are just friends."

Flor looked over to Anneya and her girls. "Look, all I'm saying is that I know there are several men here at the Lore who have sought out Anneya. Most are too intimidated by her because she is a Blade. Yet, since you two started going down to the Depths together, she spends most of her time with you."

Kaldon looked from Flor to Brenton. The Knight was looking down at the table, trying not to show his grin.

"I'm glad you think this is amusing, Brenton," Kaldon said sarcastically.

The Knight shook his head. "I never said a word. Then again, you don't seem overly seasoned with women, so you may want to listen to Flor."

Kaldon knew the truth in this. He had never even danced with a girl. In fact, he was sure Anneya was his first close female friend, other than Claude's wife Betty.

As Brenton was about to continue teasing, Kaldon lifted his arm in caution. "Wait, do you hear that?" he asked.

Brenton's forehead creased. "Hear what? You can't get out of this conversation that easily."

"No, listen carefully," Kaldon said in concentration.

Faint yells began ascending in the distance from outside the entrance of the Peak of Lore. It wasn't long before the bellows trumped the chattering of students.

As the sun lit through the entrance of the Peak of Lore, the shadow began to dim the blazing shine. The yells of a man began to climb in volume. Soon enough, it wasn't only Kaldon, Brenton, and Flor listening, but also the dozens in the Peak of Lore's entrance. All watched as a feeble man, aged in years, arrived panting in.

With a staff in his hand, the old man was out of breath. The grey wisps of hair atop his head were unruly. As eyes rested on the distraught man, the entrance hall, which was normally buzzing with chatter, was nearly as quiet as the Depths. The light mood of the Peak of Lore grew weighty with a sense of urgency.

"Great Divinity," Brenton said under his breath, now standing in concern. "That is Alden the Seer. He is Locrian's former mentor."

Kaldon stood as well, awaiting to see what the old Seer would do next.

Alden looked up to the crowd of residents of the Peak of Lore. He shouted a gnarled shout. "Bring me to Tolek immediately! I've had a vision!"

The old Seer's tone then went sombre. He said, "I saw it in a vision, the Door of the Dominion is now open. Shadow is close. Small cities in Southeast Agadin, past the Mountains of D'aal, have been attacked by Kreel. Bring me Tolek at once!"

Chapter Twenty-Three

Encountering Eternity

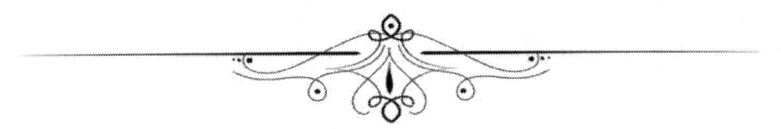

"**S**till your mind. Keep your eyes closed," the Master Healer said in a soothing tone.

Adjusting his weight, Kaldon sat cross-legged on the carpet. He was becoming accustomed to these sessions. In the quaint room, the healer sat across from him, summoning the Kingdom of Light. His task was to stay alert and remain strong amidst the weight of the presence. It took time to adjust to the flawless paradise of the Kingdom of Light.

Perfect peace began materializing around him. He knew the Kingdom of Light was entering the room. His flesh tingled at the breath of eternity.

"Do you feel that?" the Master Healer asked.

"Yes," he said, feeling the hair on his arms begin to rise.

In truth, he was struggling to still his mind. The entire Peak of Lore was in a state of panic. Flashes of the old Seer, Alden, delivering his grim message, kept rising to the front of his mind. *The Door of the Dominion is now open.* What could that mean?

The thought was unnerving, though he had no idea why.

The message struck fear and panic throughout the Peak of Lore, and he was shaken hearing that small cities in Southeast Agadin were attacked. He was thankful to learn that Rundle wasn't among them. Rumour said the Sovereign led a Swarm of Kreel into the cities and overthrew them. The Peak of Lore immediately sent warriors to help reclaim them. He hoped Rundle would remain safe, and his heart mourned for the lives already lost.

"Kal, still your mind," the Master Healer said in a sharp rebuke, seeing him grimacing, lost in his thoughts.

"Sorry," he said, refocusing. Even though his eyes were closed, he could feel her scowl.

When he wrestled to still his thoughts during these sessions, he would conjure up the image of the Owyl of Light in his mind. Visualizing the bird's flowing flames calmed him. Meditating on the fiery bird, he felt the Kingdom of Light begin to grow in intensity around him. He felt lightheaded at its touch. He sat, breathing it in.

"You may open your eyes," the healer said.

He looked at her surprised the session was already finished. The older woman sat before him, her wrinkled face grinning. Kaldon hadn't worked with this particular healer before; however, she seemed kindhearted.

"How did I do?" he prodded.

"Quite well," the woman said. "You were a little distracted, but you pressed through. It is understandable, given the circumstances we find ourselves in."

He nodded. "I am aware. The Lore has been in an uproar since Alden's prophetic message."

"Indeed," she slightly nodded, sadness evident in her tone.

"When will I learn to summon the Kingdom of Light by myself?" Kaldon asked. "I have been in numerous sessions, and it has never been mentioned."

The healer laughed. "You are likely a few years out from accessing the Kingdom yourself. It takes time to build enough belief in your link to eternity. You first need to know how to sit under the pressure of its light before you can summon it."

He figured as much. "I appreciate you meeting with me today," he said, rising from the floor.

Leaving the room, he was thankful for the training. If the Dominion was drawing closer, that meant he was running out of time to grow into a threat to the Sovereign of Shadow. He needed to be trained in any way that was available to him.

Strolling back to his room to rest for the night, he heard whispers throughout the halls; murmurs about Alden the Seer and the Door of the Dominion being opened. He heard rumours about Southeast Agadin being attacked. Although he hated seeing how frightened everyone was, he knew they needed something to break them into the reality of the Great War. The Seer's message seemed to free them from the false safety of their ignorance. They were not safe within the walls of the Peak of Lore.

Gripping the handle of his door, a shout rang throughout the stone hall.

"Kal!"

He turned to see Mikiel rushing towards him.

"Have you heard the news?" Mikiel said, nearly out of breath.

"About Alden the Seer?" Kaldon asked. "I was there when it happened."

Mikiel shook his head in disbelief. "It is unheard of for a Seer to be so out of sorts. I heard that the old man is with Tolek now, sharing his vision in greater detail."

Kaldon nodded in thought. "What do you think it means that the Door of the Dominion has been opened?"

Mikiel had a serious look on his face which was wildly uncharacteristic of him. "No one knows the full implications of the Door being opened," the young man said. "What I do know is that the Dominion of Shadow is close to Agadin. Very close."

Kaldon watched panicky students rushing by them. Brenton, Flor, and Anneya came to the same conclusion as Mikiel had. They also suspected the Sovereign of Shadow had a hand in opening the door.

"Kal, I've seen you and the Blade going to the library. Have you actually been going to the Depths?"

Kaldon's mind was still distant, meditating on the Door of the Dominion. "Yes, we have been spending time in the Depths with Fen."

Mikiel looked perplexed. "You mean you actually know the mad Philosopher? How did you accomplish something so outrageous?"

An amused look began growing on Kaldon's bearded face as his friend droned on about his concerns.

"Fen is a good woman. She listens to reason," Kaldon said, cutting him off. "She has recently been coming out of the Depths more than you would think."

"I doubt that," Mikiel said, observing his expression. "What are you smiling at? I'm legitimately concerned about you, and here you are thinking this is amusing. We already live in dangerous times, and here you are looking for more trouble. You shouldn't be spending time with people such as that woman. She isn't stable."

Kaldon looked past his nattering classmate. "Hello, Fen."

Mikiel froze.

"Why, hello there," Fen said with her scratchy voice. "Who is your ignorant friend here?"

Kaldon knew she wasn't cordial, but she was growing on him and quickly becoming a friend.

The greying woman walked forward into Mikiel's trail of sight. "Considering this young man knows nothing about me, it might be wise for him to learn to keep his mouth shut."

The Philosopher leaned toward Mikiel, looking him straight in the eyes. "After all, if I truly am mad, I could snap at any moment."

Mikiel's mouth moved as if trying to speak, but nothing came out. This was the first time Kaldon had seen the prankster without words.

"Don't mind him, Fen," he offered, trying to defuse the tension. "This is Mikiel. His mother is a professor here and an herbalist. He means well."

The Philosopher eyeballed the quaking man with a scrutinizing stare. "Fair enough. I don't have time for him anyway."

"I will see you later, Mikiel. We'll talk soon," Kaldon said, dismissing him and giving an out from the awkward situation.

Nodding nervously, Mikiel scurried down the hall. Kaldon shook his head, still amused. He knew the young man grew up sheltered within the confines of the mountain. This was likely the first time he had met a true Philosopher. He would likely be shaken up for the entire evening due to the interaction.

Fen handed him a small notebook. "Here are the next four pages. There wasn't much of interest; however, I wanted you to be able to give it a closer look."

"Thank you, Fen. I will look them over," he said, tucking the notebook in the pocket of his cloak.

She ran her hands over her simple robes. "Will you and Anneya be coming to the Depths anytime soon? As I've been interpreting, I have come across some fascinating finds."

Fen didn't surface from the soul of the Peak of Lore for no reason. He was, however, pleased to see her beginning to venture out beyond her realm of comfort, and it made sense that she had important information to share. Kaldon also liked to think that the isolated woman was beginning to enjoy the company of others.

"I was planning on coming down to visit you in the next few days, after the ceremony for Brenton's promotion. I'm looking forward to seeing what you've found," he responded.

He had been looking forward to the ceremony where his friend would be promoted from being a Knight to a Blade. He knew Brenton deserved the recognition.

Fen smiled a gracious smile, then leaned in closer. "I don't think you fully understand. Mysteries are beginning to unfold from the book you brought to me. When you visit, I have something significant to show you."

Kaldon ran his hand through his hair. "What have you found?"

"I can't say here," the Philosopher said, looking around at folk passing by. "Some truths are only safe to be voiced in the Depths. Secrets are coming to light. This book is a remarkable find."

He hoped Fen found information about the meaning of a Paragon. The Philosopher told him that she had read the word in ancient books here and there. Most references were linked to Dawntan Forlorn and her knowledge was limited. She seemed just as eager as he was to see what mysteries the book could unfold.

"I will come in the next few days, Fen," he promised.

She smiled, turning around, heading back in the direction of the library to begin her descent into the vast mountain. If it weren't so late, he would have gone down with her. He needed to rest.

Kaldon stepped into his bedroom, away from the chaos of the Peak of Lore's hectic state. Lighting the fireplace, he sat in the soft leather chair before it. He didn't light any other torches in the room. Only the beaming fireplace shone before him. He could delve into his thoughts better in the dim of night.

Pulling out the notebook, he read the words of Dawntan Forlorn.

"Over mountains, under trees. Through silver streams and upon snowed hills. I travel onward. I seek the beast, Marradus. Who would have thought a creature of such magnitude could hide so effectively? Agadin is a vast land. How I wish the brave would rise with me, yet they do not care for Agadin. They only seek their own gain. The Roeks keep to themselves. Philosophers hide in their books. Paladins are lost in their fame and riches. Agadin no longer has a shield, so I must become it. I am her protector. Since no one will stand, I travel alone. Thus is the road of a Paragon."

- Dawntan Forlorn
The First Paragon

Road of a Paragon, Kaldon thought. The words carried tremendous weight, even though their meaning was unknown to him. As heat from the flames warmed his chilled body, his mind darted from place to place. He thought of Alden the Seer. He thought of the Door of the Dominion. The Dominion of Shadow was closer to Agadin than ever before. The events of the day weighed on him. He was exhausted.

Gazing into swaying flames, Kaldon's thoughts drifted back to when he first travelled through the Mountains of D'aal to the Peak of Lore. The flames reminded him of the legendary Owyl.

As sleep pulled him in, he thought of Anneya.

Chapter Twenty-Four

The Grand Introduction

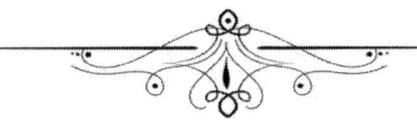

His eyelids felt heavy. It took him a moment to realize he was still in the chair.

Bending forward, Kaldon rubbed his eyes, trying to wake up. He heard rustling sounds coming from the other side of his room. Standing to stretch the dull throb in his joints, he saw the ash from the fire earlier. He felt the dampness of the room, making the pristine abode feel cold and uninviting. The notebook Fen gave him laid where it had fallen when sleep took him. The pages were still. He rubbed his eyes again, still trying to focus. A fog rolled in through the balcony window, illuminated by the moonlight. Something didn't feel quite right. He felt present, yet removed at the same time.

Then it struck him. He was dreaming.

The rustling sounded again. He gripped the hilt of his sword, looking in the sound's direction. The corner of the room was dense black, shawled in shadow. It appeared that nothing was there, but his instincts told him otherwise.

From the shadows, a man's voice softly filled the room. "I have been waiting for this moment for quite some time, Kal Wendal. I am glad we can finally acquaint ourselves."

He squinted at the shadows, unable to discern any shape or source of the voice.

"Come into the light," Kaldon commanded, rejecting the fear threatening to rise up.

A man emerged, the moonlight revealing a smooth face and average build cloaked by beige robes covered in script. Kaldon recognized the writing; it was Old Agadin. He knew by the grey in the man's hair that he must be much older than himself, but the face looked deceivingly young.

"My name is Tymas Droll. I am the Sovereign of Shadow." With that, the man stretched out his hand.

Kaldon looked at the man's deceiving face and outstretched hand. All fear left him, and anger rose up. Flashing through his mind were the multitude of lives stolen and cities destroyed by the tyrant standing before him.

"I don't shake hands with murderers," Kaldon stated unshaken.

Tymas slowly pulled his hand back, smiling. "I'm flattered you've heard of my work," he said casually.

"Your *work*," Kaldon spat out the words.

A menacing smile curled onto the Sovereign's face. "I have accomplished my greatest feat yet by opening the Door of the Dominion. This is how I can visit you in your dreams. I assure you, although we are meeting in a dream, the encounter between us is quite real."

"Have you come to try and kill me?" Kaldon asked with sternness in his voice.

"*Try?*" The Sovereign laughed a hard laugh. "If I wanted to kill you, I would simply do it."

Kaldon didn't back down. "What happened to Medric and your Kreel tells a different story."

Tymas' face grew sour. "Medric was a fool. Lucky for you, someone cannot die in a dream like this. I have come for another reason—to give you an opportunity."

Kaldon tilted his head. "I am not interested in anything you would have to offer."

"Oh, you may be surprised," Tymas said. "I can give you whatever you desire. Riches. Kingdoms. Influence. Power. Whatever you name, I can give it."

Pausing for a moment, he continued. "I know what you really want, Kal. I have the answers you are seeking."

Kaldon refused to respond.

Tymas continued, "Boy, you *bleed* insecurity. I can teach you things about yourself that you will never know otherwise. I can teach you about your foresight and train you to master it. I know everything about your father, Dolan Thain. Your whole life is a mystery to you, and I am the key. Not only am I the key to your understanding of your identity, but I am also the most powerful man in all of Agadin. You could be my direct pupil, if you choose to be. All you need to do is to commit to serving me. Embrace the Shadow."

Kaldon scowled. "I would rather die than serve you."

"Then, you shall." The Sovereign looked away, seemingly amused. "Foolish for you to turn down such an opportunity. There are those who have trained their entire lives wanting to learn under me, yet never have the privilege."

The Sovereign shook his head. "Such a shame. You know, your father was one of my greatest enemies. I hated the man. I eventually found his weakness: his connection to his past — his tie to Rundle."

The Sovereign snapped his finger. "Then it struck me. I could summon a plague. It wasn't too difficult. The Warrior General fell right into my hands and lost his life for it. I will find your weakness as well, Kal."

Kaldon refused to rise to the bait, but his mind was reeling. He knew the plagues were part of the Great War, but could this man actually summon them? His hand tightened around the hilt of his blade.

"You and I are much more connected than you realize," the Sovereign said.

"You and I have no connection." Kaldon refused to break eye contact, forcing his face to betray nothing.

"Oh, you would be surprised," Tymas said. "I have used many strategies to bring death to Agadin. Did you know that I was once trained as an herbalist? I spent years mastering the craft. I learned not only how to use it to give life, but also how to take it away."

Kaldon blinked slightly in confusion, not knowing what this had to do with him.

Tymas' soft voice growing even softer, he continued. "One day, I had a genius idea, as I often do. Why not use herbs to make a poison that appears to be a relief? Why not make it highly addictive, while giving the illusion of contentment and bliss at first? I spent hours mixing herbs to perfect the formula. Once I had it, we spread it all throughout Agadin. Its highly addictive nature ensured it wasn't long before it caught on. We even gave it an appealing name. Scethane."

Kaldon began to tremble. He forced himself to stand. The man in the room with him had not only killed his father, but had also taken the one person who loved him most. Memories flooded his mind: his mother's laugh and the way she read to him at night, the tender moments between them. He remembered her face later ravaged by the drug, and her dead body when it took her.

Tears streaming down his face, Kaldon pulled his sword from its resting place. The sword from his youth whirled from its sheath. Then, before it was even in the air, he was alone. Tymas Droll was gone. As he looked around the empty room shawled in darkness, the silence was shattered by the cries of a broken man.

Chapter Twenty-Five

From Knight to Blade

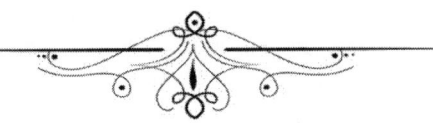

The grand stage was carved from white marble mined from the heart of a mountain. Purple and silver drapes, hundreds of feet long, regally graced the walls. Thousands of residents from the Peak of Lore were waiting for the ceremony to begin. The buzz in the room was palpable, and Kaldon was thankful to have a seat close to the stage.

In the waiting, his mind returned to the dream from the night prior, and the fury rose up again like bile. His training here was serving him well in processing the interaction. He knew the Sovereign brought up his mother's death to try and bait him into making a premature move, to seek him out. Kaldon knew he would eventually leave, but at the right time. He vowed to himself that the Sovereign of Shadow would fall.

He was fidgety, running his hands down his new clothes, smoothing out nonexistent wrinkles. The royal blue coat was a perfect fit, regal and rich-looking. He was unaccustomed to clothes such as these, fitting not only his body, but the fashion of those around him. Had the clothes not been brought to him by the Peak of Lore's staff, who insisted they were mandatory for the event, he would have worn his cloak and boots. Scratching his beard, he grinned. They tried forcing him to shave, but he was thankful he stubbornly refused.

Through the horde of students, professors, and staff, he saw Anneya. His eyes widened. The Blade didn't look like a warrior at all. She was a vision in a pale blue dress fitted to her form, her blonde hair tumbling down her shoulders.

"Hi Kal," she said, approaching.

"Anneya, I've never seen you in a dress before," he blurted out the obvious, wishing immediately he had found something else to say. Seeing her dressed this way made him feel even more awkward in his new clothes.

"You like it?" she softly smiled. "I feel quite foolish wearing it. I am a Blade, not a princess."

He could tell she felt out of sorts, but he thought her radiance shone brighter than anyone else's there.

"You look very elegant," he said, trying not to show how awkward he actually felt.

Anneya beamed.

"What do you think?" Kaldon asked, looking down at his jacket.

"Honestly, I really like them. They suit you." Anneya twisted her face. "I can tell that you hate them though. Am I right?"

"You are absolutely right," he said with a straight face.

She covered her mouth, chuckling. "Well, don't worry, Kal Wendal, you only need to endure wearing them for one day."

He fidgeted by rubbing his hands together. "Anneya, I was wondering if you were staying for the ceremony after the ball."

"I haven't decided. They are not my forte. They don't seem like they would be yours either," she replied.

Before he had seen her in that dress, he couldn't imagine her dancing. Any image he could conjure up in his mind of her would be in battle-wear. Now, seeing her in the pale blue gown with a crown of cascading golden hair, he saw her as more than a Blade.

"I have never been to a ball," he admitted. "But, if you do decide to go, I would love to have a dance with you."

Her eyebrows raised. "A dance?"

"Yes, a dance." Kaldon's nerves were raging. He immediately wished that he could pull the words back. There was a new kind of tension between them; he wondered if she felt it as well.

Chattering surrounded them, but the moment was silent between the two. Waiting for her answer, he felt like a hailstorm hit his stomach. Seconds felt like hours as he struggled to appear calm, awaiting her answer.

"Attention!" A shout rang from the stage, relieving the intensity between the two.

Everyone turned towards the sound. The host of the ceremony wore a long flowing maroon robe with gold inlay, giving a noble contrast. The room was quieting, but Kaldon was aware Anneya still hadn't answered him. He resented the man on the stage for the interjection. His heart was pounding when he risked a look at Anneya through the corner of his eye. As he caught a glimpse of her radiant smile, it told him more than words ever could. He found himself looking straight forward, beaming.

One by one, the host called those involved in the ceremony forward. Some were prominent professors, others helped govern the facility. A Knight being promoted to a Blade was a moment of great significance.

Murmurs broke out when Alden the Seer was called to the stage. The old Seer stood on the left of the stage to witness Brenton's promotion. Details of the Seer's vision still hadn't been made known to those at the Peak of Lore. There had been much speculation.

"Silence, please!" the host voiced. "There are two more guests for me to introduce. First, I invite Knight Brenton to the stage."

The crowd cheered as Brenton walked onto the stage wearing grey linens. The plain ensemble stood in stark contrast to the royal drapes and smoothed rock floor. He carried before him the folded onyx attire of a Knight of Agadin; attire that would be put to rest as he took up his new mantle.

The host paused before his final introduction. "Now, it is my honour to invite to the stage, Paladin Tolek. Master of war and battle. Head of the Peak of Lore."

The boisterous cheering for Brenton dissipated to an immediate silence at the mention of the Paladin.

A man of average height with ash-blonde hair walked onto the stage. He appeared several years older than Brenton. Not an eye in the room wasn't watching the enigmatic Paladin. Most who grew up at the Peak of Lore had never even seen the man. With a sword strapped to the Paladin's back, he was dressed in excellence. The hilt of his sword and sheath were a shining black. His scarlet ensemble was tailored to fit his build perfectly. Even though parts of his garb were loose, it was unmistakable that the body beneath was solid muscle. A white cape hung from his shoulders, gliding as he walked. His presence commanded authority.

Tolek thanked the host, taking the lead. With a deep-seasoned tone, he began. "We are here today because Brenton has chosen to live a selfless life. There was a Knight amongst us who had embraced the Shadow, serving its Sovereign, Tymas Droll."

Gasps filled the room. This was the first time many had heard of the events leading to this promotion.

Tolek continued, "Brenton purposefully went on assignment with the traitor, Medric, to expose him. He put his life at risk, travelling much of Southeast Agadin and overcoming many dangers, including near death and poisoning by a Kreel. He did this to protect the advancement of the Kingdom of Light: to protect us all. If it weren't for him, who knows what the traitor would have accomplished."

Tolek watched the crowd, allowing them to process the information. "Before I move onward, there is another here who must be honoured. The traitor was killed by a Blade from the Peak of Lore."

Anneya's eyes opened wide. She shifted uncomfortably, smoothing her dress.

Tolek gestured with his hand in her direction. "This is Anneya Padme, the Blade who slayed the Dark Knight."

All eyes moved from the stage to the unsuspecting Blade. The crowd roused once again, but this time for Anneya. She stood a little taller, looking both honoured and shocked at the mention.

"Congratulations," Kaldon whispered as he leaned towards the flustered Blade.

Her cheeks were a pink hue; she was too stunned to respond.

After a time, Tolek hushed the group so he could continue. "Now is the time we have gathered for," the Paladin said.

Kaldon saw Flor, Hayley, Haddy, and Honey up at the front watching Brenton with Tolek. Flor's face shone with pride for her husband.

Tolek grabbed the silver armour from the host. Upon the armour were a Blade's customary crimson red shoulder spikes. Brenton laid aside the black attire of a Knight and lowered himself to his knees in front of Tolek with his head bowed.

The Paladin placed the armoured shoulder blades upon Brenton. The blades suited him. Tolek lifted his sword from its sheath. The sword's blade was a translucent gold, contrasting with the onyx hilt. The golden metal shimmered in the light from the torches lighting up the room. Kaldon looked around, seeing many with their mouths open, mesmerized by the unique weapon.

Placing the tip of the golden sword on Brenton's shoulder, Tolek spoke forth a decree. "This man who was once a Knight, is now a Blade." The Paladin's words carried tremendous weight.

Cheers exploded louder than before. As Kaldon and Anneya cheered affirmations with the rest of the group, he paused. Something didn't feel right. Anxiety stirred within him. The feeling was both unexpected and staggering. It reminded him of what he felt when they were with Medric on their way to the Peak of Lore; however, this feeling didn't gradually build. It was sudden. Urgent.

Realization struck Kaldon. It was his foresight.

He looked around, trying to pinpoint what was wrong. Flor and the three girls were now on the stage hugging Brenton in congratulations. Everyone was joyous, everyone except Tolek. The Paladin carried a serious expression upon his face.

Then Kaldon saw it. A flashing image flew through his mind. The image was an arrow soaring at Brenton.

"Great Divinity, no," Kaldon whispered.

"Kal, what's wrong?" Anneya asked in concern.

Kaldon didn't have time to respond. Unapologetically pushing through the crowd, he forced himself to the left side of the stage. Before he could step onto the grand stage, the host looked at him with irritation.

The host spoke up. "No one is allowed on the…"

Kaldon pushed the man out of his way. If what he saw was correct, his actions were a matter of life and death for Brenton. He could deal with the consequences afterwards if he was wrong.

Kaldon saw the arrow; however, this time it wasn't in his mind. It shot from the back of the room. The arrow was hurled, spanning the mountain facility above the heads of those who were witnessing the ceremony.

With every eye on him, Kaldon ran towards Brenton at full speed. He needed to plan this out perfectly, or his friend's life would be lost. He knew he couldn't simply push Brenton out of the way, or the arrow would just hit him instead. He needed to improvise.

Approaching a stunned Brenton, he leaped into the air. In mid-flight, he pulled his sword from its sheath. As the arrow soared towards his friend, Kaldon's sword swung downward.

Mere inches from Brenton's chest, the sword made contact with the arrow, slicing it in two. One piece of the arrow slid upon the marble stage, and the other flew into the crowd.

Brenton was awestruck. "How did you…"

Silence wrung throughout the ceremony hall. Kaldon looked out into the crowd, seeing their shocked expressions. He saw the bewilderment on Anneya's face.

In such a moment, only one dared to speak. Through the rise of reverence, Tolek said, "Well, well. You must be the lad who defeated the Kreel."

Chapter Twenty-Six

The Paladin

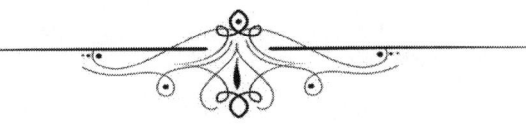

Kaldon felt their eyes burning into him. The thousands of people filling the hall were in complete shock. Time froze, and he looked around, aware of everything being in stilled motion. Brenton and Flor were astonished. He saw Mikiel in the crowd of people looking lost in wonder about what had taken place. Only Tolek seemed unmoved by the occurrence. The most confounding fact was not that he just saved Brenton's life, but that those embracing the Shadow were living amongst them. This was now clear to everyone.

Their place of refuge, their home, was no longer safe. There were enemies within their walls. These enemies could be anyone, and there was no way to tell how many.

Kaldon saw Anneya looking directly at him. Her expression told him she was concerned for him. He was no longer hidden, no longer just another student. In that moment, he was sad, realizing their dance would have to wait.

Looking back to meet the eyes of the Paladin, the man was gone. Two sizeable men stood where he had been, both wearing royal blue capes stretching halfway down their backs. The men were Bishops and outranked Blades in the tiers of fighters. Kaldon was caught off guard by the grand size of such men.

With a deep voice, one of the Bishops said, "Paladin Tolek requests your presence. Follow us immediately."

Kaldon looked over to Brenton, who nodded his head, confirming that the Bishop's words were not a request.

Slipping his sword into its resting place, he followed the men, feeling sudden relief from being away from the intense stares in the hall. As he followed, the three burrowed deeper into the mountain. The Bishops did not say a word. In turn, he didn't ask questions, simply following. Advancing through halls he had yet to travel, he glanced upon the quotes of Philosophers written on walls; however, he didn't care to read them. He didn't know what his day would hold. A Paladin wanted to meet with him.

He was ushered into a hall with walls so white and so brilliant that it caused him to blink. He was reminded of the sun coming up on the snowy landscape of the mountains the first time he'd seen them. At the end of the hall was an intricately crafted wooden door. He sensed this door led to the Paladin's abode. One of the Bishops stepped forward to open the door. Kaldon stepped in alone as they guarded the entrance.

The home was grand. The room was filled with leather couches and a table for writing. A large window in the main wall overlooked the Mountains of D'aal, while the remaining walls were covered with shelves of books. There were hallways leading off to various rooms. Weapons were spread out everywhere, some Kaldon had never seen the likes of before. Dozens of swords leaned against bookshelves. Axes and daggers laid upon furniture. He knew one of the marks of a Paladin was their mastery of all weapons. Even though menacing blades of every sort were strewn throughout the room, not one of them was as daunting as the Paladin looking out the window in deep thought.

The Paladin turned towards Kaldon.

"So, you are the one who defeated the Kreel," Tolek said slowly turning to the window again.

Weighing his words before answering, Kaldon answered cautiously. "I am. Brenton and I fought the Kreel together. When he was injured by the creature, I found a way to drive it away." He hoped his answer was sufficient. He didn't know how he felt being alone with such a man.

The Paladin didn't respond.

Kaldon ran his hand through his hair, not knowing if he should still be speaking or not.

Finally, the Paladin turned to face him. "What is your name?"

Kaldon swallowed. "My name is Kal Wendal."

"Pick a weapon, Kal Wendal," the Paladin demanded.

"Excuse me?" Kaldon said as his eyes darted to the seemingly innumerable weapons that surrounded him.

Tolek's gaze grew sharper. "You clearly have the ability of foresight. No one could stop an arrow as you did without it. I want to see what you can do with a blade."

"I do have the ability, but I cannot control it," Kaldon admitted, not yet picking a weapon. "At the ceremony, you saw the arrow as well. I saw the expression on your face when the arrow flashed through my mind. Everyone was cheering except you, because you must have seen what I saw. You must have foresight as well," Kaldon said.

"Very perceptive of you," the Paladin responded stone-faced.

"Would you have stopped the arrow?" Kaldon asked, clearing his throat.

Tolek looked out the window again. "If you hadn't split the arrow with your sword, I would have reached out and plucked it from the air with my hand."

Kaldon caught himself as he was taking a step back, forcing himself to stay planted where he stood. It was one thing to do what he did, cutting the arrow out of the air. It was another thing to have such keen senses to pluck a soaring arrow in mid-flight.

As his eyes roamed from weapon to weapon around the room, they rested upon a sword Tolek had with him at the ceremony. It was unsheathed, laying a study desk. The golden blade was vibrant. It reminded him of eternity. The sword's hilt was the exact opposite. Its darkened hilt was so black, it almost paled the vibrance from whatever surrounded it.

"You like the sword?" Tolek asked, walking over to the magnificent blade. He ran his hand over the hilt. "This sword is an ancient relic, crafted with excellence. No one knows how long ago it was forged."

He continued, "In a war several years ago, I killed the king who carried this sword. The corrupt ruler wasn't worthy of such a weapon. This deserves to be in the hand of a Paladin, rather than hanging as a decoration from a traitor's waist. The metal is like no other. It cannot dull. It is as sharp now as it was the day it was forged."

Tolek lifted the sword, looking into its reflective glow. "This sword's name is *Integrity*."

Kaldon thought it a rather odd name for such a weapon, yet was mesmerized by it nonetheless.

"Is this the weapon you choose, Kal Wendal?" the Paladin asked, gazing into the flowing gold.

Kaldon rested his hand upon his own hilt, feeling the familiar grip. "I choose my own sword," he said.

Tolek looked at him again with a questionable stare.

He repeated himself. "I choose my own sword for battle."

"This is the sword of your youth. Am I right?" Tolek said.

Kaldon nodded.

Tolek walked up to him. "May I see it?"

He handed his blade over to the Paladin. "This is a remarkable blade," Tolek said, running his thumb over the auburn-leather hilt. "Your sword has been forged well. It's a sword fit even for a Paladin, in fact. It is likely worth more than you would expect. Do you know why else it is remarkable?" he asked, handing the sword back to Kaldon.

Kaldon was thankful to have the familiar sword back in his grip. "Why?"

"Because you have history with it. It is a symbol, reminding you where you came from—what you rose from. Remembering these things helps humility shape inside of you. Humility is a prominent key for a great leader."

Kaldon let the words sink in. He didn't know what he thought of the Paladin. One moment, he seemed intimidating—threatening, even. Then the next, he was teaching him. He had never thought of naming his childhood sword; however, every good sword needed a name. Looking at the blade, he figured he had finally found its name. *Humility*.

"Now, let's see what you have in you," the Paladin said authoritatively.

Kaldon had his sword, *Humility*, ready to spar with Tolek. He wondered how different it would be fighting with a Paladin in comparison to Brenton.

Kaldon was surprised to see that Tolek laid aside the golden sword, *Integrity*, instead grabbing a wooden practice sword.

"Hit me," the Paladin challenged.

Kaldon hesitated. He didn't want to attack a man who only had a wooden sword. Then he reminded himself of who this was.

Kaldon ran at Tolek at full speed. As *Humility* came down at the Paladin, Tolek was already out of the way. Kaldon didn't hesitate, immediately coming in for a second attack. As he came in with full strength, Tolek was swift, seamlessly skirting every attempt.

Then it came. Tolek moved the wooden sword so quickly that Kaldon hardly saw it. In a blur, the wooden sword hit his arm. He heard a snap, not knowing if it was the sound of the wood breaking or his arm. Kaldon screamed out in agony. He looked over, convinced that his arm was fractured. Pain ignited a rage that seared through him.

Kaldon's scream didn't seem to faze the Paladin. Tolek stretched his hand. As he did, Kaldon began feeling a familiar sensation: perfect peace. It was the Kingdom of Light invading the Paladin's room. The arm that raged in pain began feeling light and airy until all of the pain ceased to exist.

"You can heal," Kaldon said, shocked.

"I can do many things you wouldn't be able to comprehend," the Paladin came at him again.

Kaldon grew weary attempting to block each blow that came in. Tolek moved with certainty. Each movement was intentional. No matter how hard he tried, he couldn't hit the Paladin. Tolek did not hold back. Not a single strike missed its mark.

The Paladin's fist met Kaldon's jaw. Kaldon winced, expecting to feel pain, instead, the Paladin summoned the Kingdom of Light to dethrone the pain before it was even felt. He had never seen the bridge between the realms created so quickly and with such power. He quickly lost count to how many times the Paladin had both struck and healed him.

The Paladin grew bored, throwing aside his wooden sword. "Hit me," he commanded.

Kaldon didn't make a habit of attacking someone without a weapon; however, the Paladin was as fluid as a river. Nothing could hit him. With a flash, Kaldon jumped, swinging his sword downward over Tolek.

The Paladin did not step out of the way. He watched the blade descend toward him. Before the blade hit its target, Tolek clapped his hands together over his head at a staggering speed, catching the blade in mid-swing. Kaldon's motion stopped immediately at the powerful grasp of the Paladin.

"How…" Kaldon spoke out, confused.

Before he could finish, the Paladin brought up his foot, kicking him in the chest. Kaldon flew back several feet, landing on his back. Feeling a lightness in his chest, he knew Tolek had already healed the blow. Kaldon was grateful for the healing.

Kaldon stayed down, admitting defeat as he tried to catch his breath. He thought about how as formidable of a fighter Brenton was, Tolek was something else entirely. Nothing he did could have trained him for a Paladin. He truly was a master of war and battle.

Tolek walked up to the young man who was sprawled on his back. "Consider this a lesson. There is only one reason why I beat you."

He looked up as the Paladin stood over him. Tolek continued, "It doesn't matter if you have a sword forged from iron or one crafted from wood. The effectiveness of the sword has little to do with the quality of the sword. It has everything to do with the quality of the one wielding it."

Kaldon panted, still catching his breath.

Tolek continued, "Now tell me. What is your name?"

There was no mistaking the authority in his tone.

Kaldon looked up again, this time confused. "I already told you. I am Kal Wendal."

Tolek shook his head, annoyed. "Stop lying to yourself. That isn't your full first name. It isn't even your real last name. I know who you are. I knew your father. Do you honestly think a Philosopher such as Fen wouldn't report to me?"

The Paladin spoke immediately, not giving Kaldon the chance to respond. "You say you want to learn to use your foresight, yet you reject who you truly are."

Kaldon looked down at his Legacy hanging over his shirt. It must have fallen out during the fight.

Tolek's tone softened. "You will never grasp your full potential if you keep running from your true identity. It is time to grow up and to lay aside the chains of your childhood. It is time to become the man you were created to be."

Kaldon felt pain flooding through him, yet it wasn't from the fight. It was pain from his soul; memories burned into him from his youth. Memories of Rundle, being orphaned and living on the streets. He thought of his mother. He thought of her addiction and death. Memory upon memory rushed in, like walls of a prison rising up around him. He saw them clearly for the first time as weights limiting him and trying to cage him.

"You are right," he whispered through staggered breaths.

Tolek smiled a faint smile. "Then tell me, what is your name?"

Feeling *Kaldon* was too grand a name for his circumstances, he had gone by *Kal* his entire life. Yet, Tolek was right. It was not his birth name, and he was no longer a broken boy searching out solace in a sewer. He had risen from the streets of Rundle, and now he must rise from his pain. He must rise from its limitations.

He stood, brushing dust from his clothes. He looked the Paladin in the eyes. "My name is Kaldon. I am Kaldon Thain."

With the sternness and authority that only a Paladin carried, Tolek said, "Well, Kaldon Thain, I have a mission for you."

Chapter Twenty-Seven

Geran

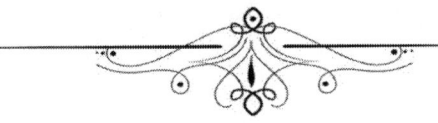

"What kind of mission?" Kaldon asked.

"Of the most dangerous kind," Tolek said dryly.

A buzz rang in Kaldon's ears. He wondered if it was from the fight, but quickly realized it wasn't. He couldn't pinpoint its source.

Tolek continued, "The Seer's vision aided us greatly, revealing the Sovereign's strategy to invade the Peak of Lore. As you know, there are traitors amongst us. Tymas Droll seeks to fortify his attack from the inside out."

"I know about the army coming," Kaldon replied. "Anneya and I heard Dark Blades speaking in the second level of the library."

Tolek nodded. "My advisors shared with me what you heard. Thank you for not keeping that information to yourself; it greatly benefited us. Unfortunately, things have progressed quicker than we hoped."

He walked to the window overlooking the mountains. "Come here, Kaldon."

Approaching the window, Kaldon saw the mountainous landscape. It was a paradise Anneya once told him paled in comparison to the Kingdom of Light. Mountains stood at remarkable heights, with numerous chasms delving to astounding depths. Looking out the window, he realized the buzzing was amplified, yet still far off. The distant ring caused him to wane, stirring his nerves.

Tolek raised a hand, pointing Kaldon off in the distance. "Do you see that large blur in the centre of that valley?"

The valley bowed between two mountains in the distance. "Yes. I see it."

"Look closely," the Paladin said quietly.

As Kaldon looked upon the faint blur, he realized it was faintly swaying. He looked up to Tolek in confusion.

Understanding struck him as he realized that he was looking at the source of the buzzing. "Great Divinity…"

Tolek rested his hand on the stone wall. "We are at war, and that is a fraction of the Sovereign's army. It is only a matter of days until that swarm of warriors, Kreel, and Nahmen arrive."

"What do we do?" Kaldon implored, hardly able to voice his question. He'd never seen such numbers, nor such a terrifying sight.

"I've already appointed the Bishops of the Lore to guard the training facility. There are many warriors here, but not nearly enough to thwart an army of this size.

"Every army is held together by its overseers. We may not be able to beat them by force, but we may be able to by dismantling their army. I am choosing an elite team to take out their leaders," Tolek said, gazing steadily at Kaldon.

"You're saying you want me to go with you?" Kaldon asked, perplexed.

"I have seen what you can do. You have the ability of foresight. You may not know how to fully use it, but you have an advantage most do not. I will be bringing along a few trusted Bishops as well as Alden. Blade Anneya Padme will also be asked to join us. Overseers of the Peak of Lore are talking to her as we speak. A Blade who slayed a Dark Knight is a formidable asset."

Kaldon knew Anneya would jump at the chance, but he wished she didn't have to be a part of such a dangerous mission. "And Brenton?"

"He will be staying behind. I can read the man. He would prefer to stay here to protect his family. I respect him for it. He will also benefit the Bishops by staying behind to shield the Lore," Tolek said with finality.

"I will help you." The words escaped Kaldon's mouth.

The blurred army loomed before him. He knew he may not live to see the end of it all; however, he also knew he had his part to play in the Great War.

"Have you ever met Tymas Droll?" he asked Tolek.

"No, but I am planning on meeting him and ending him on this mission." With tenacity in his eyes, Tolek continued. "The man is a worm. I am determined to end his reign. Still, even though this army falls under the banner of Droll, he is not the one leading it."

"Who does?" Kaldon probed.

"General Geran Rule. He is the embodiment of rage. While Tymas Droll is the mind of the Dominion of Shadow, Geran is the fist. He is the Sovereign's righthand man."

"How dangerous is he?" Kaldon queried.

Tolek's jaw set as he responded. "Geran is a *Dark Paladin*. To say he is a formidable warrior would be a dire understatement. He is one of the greatest fighters in all of Agadin."

Kaldon pondered in silence at the thought of Tolek revering someone as a warrior. He had encountered a Dark Knight and Dark Blades. The thought of a Dark Paladin chilled his flesh.

A knock struck the door of the Paladin's abode.

"Enter," Tolek said.

The wooden door creaked open. Alden, the old Seer, walked into the room looking past Kaldon, to Tolek.

"We are running out of time. The army of Shadow approaches," the Seer said in a raspy voice.

Tolek nodded. "I am aware, Alden. We will be leaving shortly."

Watching the back-and-forth interaction between the Paladin and Seer, Kaldon listened to the buzzing sound of the approaching army. He meditated on it. The low hum churned his nerves.

As the Seer and Paladin quieted, Kaldon noticed that Alden was watching him. He looked the Seer in the eyes.

"I see the scroll over your life, boy," the Seer stated.

Kaldon froze. He had never met a Seer before.

Alden looked right through him. "There is no doubting you have potential; however, I have seen many with potential lose their lives. Do you want me to tell you whether you will survive this mission or not?"

The Seer's words dripped sarcasm. Kaldon discerned his arrogance. There was a harshness to his tone that he clashed with. Alden was trying to intimidate him.

Kaldon swallowed, rising into confidence. He wouldn't allow himself to be intimidated, even if Alden was a Seer. "I will be the one who decides whether I live or die, not some vision from a Seer who doesn't know how to hold his tongue."

The Seer laughed, clearly equating the boldness to immaturity; however, Kaldon knew better than to let someone bully him. He wouldn't let Alden treat him as though he were his superior.

Tolek looked to Kaldon and the Seer, quieting both of them. "We have no time to waste. We leave in several hours, at nightfall. Meet us at the entrance of the Lore. If you are not there, we will leave without you."

Kaldon would be there. He knew before he left that there was one place he needed to go. The Depths awaited him.

Chapter Twenty-Eight

Legacy Unfolding

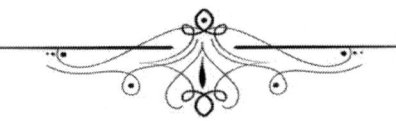

A diagram of a Legacy that Fen sketched on a rather large piece of paper laid across the table. It was surrounded by scribbled notes. Kaldon, Anneya, and Fen all stood around the sketch. Kaldon was pleased to see Anneya was already in the Depths when he arrived.

In the Depths, he felt free from curious stares and the ambush of questions throughout the Peak of Lore. Travelling from Tolek's abode to the Depths, students and professors kept stopping him, wanting to know how he knew the arrow was coming toward Brenton. They asked how he managed to cut it in half, midair, and where he'd come from. Essentially, they asked everything and nothing. He'd ignored them, persisting onward, only stopping when he ran into Brenton. He was happy to see his friend. It allowed them to say farewell before he left on his mission.

Travelling to the Depths gave him room to think about his time with the Paladin. Brushing his hand over his old cloak, he was glad to have had time to stop and change into clothes he was comfortable in.

"Kal, the book you found carries an intriguing secret," Fen said, not looking up from the diagram.

"Kaldon," he corrected the Philosopher.

Anneya turned her head, giving him a curious look. "Kaldon," the Blade spoke his formal name in thought. "I like it. It's a strong name, very suiting."

"Alright, *Kaldon* then," Fen said, shaking her head, annoyed at the interruption.

Looking at Anneya, he knew she had already been informed they were leaving. She looked up at him with fierceness in her eyes. Fire blazed within her. Even though she was physically in the Depths with him and Fen, the Blade was not present. She burned for the mission set before her. Anneya inclined her head towards Kaldon. Without a word, he knew she was communicating that she was coming with him.

Fen scrambled through her notes, unaware of their silent communication. "I must say, I did not expect that Dawntan's journal would contain such a secret. I drew this diagram to help explain what I have found."

With a finger, Fen traced the lines of the diagram. "Your book has given us more insight into the meaning of a Legacy."

Anneya piped up in surprise. "I wouldn't have thought there could be more to the symbol. It's already brimmed with meaning."

"Indeed. Look at this," Fen said, still running her finger along the diagram of the Legacy. "We know it is a symbol of the Protectors appointed by Divinity. Each of the five lines protruding from the inner circle speaks to the different protectors: Paladin, Seer, Philosopher, Roek, and Shan-Rafa. However, Dawntan taught that there was a sixth protector, a

Paragon."

"A sixth protector…" Anneya whispered.

Kaldon listened intently.

Fen looked at the two. "We have known next to nothing about what a Paragon is since this sixth Protector is tremendously rare. They are so rare that they may as well be non-existent." The telling mark of a Philosopher oozed out from Fen—the unquenchable passion for new truth.

Excitedly, she continued, "As the book's title, *The First Paragon*, suggests that Dawntan was the first Paragon to ever walk Agadin, four thousand years ago. To my knowledge, not only was he the first Paragon, but he may have been the only one to ever live. I have studied some of the most prestigious books in all of Agadin, and I have never read of anyone carrying the mantle other than him."

"So, what is a Paragon then?" Kaldon asked, knowing he had little time left to unravel the Philosopher's knowledge.

"See this outer circle intersecting with the five lines?" Fen asked, pointing to the circle. "Dawntan teaches that this circle is the symbol of a Paragon."

All three of them were transfixed by the find.

"This outer circle touches all five, because this is how a Paragon's gift functions. A Paragon is wired to pull from the gift of each protector. Dawntan explained it much better than I could," she said. Fen began quoting the translated book.

"A Paragon draws from the gifts of the five protectors. A Paragon is all five at once, yet at the same time, is none. A Paragon has the mind of a Philosopher, the vision of a Seer, the compassion of a Shan-Rafa, the skill of a Roek, the courage of a Paladin. I am a Paragon, one called to become all things to protect Agadin. Never have I heard of one such as myself. I stand alone. I do not understand why Divinity chose me to wield such ability.

Seemingly, limitless power courses through me: power not of Agadin, but from the Golden Land. I possess power that can both create and destroy: to build and to tear down. I pray this power does not corrupt me."

- Dawntan Forlorn
The First Paragon

Kaldon couldn't imagine what it would be like to have such ability, such power. Looking at the drawn Legacy, he wished the revelation pacified his curiosity. Instead, it created more questions.

"I wonder why they are so rare?" he asked. "It seems like there are numerous records of the other Protectors of Agadin."

Fen looked puzzled. "I wish I had more answers. I do know that in Dawntan's time, the Dominion of Shadow threatened Agadin in a profound way. Chaos and death draped over the land. My guess is Divinity birthed a Paragon to bring balance, so that the Kingdom of Light would take its place to shine again."

Anneya cut in. "What was Dawntan referring to when he mentioned the *Golden Land?*"

"Ah, yes," Fen responded, holding her chin between finger and thumb. "The Golden Land was written about in many texts from his time period. The term was used up until around three thousand years ago. You wouldn't hear of it in recent texts. The Golden Land was what people from the past called the Kingdom of Light."

Kaldon nodded his head in thought. The name moved him, *the Golden Land*. It seemed a name fitting for an eternal place.

"Kal..." Anneya caught herself, "I mean Kaldon. I'm sorry, but we must go. The others will not wait."

He turned to Fen. "Thank you for everything you have taught us. This is the last time we will be seeing you for quite some time."

She gave him a knowing look. "The Paladin is sending you on a mission, isn't he?"

He was caught off guard by Fen's perceptivity.

"Don't be surprised, Kaldon. I know the Paladin well. I also know better than to ask about the missions he would embark on."

Kaldon was thankful she didn't want to know the details. Still, he couldn't not warn Fen about the threat to the Peak of Lore.

"Fen, you would be wise to stay down here for the next while," he said. "Get a stock of food, water supply—anything you may need. Above the Depths may not be safe ground for a time."

Fen wore a blank look on her face. "I think I am beginning to understand the mission you two are about to endure. War is no stranger to me."

Kaldon had assumed as much from the Philosopher. "I wish we could stay to hear the rest of the translation of the journal."

Fen cocked an eyebrow. "That was one of the reasons I wanted to see you so urgently. You came just at the right time. I am finished translating."

"What did you say, Philosopher?" Anneya voiced in shock.

Fen looked Anneya in the eyes, repeating herself slowly. "I. Am. Finished." The Philosopher shook her head. "Sometimes Blades can be so thick."

Anneya rolled her eyes.

Fen rummaged through more papers, finding the last notebook of the set. "Ah, here it is." Fen handed nearly thirty written pages of translation of the book to Kaldon.

"How did you transcribe this so quickly?" he asked, flipping the pages with his fingers.

Fen seemed amused. "The hard part of translating is figuring out the intricacies of the language. Once you accomplish that, you find your flow. Once I understood the language, I simply fractioned my mind to work quicker."

Kaldon was nothing but impressed by the Philosopher. "Well, as an act of my gratitude, I will leave the original copy here in the Depths with you. I'm sure you would like to study it longer. This place is, after all, a home for priceless books."

"Indeed it is," the Philosopher smiled. "You best be on your way. Paladins wait for no one."

Chapter Twenty-Nine

Unfathomable Odds

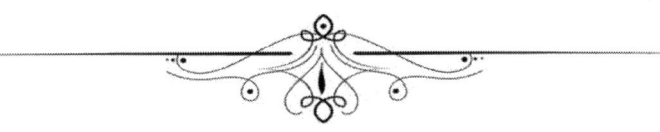

Travelling by night wasn't Kaldon's preference, especially under such circumstances. The cold stung his flesh, even though it was growing warmer than when he first arrived at the Peak of Lore. Trees hung low from the weight of the snow draping over the troop. Behind a rough outcrop of stone, the seven sat in wait. It had been several hours since they had left; however, the buzzing of the bulk of the dark army was amplifying in sound.

They drew nearer.

His back against the chilled rock, he twirled a dead twig between his finger and thumb, listening intently. The others, Alden, Anneya, two female Bishops, and one male waited for the signal to move forward again.

Pressing his ear against the cold stone, Tolek listened to soldiers' boots thudding against the snowy ground. Kaldon assumed there were close to fifty men passing by on their way to the facility. They'd already stopped several times to hide, as swarms of soldiers marched past. Luckily, mountain fog hung in the air, hiding them.

"Tolek, it is ridiculous how often we are stopping," Alden grumbled.

The Paladin remained silent, listening to the footsteps of soldiers with his ear still pressed to the stone.

"Silence, Seer," Bernice, one of the Bishops protested. "We either hide or fail in our mission."

Tolek turned towards them, giving them both a silencing glare. The Seer was quickly growing on everyone's nerves, complaining more than contributing.

As the sound of footsteps lessened, Tolek motioned for them to move onward again. Kaldon would have felt secure in the company of such warriors, but considering only seven of them marched onward into nearly a forty-thousand-person army filled with Kreel and Nahmen, his nerves were on edge.

Tolek led the troop. The man was fearless. Behind him was Alden, using a staff to help him keep up. The three Bishops were usually within several hundred feet of the group, scouting for threats.

Kaldon and Anneya walked side by side, her armour matching her countenance. Through the filter of the fog, he saw her confidence illuminated with each step she took.

He whispered toward her. "Have you been on such a mission before?"

Still looking onward, Anneya answered. "I have been on many missions: both dangerous and life-threatening. I can't say I have ever walked head-on into a sea of forty-thousand opponents."

"Are you afraid?" Kaldon asked.

"Yes." Her face betraying no emotion, she kept moving.

Her voice was steady. "Are you afraid, Kaldon?"

He swallowed, gripping the hilt of his sword, *Humility*. "I am."

Through the breath of silence, he continued speaking to lighten the mood. "I know we will survive."

"How do you know?" she asked, finally looking over at him.

"Because... you still owe me a dance."

She looked away, smiling. "I suppose I do."

Anneya's smile warmed him, shining in stark contrast to their dire situation. It gave him courage to believe that they may actually survive.

Their momentary ease evaporated as the sound of a mournful weep filled the night. Anneya's face turned grim once again as she saw Tolek stop ahead of them. Everyone quietly approached the Paladin to hear his instructions. Everyone other than one of the Bishops was together.

"Where is Bernice?" Tolek asked, looking at different assortments of trees as he tried to pinpoint where the noise came from.

The male Bishop, Troy, stepped forward. "I saw her minutes ago scouting, Paladin Tolek."

Tolek nodded, waiting.

A rustling of twigs sounded to the side of the troop, followed by the grunts of a man.

"Keep walking," the troop heard Bernice say authoritatively, as she pushed her way through trees. The Bishop came out with her prisoner shuffling in front of her.

The gruff Bishop pushed the young man to the ground. "I found this poor excuse for a man following us."

Kaldon peered at the young man. The moonlight revealed his mopped hair and spindly body.

It was Mikiel.

"Why are you following us?" Tolek demanded.

Mikiel began stuttering. His eyes darted from person to person. "I saw you all leaving the Lore," he fumbled, his panic evident. "I was curious where you were going, so I followed. I knew I couldn't turn back once I saw soldiers passing by who were not our own."

Tolek shook his head, rubbing his eyes in frustration.

"Should we send him back to the Lore, Paladin Tolek?" Bernice asked forcefully.

"No," he responded in annoyance. "They will have sealed all entrance points by now. The landscape behind us is filled with soldiers from the army of Shadow. He will be killed if he tries to go back."

Mikiel's eyes widened.

The Paladin turned to the other female Bishop named Shar. "Bishop, give him one of your spare daggers."

The Bishop pulled a dagger out from her belt loop, spinning it in her hand. Walking over to Mikiel, the Bishop thrust the dagger towards him. He took it reluctantly.

Looking at the frightened young man, Tolek continued. "You will surely die if you return; that is the only reason I am not sending you back. Your curiosity made you a volunteer for a mission that will likely cost you your life."

Mikiel gulped.

"What were you thinking?" Kaldon asked his shaken friend as the small troop trudged closer to the sound of the buzzing army.

"When I saw you leaving, I had to follow," Mikiel said. "I have been restless for years. I grew up in that mountain. It's all I know. I want to see Agadin, and this was my chance. What better way to leave than following a Paladin?"

As he shared, Kaldon looked ahead into the distance. Five bulked trees darkening the path caught his attention. With the moon behind the trees, he could only see their outline. They were hazy through the clouded fog. He thought it was odd for trees to grow so close to the drop-off of a ravine.

"I'm sorry to disappoint you, Mikiel," he said, pulling his attention back to their conversation. "You may not see much of Agadin. We may not even see tomorrow," Kaldon explained.

Mikiel shook his head. "I know it wasn't a wise decision, but I needed to come. This might sound strange, but I've always felt like I have a part to play in what is taking place in Agadin; a role in the Great War between the Kingdom of Light and the Dominion of Shadow."

Kaldon understood Mikiel's longing to accomplish great things. He supposed everyone carried a desire to make an imprint on the world; to leave a legacy. Still, he wished the young man would have stayed safe within the fortress.

"Just keep close," Kaldon said with his eyes on Tolek. "And for Divinity's sake, don't even think of pulling any pranks with this troop."

Mikiel bobbed his head in adamant agreement.

Seeing the five trees dawning closer, Kaldon moved his eyes to the Paladin. Tolek stopped before the bulky trees. Kaldon thought it was odd to rest in plain sight and so close to a cliff's edge. Alden the Seer took a step beside Tolek, gazing at the distinct trees. Kaldon and Mikiel quickened their pace to see why they stopped.

Nearing the trees, their features became more distinct. As their sharp features cut through the fog, he saw what looked like a thick branch lift into the air. Realization struck him. Kaldon's steady pace progressed to a sprinting stride toward them. He stood beside Tolek and Alden as five adult Kreel looked back at them.

One of the Kreel snarled. The sound pulled memories of Ont's death into Kaldon's mind. Nerves swelled as he looked upon the snarling bat-like faces.

In unison, all five Kreel raised their sword-like claws. Their reptilian tails swayed at the sight of their prey. Shrieks filled the night. Anneya snapped out her bow and arrow, firing at one of the Kreel. The arrow bounced off its shoulder.

"Stop!" Tolek commanded. "Every one of you, get behind me!"

They all looked at one another in confusion. The only one who didn't seem dismayed by Tolek's remark was Alden. The Seer had an impatient look written on his wrinkled face.

"Tolek, we will fight to the death alongside you," Bernice voiced with passion.

The Paladin looked to the overconfident Bishop. "I *said*, get behind me." His tone was severe.

At his command, the troop backed up, allowing him to stand alone before the Kreel. Each of the creatures loomed over the Paladin. Their talons shone in the light of the stars. Before any could charge him, he summoned *Integrity* from its sheath. The Paladin lunged toward the Kreel.

Jumping in the air, his sword swung toward one of the Kreel. Simultaneously, his foot came up to another one, striking its eyes. The Kreel stumbled away, wailing a shrill cry while covering its monstrous face with its talons.

Kaldon watched in disbelief as Tolek swung his sword and spun his body around Kreel that were twice his size. There were times when he was so quick that Kaldon could not distinguish his movements.

Tolek darted around and through the creatures while the blinded Kreel stumbled around swinging its claws and tail. The other four surrounded the Paladin, trying to trap him. Tolek, discerning the intents of the Kreel began striking the beasts with ferocity, specifically targeting their eyes and wings.

It was mesmerizing to watch. The Paladin was a hurricane of warfare. The seemingly indestructible beasts were overwhelmed by the seasoned warrior. With every attack that came at him, he countered in an unexpected way, confusing the beasts.

As the blinded Kreel stumbled off a nearby cliff, Tolek struck another in the eyes, killing its sight. The Paladin swung his golden blade at the wings of the Kreel, preventing flight or escape.

With only three Kreel left to cause harm, Tolek charged two who were nearing the cliff. The Paladin leapt, planting a foot on each of the Kreels' chests, launching them off the mountain's edge. The two Kreel attempted to flap their shredded wings as they fell into the rocky chasm, screeching.

The final Kreel roared with rage at the Paladin. Tolek stood still, inviting it to attack. As the creature pounced, he gripped its fur, using its body weight against it to pull it to the ground. As it laid upon the mountain stone, the Paladin reached below its jaw and yanked up its chin.

Looking into the eyes of the beast, he knew a Nahmen was on the other side, watching him. "Nahmen! I just defeated five of your Kreel single-handedly. Tell your Sovereign and the Dark Paladin that I am coming for them next!" Tolek brought the hilt of his blade down upon the Kreel's head, rendering it unconscious.

Three Kreel laid at the bottom of the chasm, another was unconscious; the last stumbled around blindly. Tolek looked up to his troop. All that met him were expressions of mesmerized shock.

Through the awestruck gazes, the voice of a young man arose. In sheer disbelief, Mikiel said, "We may actually stand a chance on this mission."

Chapter Thirty

An Unexpected Meeting

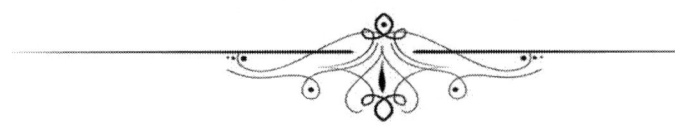

"I, Dawntan Forlorn, tracked the demon dragon, Marradus. Through forests and streams, I found the hiding place of Furion's beast. The creature hid at an isolated mountain, surrounded by barren land. The mountain towered before me. Above the mound of rock, I saw it hovering in the open skies. The creature cracked throughout the expanse of air. I vowed in my heart that this beast would fall. One of the most strenuous fights of my life had just begun."

- Dawntan Forlorn
The First Paragon

Slowly, Kaldon closed the book.

Just as Dawntan had an obstacle before him, so did they. While Dawntan's was a dragon from the Dominion of Shadow, theirs was an army of forty thousand.

Morning light crested the distant peaks. The night's journey had been long. He was grateful for the few hours of rest. The troop was awake, scurrying about, getting ready for their travels. Alden was packing. Mikiel was uncharacteristically silent as

Anneya ordered him about to make him useful. Today, they would reach the dark army.

From their vantage point, they could see the enemy camp in the distance. There were so many dark warriors that they reminded him of locusts swarming low to the ground. It was impossible to see the ground under them. Above the army, countless black dots littered the skies. Kaldon knew exactly what they were. Tolek had defeated five of the Kreel the night prior, but the creatures now seemed endless.

"Has your foresight sparked at all since we left the Lore?"

He realized Tolek was speaking to him. "No luck yet," Kaldon responded honestly, still watching the Kreel.

"There is your problem," Tolek said, running his hand over the hilt of *Integrity*. "You think it has to do with luck. It doesn't. It is in your control."

Kaldon held back a laugh. "I wish that were so. It only sparks at random. I can't control it."

Tolek held his chin in thought, watching the army in the distance. "You know Kaldon, I knew your father quite well. He had a brilliant mind, unmatched by any I've ever known. He had the ability to be numerous steps ahead of any problem or situation."

Listening to the Paladin reminisce about his father, Kaldon was hungry to know more about him.

Tolek continued, "One time I was with Dolan and asked him what he believed the key to unlocking an individual's potential was. He said, 'There are many keys to unlocking potential. One of the greatest keys is to reject the lie that fate is your master. Never believe your life is defined or determined by circumstances. Potential has nothing to do with luck. It has everything to do with choice. One who doesn't feel in control of their potential is one who lacks control of their confidence."

Kaldon felt the weight of his father's words. "So, you believe I can't control my foresight because I lack confidence?"

"I'm saying you can't control your foresight because you don't feel in control of your life. You have learned to speak confidently, as you did to Alden in my chamber, but down deep, you believe circumstance dictates your path. In reality, it doesn't. You do."

Tolek looked at him, saying, "You've had terrible circumstances throughout your life, but they do not define you."

Receiving the words Tolek spoke felt like trying to swallow a mountain; he simply didn't know how to. At the same time, he knew it would be foolish to dismiss the words of a man such as this.

"I will think on what you have said, Tolek. Thank you," he said with sincerity.

Alden hobbled over to them. "You two could prattle on all day about foresight, but it won't get us anywhere. What is your grand scheme to find the Sovereign and Geran in that mess of an army?" he asked, pointing to the crowd of soldiers.

Tolek watched the moving specks of warriors, Kreel, and Nahmen. "It won't be hard to find them. I suspect their vanity will give them away. There will be tents scattered throughout the camp, but theirs will likely be the most prominent and polished. They wouldn't subject themselves to what their soldiers endure. The hard part will be going about unseen by those who serve the Sovereign. We need to stop this army, or the Lore will be devoured."

"How can we stop an army so large?" Kaldon asked.

"We can't," Alden complained. "As I've been saying, it's impossible."

"It isn't impossible," the Paladin said with certainty, unswayed. "An army that large must be divided. Taking out the Sovereign and Geran will wreak havoc amongst them. We will need a more strategic approach to fully divide them. I haven't yet figured that out."

Alden grunted his disapproval.

As Kaldon listened to Tolek and Alden, he saw something dart past him out of the corner of his eye. Adjusting his sight, he watched Anneya running at full speed from a horde of trees.

"Come with me!" she shouted at them, exasperated, stopping dead in her tracks. "You will never guess what I have found. Follow me!"

Before anyone could even ask a question, the Blade was gone, lost into the trees again.

Alden sighed.

Tolek was already following her into the forest. Mikiel and the Bishops were not far behind. Alden trailed behind, walking slowly.

With everyone but Alden past him and out of sight, Kaldon followed the sounds of running footsteps. He ran as fast as he could without tripping over scraps of wood on the ground beneath him. Dodging trees and branches zipping past him, he finally caught up with the rest of the troop. At the bottom of an outcropped hill, everyone stood with their heads tilted up, gaping at the unassuming sight.

Atop the snow-covered hill stood a man with the radiance of the sun beaming from behind him.

"Great Divinity... It can't be," Tolek whispered.

The charcoal-linen cloak drifted in the morning air. With a silver staff in his hand, the hairless man looked down from the hill to the troop.

As the troop watched, Anneya raced up toward him. "Locrian! I can't believe it's you!" she shouted.

The young Seer descended down the hill to meet the Blade. With each step, his staff struck the ground.

"Did I make it in time?" Locrian asked.

Tolek strode toward the young Seer. "Locrian," the Paladin said, grasping the man's forearm in a firm greeting. "It is good to see you again, my friend."

Before Tolek even let go, Anneya leapt at the Seer, embracing him in a hug.

"Ah, the fugitive from Gallaway Morgue. I'm glad to see you are doing well, Anneya," Locrian said lightheartedly.

"Oh, Locrian," she said in response. "I didn't know if I would ever see you again."

He smiled a genuine smile.

As he said his greetings, his eyes swept over them, stopping on Kaldon.

As Kaldon watched the Seer, he knew Locrian carried an intensity to him, such as Alden did. However, there was something unique about Locrian that made him differ from the elder Seer. Kaldon knew insecure men avoided eye contact. Arrogant men would look through you. However, men of depth looked into the core of who someone was. Locrian was such a man.

"You are him," the Seer said, slowly walking toward Kaldon.

"Him?" Kaldon said, feeling uncomfortable being singled out.

Locrian began quoting his oracle. "*You were created for more than the depths of the sewers. One day, you will soar among the stars. One day, you will be someone great.*"

Chills glided over Kaldon's flesh. This was the man who decreed the order for the three Knights of Agadin to find him in Rundle. Everyone in the troop was confused at the prophetic utterance. No one but Anneya knew its meaning or how it was linked to his past.

"You are only on the brink of your potential, Kaldon Thain. You are the one who was destined to rise from the sewers to become a Protector over Agadin," the Seer decreed with an intense gaze.

As the troop stood around the Seer and Kaldon, the weight of the words spoken were tangible. The declaration created a reverence amongst the group—a solemnness.

Tolek spoke quietly. "Locrian, I don't want to interrupt, but our time is short."

Locrian turned his eyes to the Paladin as Tolek continued. "Seer, I know your steps are guided by time. Tell me, why have you come to us?"

"Tolek, I admire your courage to lead seven into an army this size. As you know, your odds are weak. Even with the certain advantages you carry," Locrian said, motioning to Kaldon.

"You will not succeed without a prominent key," the Seer added, resting on his staff.

Tolek crossed his arms, waiting for the Seer to continue.

"I am here because I have had a vision," the Seer announced. In my vision, I received a strategy for you. I am now going to teach you how to turn a forty-thousand-person army against itself."

Chapter Thirty-One

Lost Ability

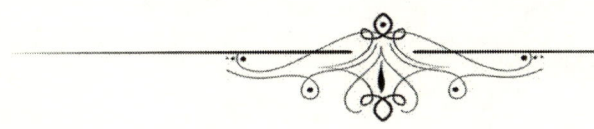

Troy, the Bishop, swept into their camp and drove his sword into the snowy ground. His blue cape traced behind him, filthy with blood. "I've taken out twenty-three of Geran's soldiers so far. How are the others doing?" he asked Tolek.

The troop had travelled for most of the day, making camp at a safe distance away from the army. A barrier of trees and bush shielded them from sight. Troy, Bernice, Shar, and Anneya guarded the perimeter which proved to be harder than they initially thought. Soldiers were consistently buzzing around and the four were regularly eliminating potential threats.

Tolek spoke up. "Twenty-three, Troy? Not bad. You are beating Anneya and Bernice; however, Shar is at thirty-six kills."

"Thirty-six?! How did she manage that?!" Troy asked exasperated.

"Sorry, Bishop, you must be slacking," Tolek laughed out.

Pulling his sword out from the ground again, Troy grunted. "I won't be bested by another Bishop." He headed back through the veil of trees, looking for more threats.

Kaldon was thankful for the protection, but preferred to be with them to help. When he'd offered to go with them, Locrian stopped him. He played too crucial a role in Locrian's strategy for his life to be gambled.

As Kaldon watched, Locrian was preparing for the mission from the tree stump he was sitting on. To the left of the Seer was a pond, only partially frozen as spring neared. The water rested calmly beside him. The tranquil scene contrasted with the mission before them.

The Seer's face contorted in concentration. What such a man would ponder was beyond him. Kaldon assumed he was meditating on unravelling the mysteries of Agadin, or the Kingdom of Light. He had what felt like a multitude of questions for the Seer.

His attention was pulled to the ground in front of Locrian, where small pebbles shook upon the rocky floor.

He observed the environment. Kaldon knew the rumble of footsteps from the army wasn't moving the stones. It also wasn't an earthquake, considering no other ground shook. Looking over to Mikiel, he could see him watching also.

Both of them edged closer, drawn in by curiosity. As the distance between them and the Seer was bridged, they watched in amazement as a pebble slowly lifted from the ground. The stone rose, hovering weightlessly in the air before Locrian's face.

"How is that possible?" Mikiel whispered.

Kaldon didn't answer as he continued toward the Seer.

"Locrian…" Mikiel said, stumbling over his words. "Are you Commanding Creation?"

"Yes," the Seer stated casually with a flick of his hand. Locrian didn't take his focus off the stone as it hovered at eye level.

"How is that possible?" Kaldon asked. "I thought only Roeks could Command Creation."

"That isn't quite true," Locrian said, looking over. "My Commanding Creation as a Seer is similar to how a Paladin can see visions with foresight. A Paladin taps into a small aspect of a Seer's ability; however, they have not mastered it by any means. Roeks are those who have mastered the art of Commanding Creation. I have not. In comparison to a Roek, my ability with the craft would be like a child's."

Kaldon and Mikiel were in awe. They sat on the ground in front of Lorcian. Their eyes were fixated on the stone.

Mikiel finally piped up. "How does this work?"

Kaldon could see Mikiel's eagerness. Back at the Peak of Lore, he didn't often see Mikiel take much interest in studies. He seemed enthralled by the topic of Commanding Creation.

Locrian paused before answering. "I cannot come close to explaining even the most elementary of those truths in the time we have; however, I will try to give you some revelation."

From atop the wooden stump, he began. "The concept of Commanding Creation is based on the principle that Divinity created Agadin. Not only did he create it, but he entrusted it to man and woman to rule and reign. Those who grasp Commanding Creation understand this partnership between themselves and the land. There is a connection. This isn't a link you can see with your eyes. It is woven in the fabric of who we are."

"So, this connection needs to be strengthened to Command Creation?" Mikiel asked.

"Not quite," Locrian answered. "The link is definitively there. Nothing can change that. It is the belief in the connection that needs to develop."

Kaldon thought about what the Seer said. "Wait, this sounds familiar. Is this similar to our connection with the Golden Land?"

Locrian's face warmed. "The Golden Land," he stated. "I haven't heard the Kingdom of Light being called that in a very long time."

Mikiel looked puzzled, clearly having never heard the term before.

"Yes, it is exactly like our connection to the Kingdom of Light, Kaldon," Locrian responded. "Each of us has a link to eternity. One gifted in healing has a greater belief in that link. This is how they bridge perfect health from the Kingdom of Light and bring it into this realm. As a Seer, I understand this link to the Kingdom of Light as well. I have mastered my belief in my link to the Kingdom of Light to see the River of Time. Roeks are similar, though altogether different. They haven't mastered their belief in their link to the Kingdom of Light. They have mastered their belief in their link to the land. The land is their link to creation, which was given to them from Divinity. They understand their reign over it, so therefore creation obeys them."

"So, Commanding Creation is having power over the land?" Mikiel asked, intrigued.

"Again, not quite. It isn't power. It is having authority over it. There is a distinct difference," Locrian said.

"What is the difference between power and authority?" Kaldon asked.

A smile curled onto Locrian's face at the sight of students so hungry for truth. He pointed to the levitating stone. "You may think I am lifting this stone. I am not. In fact, what I am doing has nothing to do with the stone."

Both students leaned in.

"I have told the wind to hold the stone in place," Locrian said.

Mikiel's mouth hung open. "You spoke to the wind?"

"Yes, but not with my voice. I spoke to it with my mind," he said, tapping his head with his pointer finger. "This is how the connection works between us and Agadin. We can command the land. We can wield it by word or thought."

"Why not just tell the stone to move, instead of commanding the wind to do so?" Mikiel asked.

"I haven't built my belief enough in my link to earth; I have focused on my link to wind. Roeks from the past would build their belief to mastering one element, whether with fire, water, wind, or earth. They may have possessed a general knowledge of their connection to other elements, but were most focused on mastering one."

Kaldon nodded. He saw the wisdom in becoming a master of one thing, rather than becoming average at many.

Locrian regarded the stone again. "Now, I will teach the difference between power and authority. To exert power, all I would need to do is grab this stone with my hand and throw it into the pond next to us. That is power. It is simply strength or force. Authority is completely different. Authority is me telling the stone to throw itself into the pond, and the stone obeying. In my case, I would tell the wind to throw the stone."

Suddenly, without anyone touching it, the stone shot from hovering before Locrian. The pebble soared through the air and slashed into the nearby pond.

Locrian looked back at his pupils. "This is the difference between power and authority. This is how to Command Creation. Roeks from the past could move mountains. They could command even the ocean because of their link to the land, their belief in it, and their authority over it."

Kaldon and Mikiel sat in near disbelief at the philosophy of mankind's link to creation.

Mikiel's voice rose, filled with anticipation. "I have lived at the Lore all my life. Why wasn't this taught at the training facility?"

Before Locrian could answer, a gruff voice cut in. "Because it is useless information," Alden said in a stern voice, approaching the three.

Locrian tensed at the sound of his former mentor's voice.

The old Seer stood with staff in hand, overlooking the three. "What is it you are teaching these boys, Loc? More of your petty tricks? What use is there in focusing on such things?"

Locrian sat tall, not wavering under the ridicule. "The purpose is so we don't forget what has happened in the past. As soon as we forget what was, it can never become present again."

Alden sighed sarcastically. "The Roek have been extinct for over two thousand years. They will never be present again. The sooner you get that in your thick head, the better."

"Well, Alden, I thank Divinity I'm not as cynical as you. The Roek will rise again in Agadin," Locrian said with certainty.

"You truly believe that?" Mikiel said with hope ringing through his voice.

"I do," the young Seer said.

Alden waved his hand in annoyance. "You will never change, Loc. You have always shaped your beliefs around fairytales."

Locrian looked deep into the old Seer, silencing him with his stare. "Imagination is a gift I will never forsake. It gives us the ability to look past limitations. It is the birthplace for new ideas and fresh revelations."

Alden rubbed his forehead, clearly frustrated. The old Seer turned away, not hiding his disdain. Before the young Seer could continue, Tolek called from a distance, his words cutting through the tense moment.

"Locrian, it's time for us to send out the first group into the army," the Paladin commanded. "Are you ready?"

"I am ready," the Seer announced as he stood. The time had finally arrived.

Locrian looked to his two pupils. "It was an honour teaching you both, even if briefly."

Kaldon was disheartened their lesson was cut short—not only because he wanted to learn more, but because he knew their day was about to take a dangerous turn. At the sight of Locrian walking away, Kaldon felt shivers rushing over his body. It was beginning. His fear rose knowing that Anneya was part of that first group.

The young Seer stood next to Tolek, before the assortment of trees that lead to the army camp. Anneya and Shar, the other two members of the first group followed him.

As bleak as their circumstances seemed, Kaldon was impressed by the plan. They had been divided into three groups. The first would leave immediately. The second group which consisted of Alden, Mikiel, Bernice, and Troy would leave much later. The last group would be Kaldon and Tolek. The first two groups had a crucial objective to track down the Nahmen. As daunting as the first and second groups roles were, Tolek and Kaldon's were far more dangerous.

Tolek assembled the first group. "You three need to succeed for our plan to work. There isn't room for failure," the Paladin said.

They nodded adamantly in unison. "We will not fail you, Paladin," Anneya responded militantly.

Tolek acknowledged the pledge, then turned to Locrian. "Locrian, do you know where the Nahmen are in the camp?"

Locrian pulled out a map. "This is a map of the enemy's camp."

"I saw the army's camp in a vision by looking into the River of Time," the Seer said, running a finger over the illustrated map from tent to tent. "Here are the different tents throughout the camp. These ones with the X's hold the Nahmen. They are protected by soldiers. I will have Anneya and Shar with me, so that shouldn't be an issue for us. The three of us need to leave sooner than the second group, because we need to take out the Nahmen who are deeper within the army first. The second group's targets are much closer, near the outskirts of the camp. If we were to attack the nearby Nahmen first, we would never be able to work our way into the core of the army for the others."

Tolek observed the map. "This whole map is based on what you saw in visions?"

"Yes," Locrian responded, not taking his eyes off the map.

"Very impressive," Tolek admitted

Kaldon noticed that Alden kept quiet while looking at the map. The tension rising from the old Seer toward Locrian was evident.

"You have the tent marked for the second group as well?" the Paladin asked.

"Yes, and I have Geran and the Sovereign's tents marked for you and Kaldon," the Seer said.

"Excellent," Tolek responded.

Kaldon found Locrian's plan concerning the Nahmen quite brilliant. The Nahmen were connected to the Kreel and controlled them. If the Nahmen were killed, the Kreel would give in to their natural instincts, killing whatever was in sight. It didn't matter if the Kreel were around Geran's soldiers. Locrian said the beasts would attack them. Kaldon hoped he was right. The aftermath of such an event could very well tear apart the entire army.

Group one was ready to enter the enemy's territory, a place from which they may not return. As Locrian and Shar turned into the darkened forest, Kaldon stopped Anneya before she left.

He grabbed her hand. The Blade looked caught off guard by the gesture. "Anneya, I need you to…"

Anneya cut him off. "Kaldon, you can't ask me to be safe right now. Nothing about this mission is safe. I may need to give my life for Agadin today. If I need to, then I will. You may need to as well."

He knew she was right.

"No, you misunderstood me," Kaldon said. "I wasn't going to say, 'be safe'. This is who you are. You are a Blade. I was going to tell you, 'I am proud of you.'"

She looked at him with a curious look.

He continued, "I am proud of you for standing for what is right; for taking a stand in the Great War. You didn't need to come on this mission, but you chose to. I won't lie and say I'm not worried that I won't see you again, because I am. But I need you to know I am proud of you for who you are."

Anneya could read the sincerity on his face. She could also see his concern.

The Blade smiled, looking at their hands woven together. "You know, I don't remember the last time someone worried about me."

Kaldon smiled back at her.

"As I said, I cannot promise I will be safe," Anneya said. "I may not live, and you may not either. From the sounds of it, your mission in Locrian's plan is far more dangerous than mine."

He knew that much.

Anneya continued, "I believe I will see you again."

She leaned in and pressed her lips against his. Kaldon felt the tears on her flushed cheeks. Her tears matched her teardrop scar.

Before he could respond, the Blade turned away, following Locrian and Shar into the darkened forest.

"I believe I will see you again as well, Anneya Padme," he said in a faint whisper, as she disappeared into the abyss of trees toward the enemy's camp.

Chapter Thirty-Two

The Raid

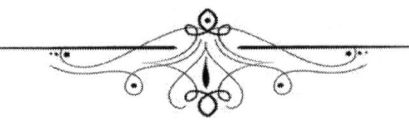

Dashing through the halls at the Peak of Lore, Brenton felt his new armour shifting upon his body. After retiring the cloak of a Knight, his new armour would take time adjusting to.

At the sounding alarm, heralding the imminent attack, all the warriors rushed to their posts. Brenton did the opposite. He was thankful he had enough time to make sure Flor and the girls were safe. Now, he ran to make up for lost time.

Father and husband first, a Blade second, he thought to himself as he sprinted through the halls.

He could still hear his daughters' cries in his mind. He was thankful that the Peak of Lore's design included numerous emergency rooms in case of an attack. There were also several secret exits in case things turned for the worse. Brenton was thankful his family was safe for the time being. It gave him the liberty to think of the task before him.

Entering the great hall, he saw that it was empty of students and study books; it was prepared for battle. Nearly twenty Bishops secured the entrance door, many shouting commands to Blades and Knights stationed within the foyer. Dozens of Blades and nearly one hundred Knights were ready to defend their home.

The tough wood clattered as blows struck the mighty door from the exterior. Shouts of many were heard from the other side. Unearthly shrieks echoing from outside churned the nerves of those in wait. With each shriek, Brenton remembered the sting of the Kreel's claws.

"Draw your weapons! The door can't hold any longer!" a Bishop shouted from the front lines.

Drawing his sword, everything slowed down around him. His training told him this was the calm before the chaos. He didn't know how many were behind the door; however, every person present was willing to die to stop the dark forces from burrowing into the Peak of Lore.

"Great Divinity, help us," Brenton whispered under his breath.

A shard of wood broke loose from the door, shooting through the air. The shouts were more aggressive. The shrieks amplified.

The door splintered and crashed in.

Soldiers swarmed in. Bishops at the front line immediately attacked. Kreel flew in through the top, darting through the entrance room.

Brenton quickly counted eighteen of the winged beasts. As soldiers forced their way into the room, the Kreel flew about and crawled upon the ceilings like bats in a cave. The creatures dropped down on their prey. The reverb of their cries filled the circular room as gutting screams began to rise up from their victims. It was deafening.

A sword swung at Brenton. The Blade was surprised at how quickly one of the soldiers made it to him. Then he realized that the enemy wasn't one of the soldiers coming through the door. Several professors and students had weapons in hand, attacking the defence force. Traitors.

Looking into the eyes of his nearest assailant, he saw the frothing rage within him. The man came in with a strike. Brenton dodged it, cutting the man down effortlessly.

Brenton knew the soldiers were driven by fury, consumed with the emotion of their cause. The Blade knew this could work to his advantage. Passion could give you strength to do things you couldn't do otherwise, but it could also prevent you from thinking clearly.

He saw an ensemble of soldiers eyeing him. Five men, filled with sheer hate, strolled toward him. "I suppose it's time to get serious, isn't it?" the Blade said to himself, while unsheathing a second sword. The ring of steel was muffled by the cries of men and sheiks of Kreel.

Preparing himself for the attack, he watched as four Kreel stopped in mid-attack simultaneously.

The four beasts jumped into the air with their bat-like wings spread. Each darted down a hallway deeper into the Peak of Lore, letting out shrill cries. The defence force was losing its battle right as it had begun.

Through the shrill howls, cries and screams, Brenton stood ready as five soldiers approached him with swords drawn.

"I love you, Flor," Brenton whispered into the shrill sound of war.

Chapter Thirty-Three

Amidst the Enemy

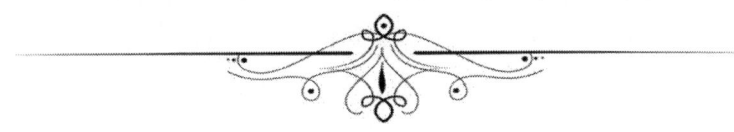

They looked over the shielding boulder, watching the Dark Paladin's soldiers. After travelling into the core of the enemy's camp, the buzz from the sheer multitude of them was now thunderous.

The cold stone chilled Anneya's bare arm as she crouched next to Shar and Locrian. Seeing the beige tents, muddy from travel, they knew the Nahmen dwelled in one of them.

A portion of land brimming with soldiers laid between them and the tents. The camp was disorderly, hollering and brawling continuously breaking out. Most of the soldiers were common warriors, but there were a generous number of Dark Knights amongst them. Anneya noticed the occasional Dark Blade, former comrades, now consumed by the Shadow. Kreel soared above the army, while several walked the land with the soldiers.

Anneya jerked, feeling something brush past her foot. Looking down, she saw a *caw* waddling past. She shifted her foot, scooting the bird away. She didn't mind birds; however, she didn't find caws appealing. Their greyish body made them look unclean, while their stomachs were covered in purple feathers. They were remarkably quick, and another sign of winter losing its bite. Caws were scattered all throughout the army's camp. The caws provided food for the Kreels, she figured.

Locrian spoke aloud, knowing his voice was drowned by the army's racket.

"Five."

"Four."

"Three."

Anneya was accustomed to Locrian's method of partnering with time and knew her group had an advantage with him being there.

"Two."

"One."

The three rose from behind the boulder. Anneya and Shar blended into the camp rather well, considering their ensemble matched that of warriors. Anneya didn't consider herself short, but Shar was at least six inches taller than her and broader in mass. The Bishop's curled, raven-coloured hair made her appear non-threatening. Anneya knew differently. In her opinion, the Bishop was the true definition of a threat.

The Dark Blades throughout the army wore the same crimson shoulder blades as Anneya did. Shar was simply mistaken for a Dark Bishop. The only thing differentiating them was the deception burning in each of the Sovereign's warriors' eyes. Locrian was a different story. The Seer was renowned throughout Agadin. Nearly any one of the soldiers could recognize him.

Locrian flipped his charcoal hood over his head, masking his face. The three rushed past warriors, weaving through brawls and chaos.

Anneya was nearing one of the Kreel lurking on ground. She looked down, avoiding eye contact. The Kreel's snarl was heard even above the noise of the army. Its beady eyes darted about. She was unnerved seeing a Kreel being civil amongst humans. She knew the Kreel wasn't giving in to its instincts to attack the soldiers surrounding it, simply because they were controlled by the Nahmen. As they persevered towards the tents, soldiers continually bumped into them due to a lack of space and order.

Four warriors walked in their direction. She watched Locrian lift his eyes to look past his hood at the men. The Seer's gaze met one of them who looked no more than eighteen years of age.

As the young man's gaze met the Seer's, his eyes widened. Anneya knew that look—he'd recognized Locrian. With lightning speed, Locrian's metal staff spun into the air, striking the young warrior on the head.

The young man dropped unconscious.

Luckily, such violence wasn't out of place in a camp of war. In fact, being amidst the brawls of soldiers, Locrian's defence helped them fit right in. The three others who were with the young man simply laughed and carried on their way.

Anneya was surprised to see how swift Locrian was with his metallic staff. She had seen him take out several soldiers already. She was even more impressed by Shar's skill with her daggers. Since they left their troop, the Bishop cut through more soldiers than Anneya could count.

The three ducked behind one of the tents.

"This isn't the tent with the Nahmen," Locrian stated.

"Which one is it?" Anneya asked, forcing her nerves to steady.

The Seer nodded his head to his left. "It's that one over there."

She looked over to the large beige tent. It was guarded by five Dark Knights and two Dark Blades.

"You have got to be kidding me," she said. "I suppose I can take them out with arrows. They wouldn't expect it." The Blade pulled an arrow from her quiver.

"No," Shar said, placing a hand on Anneya's arm. "Arrows fired from this far away will look like an ambush, drawing too much attention. Our cover will be forfeited. The tent they are guarding is secured by trees. The cover of trees may allow us to take them out without being seen."

Locrian nodded his agreement.

"Won't whoever is in the tent hear us fighting them?" Anneya asked.

He shook his head. "No, it will just be mistaken for those in the army squabbling."

Anneya nodded. "Let's go."

Before she finished her sentence, Shar was already gaiting toward the Dark Knights and Dark Blades. The Bishop pulled out two daggers, one in each hand. Before Anneya was even at a steady run toward those guarding the tent, Shar had already taken out two Dark Knights. Her aggressive approach drew the attention of the others.

Shar was surrounded by three Dark Knights and two Dark Blades. As they came in with attacks, Anneya knew they wouldn't expect her approach. Running full speed at one of the Dark Blades, she leapt in the air, bringing both legs up. Planting her boots in the centre of the Dark Blade's chest, she thrusted him forward. Shar lifted her dagger, ending the man.

Four left, Anneya counted, pulling out two metal arrows.

A Dark Knight came at her, swinging his sword. She ducked, then brought up her elbow. Anneya felt his nose break on impact. The Dark Knight faltered for a moment, then persisted. Before he could swing again, she shoved her foot into the man's stomach, forcing him back. Before he could recover, she locked one of her arrows in her bow, then fired. He sank to the ground, dead.

She was prepared for more, but when she looked to Shar, the final three warriors were already sprawled on the ground.

"How did you do that so quickly?!" Anneya protested.

Shar stood tall, her blue cape shawled over her back. "I did it so quickly because I am not a Blade. I am a Bishop."

"A cocky Bishop," Anneya laughed. "It seems like I have found someone I can learn a thing or two from."

Shar threw her head back in a laugh.

"Who are you!?" The question cut off Shar's laugh. Anneya and Shar could hear the sound of a sword being drawn.

They looked up towards the man standing before the entrance. Neither had even seen him approach. The blue cape he wore made it clear who he was—a Dark Bishop.

The Dark Bishop had a menacing glare. He released a shout as he moved toward them, clear on his intent to kill.

Anneya and Shar readied themselves. Defeating a Dark Knight or Blade was one thing; defeating a Dark Bishop was another entirely.

Before they could respond, Locrian emerged from between them. The Seer slammed his metal staff into the ground.

"You will stop!" Locrian demanded the Dark Bishop.

The Dark Bishop persisted toward the three.

Locrian looked deep into the man. Anneya watched the Seer. Locrian was not simply observing him. It looked as though the Seer was reading him.

He spoke with more aggression. "Gregory Scheel, you will stop at once!"

The Dark Bishop stopped. "What did you call me?"

"I called you Gregory Scheel," Locrian said.

"How do you know my name?" The man frowned in confusion.

"I know plenty about you," the Seer said with certainty. "I know you have travelled with the Sovereign's army for nearly three years now."

The man was silent.

The Seer continued as he stared into the man's eyes. "I also know that since being with the army, you haven't seen your son or daughter. It has almost been three years since you held your children."

The man's eyes swelled with tears.

Locrian's tone softened. "I have seen your life in the River of Time, in a vision. If you turn from the Sovereign's hand, from the Shadow, you will see them again," he said with a nod.

The man was overcome with emotion. He tried to speak, yet could not push words past his sorrow.

"Tori and Leopold miss you, Gregory. It is time to go home," the Seer said, driving his message deep into the man's heart.

The man crumpled to the ground, sobbing uncontrollably.

Anneya watched in disbelief. Only a moment ago, this man was intent on fighting to the death, and now he was broken on the ground.

"What did you do to him?" Shar asked, visibly stunned.

"I gave him an opportunity. I unlocked his heart," Locrian said. "Everyone has tender areas within their soul, even those who have embraced the Shadow. I saw his heart. At his core, he is a good man. He was simply deceived by the doctrine of Tymas Droll."

Locrian looked over at the man, now curled in a ball on the ground, weeping. "He will now have to face a choice, to either continue walking in the way of the Shadow or to choose to take his life back. I sincerely hope he chooses wisely."

Anneya didn't know what she thought about this man getting a second chance. He wasn't just an ordinary warrior: he was a Dark Bishop. She could only imagine what horrors he had likely done. Until now, she hadn't realized that not all of these men and women were mindless zealots. Some were simply deceived by corrupt doctrine, like Gregory.

"Locrian, I know you mean well for this man, but time is not on our side. We are finally at the tent. We need to eliminate the Nahmen, now," Shar said.

As the Bishop began walking to the tent's entrance, Locrian grabbed her shoulder.

"Don't let your passion move you prematurely, Shar," the Seer stated like a teacher giving a lesson.

He continued, "I know the Nahmen are right on the other side of the cloth of this tent, but we can't eliminate them just yet. First, we need to trap and corner them. Otherwise, we may fail," Locrian instructed.

"Aren't they already cornered in the tent?" Anneya asked.

"The Nahmen are from the Dominion of Shadow," Locrian stated. "A mere tent won't hold them. They can transport. We need to be clever to defeat such creatures. We need to trap them."

A curious smile spread across Shar's face. "I won't lie, Locrian. I am interested in seeing how you will accomplish trapping Nahmen. This sounds like it promises to be quite entertaining."

Chapter Thirty-Four
Divine Strategy

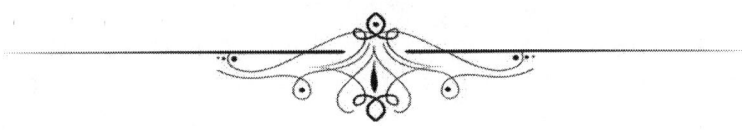

"This is dreadfully boring," Shar complained.

Both she and Anneya were ready to move into the tent, but Locrian had them wait.

"Locrian, we need to move!" Anneya said. The bodies of the fallen guards were already hidden, and both women were zealous to move on.

"I agree," Shar said. "We are literally right outside the tent where the Nahmen are. Time is running out."

"Don't talk to me about time," Locrian snapped, watching the caws puttering on the ground between soldiers and Kreel.

"You've been looking at those birds for nearly three-quarters of an hour! We could be seen at any moment," Anneya protested. "The worst part is that you won't even tell us why!"

"I don't need to tell you why I am watching these birds. You will see why soon enough," he said, undistracted in his intense focus.

Anneya ran her hands through her hair in frustration.

Her only time of interest while waiting for Locrian was watching the progression of Gregory, the Dark Bishop's state. The man wept for half an hour straight, until his cries calmed. He eventually rose without acknowledging any of them at all. He simply dropped his sword to the ground and walked into the forest. She wondered if he truly gave up the doctrine of the Shadow to go home to his children.

"Look there!" Locrian said, pointing his finger. "Do you see that bird?"

"Yes, what of it?" Shar asked melancholically.

"That is the mother bird," Locrian explained. "Caws aren't disorderly birds. They follow the lead of one, the mother bird. I've been watching the caws to see who they follow. I'm certain that is the mother bird."

Anneya and Shar looked at each other, clearly annoyed at how much time they'd wasted while Locrian was bird watching.

"It's time," the Seer said, cracking his fingers.

Locrian closed his eyes and stretched forth a hand. As he did, an unexpected gust of wind brushed past them towards the bird. The bird shuffled its feet at the feel of the wind Locrian wielded. It simply kept puttering along the ground.

"Come on, you ridiculous bird! Fly already!" he shouted.

Anneya watched Locrian Commanding Creation, genuinely intrigued. The Seer rolled up the sleeves of his cloak. He closed his eyes again. This time he was holding out both his hands. Another gust of wind shot through the air, hitting the mother bird.

The bird, made uncomfortable by the wind, stretched its grey wings and leapt into the air. They watched as the mother bird took flight.

"Come on. Follow her," Locrian whispered.

As the caw flew away, other birds on the ground began stretching their wings. Thousands of birds followed the mother's lead, lifting themselves into the air. Caws flooded the air, soaring above the army's camp.

Then, something took place that the Blade did not expect. Kreel, throughout the enemy camp, launched from the ground in a rush, targeting the birds soaring into the sky. The caws darted about, besting the Kreel in speed. The Kreel were ravenously trying to catch the small caws.

Locrian smiled coyly. "You can always depend on a predator to prey."

"Impressive," Shar said. "But, how does this serve us?"

"It traps the Nahmen," Locrian said, brushing dirt off his robe. "If we had gone straight into the tent to kill the Nahmen, they would have used their link to the Kreel to transport to where the Kreel they oversee are. Now, if they try to transport, they will fall from the sky. Nahmen can't fly."

Anneya's eyebrows raised. "Genius…"

"I am aware," Locrian said with a steady face. "Now let's go." The Seer strode into the tent.

Upon entering, they saw that the tent was void of furniture. All that stood were nearly thirty Nahmen.

Anneya cringed at the sight of such creatures. Their grey and hairless appearance made them look both human, yet not. The hollow eyes of Nahmen looked upon the three.

"We don't have time to delay. Shar, begin what needs to be done," Locrian ordered.

The Bishop pulled forth her two daggers without hesitation. At the sight of the daggers, a handful of the Nahmen vanished into nothingness.

Anneya had never seen someone disappear before. The sight of something so otherworldly made her stomach turn.

Moans sounded from outside the tent. The moans were followed by loud thuds. Out of panic, the Nahmen were transported to the Kreel, which they controlled, assuming they would be safe from harm. Little did they know, the Kreel would be in flight.

Absolute genius, thought Anneya.

"They are all trapped," Locrian said, turning toward the tent's exit. "Anneya, come with me," he beckoned.

The Blade and Seer began leaving the tent when Locrian called back to Shar. "Bishop, you know what to do."

As they left the tent, they heard the ring of steel from Shar's daggers.

Standing in the sunlight, Anneya and Locrian watched the Kreel soar throughout the skies. There was still the occasional Nahmen who would suddenly appear in the sky before falling to its demise.

One by one, Anneya watched the airborne Kreel begin to jerk about in an unnatural fashion.

"Did you see that?" Locrian asked, pointing to the sky.

"I did," Anneya answered.

"For every Nahmen that dies, their link to the Kreel they controlled is shattered," Locrian said, holding his metal staff. "The Kreel become their own masters. They are immediately taken by instinct."

As each Kreel was set free from the control of the Nahmen, they could see their instincts overtaking them. Chasing the caw wasn't working to their benefit. The birds were too quick. The

Kreel decided to target easier prey.

The winged beasts began descending. Soldiers screamed in terror as the Kreel turned against them. Several attempted to fight them, but quickly failed. The place became a mess of panic. The Kreel took no sides in war without being controlled by a Nahmen.

Locrian and Anneya watched the mayhem taking place. With his hands resting on the top of his staff, the Seer said, "And that, my dear, is how you turn an army on itself."

Chapter Thirty-Five

The List

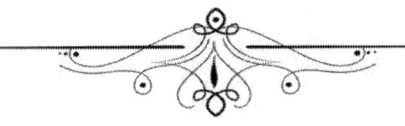

Loud screams and shouts filled Kaldon's ears. They had been hearing the screams from the camp for nearly two days. He hoped Anneya was safe.

Though the piercing screams were palpable, something more tangible demanded his attention. A man was running at a steady pace towards them.

His beaming-red face conveyed urgency as he dashed around scores of trees. Kaldon had never seen him before. His clothes made him look like one fit for travel, but his shaven face betrayed a short journey. The man's dark hair was slicked back with sweat. Drawing his sword, he watched the man run towards them.

"Put that thing away," Alden hissed. "It is a messenger from the Peak of Lore."

Kaldon sheathed *Humility* as alarm rose up like a hot flame within him. A messenger would need good reason to risk his life coming this close to the sizeable army.

"A messenger…" Tolek said quietly, the strain on his face showing concern.

The man stopped before them, bending over in a pant. He staggered, trying to find his breath before beginning. "Paladin Tolek, your Bishops sent me with a message," the messenger said between forced inhales and exhales.

The Paladin's demeanour had hardened. "Speak, messenger."

Before the messenger could answer, Mikiel wandered up. "Who is this?" Mikiel asked.

"Quiet!" Alden snapped. "Don't speak when a Paladin is awaiting a response."

Mikiel quieted.

The messenger uncomfortably cleared his throat, then said, "The Bishops told me to tell you that a raiding party from the Dark Paladin's army have broken through the entrance way of the Lore. Warriors and Kreel swarmed the facility. Those who were undercover among us came out of hiding, attacking as well."

Tolek's fists tightened.

The man continued, "Numerous lives were lost; however, the raid was brought to a halt."

"How was it brought to a halt?" Tolek demanded.

"The Kreel turned on the Sovereign's men. It was as though they lost control of themselves. Thank Divinity, it tipped the odds in our favour. The Bishops were then able to defeat and drive out most of the Kreel. The soldiers weren't an issue for our defence units without Kreel as an obstacle," the messenger said.

Kaldon was relieved to hear Locrian's plan worked properly. They had found the Nahmen in the core of the camp. It also meant Alden, Mikiel, Troy, and Bernice would need to leave soon to hunt the remaining Nahmen. He and Tolek would be leaving shortly as well. Anneya's face came to his mind.

"What do you mean they defeated *most* of the Kreel?" Tolek asked.

"Eighteen Kreel were counted breaking into the Peak of Lore. Only fourteen were either destroyed or vacated from the facility. We cannot find the remaining four," the man relayed hesitantly.

Tolek shook his head in frustration. "Did any of my Bishops lose their lives?"

The messenger was nearly shaking. "Yes, sir. Several lost their lives. There are some still alive, though I have no count on that."

The news was grim. Bishops were the Peak of Lore's primary defence.

"Did you bring a list of those whose lives were lost?" Tolek asked quietly, forcing his emotions to harden.

"I did, Paladin. It is preliminary at best," the messenger responded, rummaging through his tunic. "You should know, the raiding party made it deeper into the Lore than we hoped. We tried to hold them at the entrance, but they were too strong. It wasn't only soldiers who lost their lives."

Kaldon was nearly trembling, thinking of the friends who were quickly becoming family to him.

Tolek read the list silently, his face unreadable. No tears were shed.

The list travelled from person to person in the troop, so everyone could see if a loved one was lost.

It finally arrived in Kaldon's hands. His eyes shifting from name to name, he could feel his anxiety rising as he searched for his friends. Reaching the end of the list, he sighed in relief. Brenton and his family were not on the list of the dead.

"The plan worked," Tolek said in a sombre tone. "He broke the Sovereign's control over many of the Kreel."

The troop nodded in silent agreement. A moment that should have been celebrated was dampened by reverence for the lives lost.

Tolek continued, "Now is not the time to mourn. We have tasks at hand. It is time for the second group to leave. There is still one more group of Nahmen. Kaldon and I will need to leave shortly as well."

"No!" a voice shouted, breaking through the Paladin's words.

"No! It can't be! No!"

Turning back, they saw Mikiel on his knees with the list of the deceased crumpled in his fist.

Kaldon rushed to the young man, placing a hand on his shoulder. "Mikiel, what's wrong?"

Shaking with emotion, he looked up at Kaldon.

"It's there," Mikiel said, despite his tears.

"What's there?" Kaldon asked, not understanding.

"My mother's name…" the young man wept out.

Kaldon stepped back in disbelief. "I'm so sorry," he said, knowing from experience there was nothing he could say to ease his friend's pain.

Mikiel didn't respond. He was trembling. His eyes roamed, looking from person to person, seeing sympathetic faces staring back at him. His eyes rested upon Alden.

"You knew, didn't you?!" he blurted out to the old Seer.

"Excuse me?" Alden said.

Mikiel rose from the ground. "You came to the Lore because you had a vision. Did you know it would be attacked? Did you know lives would be lost? Did you see it in your vision?"

Alden began stuttering.

Tolek spoke up. "This isn't Alden's fault."

"Did you know?!" Mikiel asked pointedly of the Paladin.

"We knew the Lore would be attacked," Tolek stated. "We didn't know what the outcome would be. We didn't even know if Geran's raiding party would breach the door. Either way, we knew we needed to move on with this mission or risk the Lore facing the Dark Paladin's entire army. The whole facility would have been taken over. No one wanted your mother harmed, believe me."

"You knew," Mikiel said, dumbfounded. The young man looked at Alden. "You saw it in a vision? The Lore being threatened with the attack?"

"I did," Alden said in honesty. "I'm sorry about your mother. It wasn't a decision we made lightly. The choice was to risk a few lives or sacrifice all. We tried to protect as many as we could."

"A choice for the *greater good*." Mikiel's words dripped with venom. "I will remember your apathy, old man."

Mikiel diverted his eyes from everyone to the ground beneath him.

Tolek stepped in again. "We have all experienced loss, Mikiel. Right now, we don't have time to mourn. We need to focus this anger on the enemy at hand, where it belongs."

Tolek placed his hand on Mikiel's shoulder. "Mikiel, the second group of our troop needs to leave now to find the remaining Nahmen. You have an opportunity to avenge your mother's life right now; to stand for life. If you need to stay behind, I understand. Alden, Bernice, and Troy will leave without you; however, you not going is putting us all at a disadvantage. We could use your help."

Mikiel looked up at the Paladin with glazed eyes and then to the forested path leading to the army's camp. "I have nothing left to lose," he said. "There is nowhere to return to. Now that my family is gone, I find the fear that was within me is also dead. I will go with them."

Chapter Thirty-Six

Master of Warfare

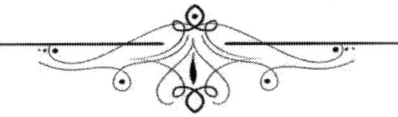

Morning light shone in stark contrast to the scene before him. Warriors darted past Kaldon, running for their lives. The closer they came to the back end of the camp, the more condensed the terrain became. The forest was dense with trees climbing nearly one hundred feet into the sky, preventing clear vision. It was the perfect place to hide the Sovereign of Shadow.

"Geran should be close," Tolek said with certainty. Kaldon could see his determination. The closer they moved in, the more he hardened.

The deeper they delved into the army's camp, the more unorganized the Dark Paladin's soldiers became. Warriors were scattered everywhere and Kreel were rampant, attacking those who served the Sovereign. It was an absolute massacre. This gave Kaldon and Tolek more freedom to move around quickly. They could advance openly with the soldiers focused on escaping the Kreel.

"Their entire army seems to be dismantled," Kaldon said.

"Yes," the Paladin nodded. "Still, we need to find Tymas and Geran quickly. The Sovereign and his General are skilled leaders. It isn't outside of their ability to bring this mess back into order."

One of the soldiers ran past a barricade of trees towards them in a state of frenzy. The enemy warriors were so terrified of the Kreel that they weren't thinking clearly. They simply attacked at random.

The warrior lunged at Tolek, sword in hand. Drawing his sword, *Integrity*, he cut him down. As the body thudded to the ground, Kaldon thought back to how unnerved he was when he first saw his first killing, Ont. Now, he had seen many fall before him. The sight of death was losing its impact.

Through the maze of forest, Kaldon and Tolek rounded a stage of towering trees. "Tolek, look!" he said, pointing to a grand tent in the distance.

While other tents around the camp were a beige colour, this tent differed. It stood taller than the rest and was made from richer fabrics: blacks and purples. The tent appeared menacing and royal all at once.

"The Sovereign's abode—right where Locrian's map said it would be," the Paladin noted.

A company of Dark Knights, Blades, and Bishops circled the tent's exterior. Before the human shield laid the slain, those who attempted and failed to penetrate the tent housing the Sovereign.

"How are we supposed to get past them? There are about two hundred of them," Kaldon said.

"I need to take out the Sovereign's shield of defence," Tolek said, stone-like.

What he was suggesting was unfathomable. "We are only two men. We can't beat two hundred," Kaldon said.

"Who said anything about you?" Tolek sternly replied. "I will distract them while you go to the Sovereign. I stand a better chance against two hundred than you do."

Watching the warriors, a question stirred within Kaldon. "Is it true you once killed one thousand men single-handedly?"

The Paladin looked at him curiously. "Where did you hear such a thing?"

"On my journey from Rundle, the Knights who brought me to the Peak of Lore told me," Kaldon responded, not lifting his gaze from the men.

The Paladin grunted. "It was a long time ago, but yes, it's true."

Kaldon was in near disbelief. "How is that possible?"

"The key is perseverance and stamina," the Paladin responded. "Perseverance and stamina are two of the most prominent lessons you must learn in training. No matter how large a group you are fighting, only five men can get to you at once. If you know how to fight five, then as long as you don't tire, you can defeat an entire army."

Fighting five men at once sounded daunting to Kaldon. He supposed if his foresight sparked, he would stand a better chance; yet, these weren't average men. Each one was trained for war.

"You confidently believe you can defeat these two hundred men?" he asked, testing the Paladin.

"There is a risk of death; however, I am a Paladin. I am trained to defy impossible odds."

Kaldon could hear conviction in his words.

"Then so be it," Kaldon said.

Kaldon could see the light of Agadin's sun shimmering from *Integrity*. The gold hue burned like a star from the heavens. The Paladin's fist tightened over the blackened hilt.

"You must move quickly and get into the tent, Kaldon. Don't allow yourself to be seen by anyone." Tolek didn't hesitate. He began approaching the two hundred men starting with a walk, then accelerating into a sprint. The eyes of two hundred warriors were on the approaching Paladin.

Kaldon watched from a distance as arrows shot at the Paladin. Tolek cut several arrows right from the air. The rest he simply dodged. Leaping into the air, he cut through numerous warriors before landing.

The battle began.

Seeing the men distracted, Kaldon darted into the section of forest. The trees provided camouflaged access to the tent. He hid from tree to tree, avoiding sight.

Tolek was surrounded. The Paladin fought with ferocity like a hurricane of warfare. His skill with a blade was unmatched by anyone Kaldon had ever seen. A pile of fallen warriors quickly began building around the Paladin. It didn't matter if it were a common warrior or a Dark Bishop, Tolek bested them without fail.

Kaldon unsheathed *Humility*. He saw his chance, bolting to the tent. He hugged close to the tent, hidden. He watched the entrance, only a few feet away. All he needed to do was slip in unnoticed.

Kaldon crept towards the entrance. Mere steps from his destination, a warrior's gaze lifted, spotting him.

"Not now…" he whispered to himself.

The warrior rushed him, swinging his axe. The man's stale eyes were death itself.

The warrior's axe soared mid-swing. Its weight threw the overconfident soldier off balance. Kaldon seized the opportunity, bringing in *Humility* to cut down the man. The warrior slouched over, hitting the ground.

Kaldon looked towards the tent housing the murderer of his father and mother, the man responsible for countless deaths throughout Agadin.

He stepped into the tent.

"I climbed the isolated mountain, persevering to the top. All that was above me were the darkened clouds and Furion's beast. The demon dragon's magnitude felt like a castle flying over me. I feared I would become another victim of its fire."

- Dawntan Forlorn
The First Paragon

Chapter Thirty-Seven

Tymas Droll

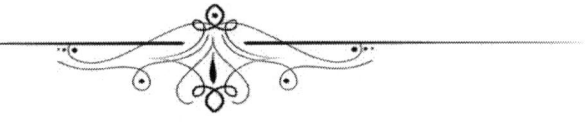

The fabric of the tent was illuminated by the sunlight beaming upon it. A desk stationed in the back-centre of the tent had a Nahmen standing on each side.

Kaldon thought all the Nahmen were defeated. He was wrong.

He felt the dead eyes on him. He had never seen the creatures until that moment. They seemed lifeless, stale creatures of decay from the Dominion of Shadow.

"It is nice to finally see you somewhere other than in your dreams, Kal Wendal," Tymas said from behind the desk. "However, I can't say I expected to see you here."

With a Nahmen on each side of him, the Sovereign of Shadow sat casually, not seeming at all threatened that someone had stormed into his private abode.

"My name is Kaldon Thain," Kaldon corrected him.

"Ah, I see," Tymas said amusedly. "I assume you are here to try and kill me. Correct?"

"Yes," Kaldon said, clenching *Humility* tightly in his hand.

The Sovereign stood, coming around the table. His beige robes swayed as he walked. The robes bore writings of Old Agadin, just like in Kaldon's dream.

"So much like your father," Tymas said, tisking. "Your passion makes you believe you are much more capable than you actually are."

Kaldon felt heated standing before the man who killed his parents—killed so many. "You will pay for what you have done to Agadin."

"You know, Kal. We are not so different, you and I," Tymas said. "We are both simply trying to heal Agadin of its brokenness."

"Heal? You are destroying Agadin!" Kaldon spat out, feeling his hands beginning to tremble.

"Oh no, you misunderstand, boy," Tymas said with certainty, stroking his smooth chin. "Let me explain. When I was a child, no older than five years of age, our people in Gorath were hit with a dreadful plague. Nearly one quarter of the population died. Thousands of lives were lost. I remember watching my father and mother grow ill. My father, a blacksmith, was reduced to a weak man. My mother lost her strength as well. They knew their lives would be gone in only a matter of time, yet they held onto hope since I, their beloved son, was still healthy.

"One day, black spots appeared on my skin. The plague took hold inside my body. I watched my father and mother fall to their illness. Even at the age of five, I knew the taste of death. It reigned in my body. Some of the city folk took pity and tended to me. Then, something strange happened.

"I began to glow," Tymas said with reverence.

"My skin shone like the sun itself. I watched as the sores melted from my body. The plague no longer had a hold of me. It was then when I knew I was called to be a healer, and a gifted healer, at that."

Kaldon paused, as realization struck him. "No... You can't be."

"Oh, yes," Tymas said, smiling. "I am a Shan-Rafa, destined as one of the five types of Protectors of Agadin. I am the only one born in thousands of years. I am the most proficient healer in all of Agadin. It is only unfortunate that I learned this after the death of my parents. I wasn't experienced enough then to do what only a Shan-Rafa can do—to raise the dead. However, I did use my gift when it was discovered. At the age of five, I used my gift to stop the plague that took thousands of lives in Gorath."

Kaldon was dumbfounded.

"After discovering my gift, Furion herself began visiting me in dreams. She taught me that as a healer, I could heal Agadin. I could usher people into eternal healing by inflicting temporal pain. I take life to give it. I do this by being a bridge for the Dominion of Shadow to come to Agadin."

"You are mad..." Kaldon said, raising his voice. "You're not healing by taking innocent lives. You're leading a genocide!"

The Sovereign's face soured. "What do you know, *Kal Wendal?* Are you so arrogant to think you can teach a Shan-Rafa? You are a sewer rat who has taken it upon yourself to try to save Agadin. You may have a renowned father, but your name will never be remembered. Men like you *aren't* to be remembered."

Kaldon's breathing quickened. He could feel heat rising to his face. He was finished with words.

Tymas Droll had no weapon in hand. It was the perfect opportunity to strike. In a flash, Kaldon stepped toward the Sovereign. Lifting his sword, he swiftly moved in. *Humility* whirled sideways at the Sovereign of Shadow, cutting into his midsection. Kaldon watched the sword swipe through Tymas' linen robe, cutting skin. Such a gash to the stomach would kill anyone. He stood back, awaiting the Sovereign's fall.

Kaldon's gaze widened. "No..." he stammered, backing away further as he watched the fatal gash begin to glow in translucent light, mending like flesh being stitched back together. The Shan-Rafa healed himself as quickly as he was cut. Tymas smiled, completely intact.

The Shan-Rafa unsheathed his sword. The curved blade was nearly as long as he was tall. He charged in. The Sovereign's sword clashed against Kaldon's. His quick movements proved Tymas had clearly mastered the blade.

The Sovereign released a loud shout, crashing his sword into Kaldon's, casting it aside. Without a weapon, he was completely defenceless. The Shan-Rafa swung his sword with precision, piercing Kaldon's shoulder.

Crumbling to the ground, Kaldon gasped. He felt his face smack against the hard floor. Breathless, he watched the Sovereign's feet coming closer.

Tymas sighed. *"Pathetic."*

Kaldon felt his clothes growing wet, stained with his own blood.

Tymas loomed over him, shaking his head. "I expected much more from the son of Dolan Thain."

As the Sovereign of Shadow took a step closer to Kaldon, one of the Nahmen approached him, leaning in to whisper in his ear. The Sovereign's countenance immediately changed from menacing to urgent. The Shan-Rafa backed away from Kaldon, quickly sheathing his sword.

"I'm sorry to cut our meeting short, Kal Wendal. I was just informed that I must be somewhere immediately," he said in a strangely pleasant tone.

Kaldon was dizzy from his loss of blood. He knew the cut was severe. If it weren't tended to, he would bleed to death.

Tymas continued, "By the way, my sword is laced with poison made by my own hand. You will have no life left in you within the hour. Sorry to spoil the surprise, but I can assure you, your passing won't be painless," he said with a laugh.

Kaldon saw *Humility* lying beside him. "You will not leave, Tymas Droll!" Fury pounded through him as he struggled to sit up.

Tymas laughed mockingly. "You cannot hold a Shan-Rafa back from fulfilling his duty, sewer rat. You aren't worth my time."

Delight stretched across the Sovereign's child-like face. "Shan-Rafa are known to be able to heal anything. However, now I must fulfill a more important mandate—one to raise the dead."

Tymas placed a hand upon each of the Nahmen's shoulders. "Nahmen, your Kreel are in the Peak of Lore. Take me there."

In a flash, Kaldon was alone in the tent.

"No!" he shouted. Frustration raged through him as pain coursed throughout his shoulder. He knew the poison was settling in his body.

Picking up his sword, he rose to his feet. His shoulder burned. His head spun as he fought blacking out from the pain.

The Sovereign is at the Peak of Lore, he thought to himself. "I failed," he said faintly to himself as he looked upon the empty tent. Tymas Droll had been right before him, and now Kaldon's moment was lost.

Silence washed over him.

"Wait, why is it silent?" Kaldon asked himself in a whisper.

Realization gripped him. The battle outside the tent had ceased.

Tolek!

Paying attention to his steps, he moved slowly so as not to faint from the rush of pain. The silence outside was eerie. He heard no sound other than the wind coursing through trees. He moved the tent flap and stumbled out. Two hundred bodies were strewn upon the ground. Not one was left standing. Tolek had slain them all, completing his part of the mission. Regret washed over Kaldon. He wished he could say the same.

Beyond the tent that once held the Sovereign of Shadow stood two figures. Tolek and Geran had their swords drawn.

A battle between two Paladins was about to begin.

"Time and time again, Marradus lunged at me. Its talons were fierce, yet I eluded them. I tried summoning fire, yet the demon dragon was immune to it. I commanded the rock of the mountain beneath me to be hurled at the beast, yet the dragon was too swift."

- Dawntan Forlorn
The First Paragon

Chapter Thirty-Eight

A Battle Between Light and Shadow

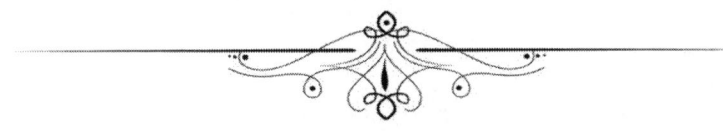

Tension roared between the two Paladins. Tolek wielded *Integrity*, the gold blade gleaming. Geran's sword curved much like the Sovereign's, except not nearly as long.

Seeing the two fight was like watching a dance of excellence. They were masters of the art of warfare. Back and forth, every lunge was strategic. Each strike held tremendous force and staggering speed.

Kaldon approached with *Humility* in hand. He doubted Tolek would invite help from him, but he also knew Geran had the upper hand in battle since he was rested. Tolek would be fatigued after slaying the two hundred soldiers. Whether he wanted it or not, the Paladin would need help.

Nearing the fight, a kick suddenly exploded into his stomach. He coiled over with a grunt. Three men with blue capes hanging down their muscular backs surrounded him with weapons drawn.

"Kaldon! Stand your ground!" Tolek shouted from between blocks and attacks.

Listening to the Paladin, he stood to avoid hitting the ground. Three Dark Bishops surrounded him, ready to pounce.

Remain calm, Kaldon reminded himself. His stomach quaked. His shoulder throbbed. At the very least, he was thankful his wounded shoulder wasn't the arm he used for battle. He could still fight.

His thoughts quickened. He had never bested Brenton even before he was a Blade. Bishops trained Blades. He waited for his foresight to spark. He hoped it would, yet doubt shrouded his expectancy. As nothing came, he grew frustrated.

He needed to move. Deciding to take the offence, Kaldon rushed in to one of the Dark Bishops. The metal of swords clanged. When the first Bishop deflected his attempt, Kaldon spun around to attack the man behind him. His mind swirled, trying to think of fighting three experienced warriors at once. He could feel his movements were erratic, much slower than usual. The poison was already taking effect, making him stiff. As attacks came, he dodged and blocked accordingly, trying to counter quickly in an attempt to throw the men off guard.

Then it came. One of the Dark Bishops pounded his fist into his wounded shoulder.

Shouting, he dropped to his knees. Kaldon held his wound as he felt his face beginning to flush. His hand was soaked in his own blood.

Dread and anxiety drifted through him as he looked up at the three enemies before him. He should have known he stood no chance against one Dark Bishop, let alone three.

A boot slammed into his face, knocking him on his back. He laid in a disorientated blur. Behind the laughs of the three Dark Bishops, he could hear the crashes and clangs of the Paladins battling. The sounds were filtered through the ringing in his head, muffling it.

"Kaldon!" a voice echoed. It was Tolek's.

The Paladin's concern warmed Kaldon, yet there was no way out for him. The Dark Bishops loomed over him. Even at his best, he knew he could not beat such formidable warriors. Even if they didn't take his life, he knew the poison soon would. Looking up to the Dark Bishops, the three were blurred. He awaited his death.

Looking past the hazy Dark Bishops, he saw the sky above them. The moment was still. Clouds drifted softly. The wind hummed gently. He supposed the calm peace was fitting in the moment where he would pass from life to death. He contemplated his life. He thought of Rundle, his father and mother, the Peak of Lore. He thought of Anneya.

Far past the drifting clouds, Kaldon saw a blaze of light. He knew it was not the sun. He lifted his hand into the sky, trying to reach the light. He supposed it was a glimpse of eternity, a place he would soon know far more intimately.

As his sight narrowed in, clarity came. Kaldon could see that the light was in fact a fire soaring in the skies. It was the Owyl of Light, the bird from eternity. He wondered if the bird of fire was bidding him a distant farewell before he drifted into the Kingdom of Light.

Then he paused.

The Kingdom of Light, Kaldon thought.

As one of the Dark Bishops raised his sword to end his life, Kaldon kept his eyes on the bird of fire illuminating the skies above them. He was taught that Divinity created every individual to have a connection to the Kingdom of Light. We simply need to build belief in that connection. He now needed belief in that link more than ever before.

He shut his eyes, focusing on how Anneya once described the Kingdom of Light during their travels to the Peak of Lore.

"If the Mountains of D'aal were a drop of water, the Kingdom of Light is an ocean. If these mountains were a flicker of flame, the Kingdom is the sun. There is no sickness or disease there. There is no anxiety, sorrow, or depression. It is an abode of perfection—flawless."

He focused on the place where there is no anxiety, sorrow, or depression. The place where there was no sickness, disease, or pain.

His eyes snapped open. Tremendous heat invaded his body in a sudden jolt. As light flashed, Kaldon's body jerked.

The three traitors launched backwards at the impact of the Kingdom of Light. Each grunted as they hit the ground.

Kaldon sat up, moving his shoulder to test for pain. The dizziness in his mind evaporated. The pain in his shoulder disappeared. His wounded flesh was mended. The stiffness in his body was gone. The poison had been dethroned.

"Great Divinity, I healed myself," Kaldon said, still unsure of how he was still alive. He slowly rose to his feet.

The Dark Bishops stood in confusion. One of the more outspoken warriors piped up, his fists trembling. "I don't know how you did that, but I don't have time for your tricks!"

Kaldon didn't have time to wrap his mind around what just happened; he needed to fight. He needed his foresight. If he could access the Kingdom of Light, he should be able to spark his gift.

Shutting his eyes in concentration, he summoned his unpredictable gift.

"I am in control," he muttered quietly.

"What is this fool doing?" one of the Dark Bishops spat out.

Another drew his sword, approaching Kaldon. "I've had enough of this."

With Kaldon's eyes still closed, the moment became still. Quiet.

In his mind, he saw a blade swinging downwards toward him. The descending sword whistled through the air. He stepped to the side as the Dark Bishop's sword whirled past him.

The Dark Bishop growled in frustration. Kaldon began seeing several attacks from the three warriors in his mind, like visions streaming through his thoughts. He responded to what he saw, dodging each attack.

When Kaldon first encountered them, he found their attacks sporadic and threatening. With his foresight active, their moves became predictable. He understood the flow of battle in a way he never did before.

Evading swords whirling around him, he dodged their attacks. A moment ago, he reached for the fire in the sky. All he needed to do now was to reach the weakened areas in the enemy's defence. As they drove at him, he moved to position himself to drive his sword into their vulnerable spots. He vowed they would fall. Every last one of them.

Wielding *Humility*, he cut, stabbed, and sliced with precision. One by one, the Dark Bishops thudded to the ground, lifeless. They were defeated under his blade.

At Geran's shout, Kaldon knew it was not a time to take in the moment of what just occurred. He watched as the Dark Paladin tirelessly thrashed his sword at Tolek. Kaldon could see Tolek was beginning to wilt under the incessant attacks. Approaching the battling Paladins, Kaldon pointed his sword at Geran.

"Kaldon, get back!" Tolek shouted between pants.

Kaldon's focus was locked on Geran.

"No," Kaldon said, unmoving.

"Another one?" Geran bellowed, briefly stepping away from Tolek. "It would be my honour to eliminate another who opposes the way of the Shadow."

With one aggressive pull, Geran ripped his shirt off from concealing his barreling chest. His bulk was intimidating.

"I don't tolerate my men being killed by petty tricks," Geran directed his comment at Kaldon. He pulled out a second curved blade, pointing one at Kaldon and the other at Tolek.

"You may have beaten my Bishops, now you will fall by my blade," he snarled.

Geran jumped, spinning in the air, thrusting his blades toward Kaldon and Tolek simultaneously in unpredictable movements. Kaldon's foresight sparked while fighting the Dark Paladin; however, Geran was difficult to read in combat. There were times when it looked like Geran would strike from one angle, but would immediately change his course of attack. He masked each attack in mystery. Kaldon's foresight was being thrown off drastically by the confusing movements. Geran came in with steady strikes and frothing rage.

As they fought the Dark Paladin, the buzz of oncoming warriors began rising. Twelve warriors stormed the battlefield.

"What do we do?" Kaldon asked Tolek in a shout.

Tolek didn't answer. Sweat streaked down the Paladin's tired face. He was wavering. Geran let out a boisterous laugh at the sight of his oncoming men.

The Dark Paladin brought his boot to Tolek's chest in a jolt, forcing him to the ground. With the Paladin down momentarily,

Geran approached Kaldon. From the other side of Kaldon, a Dark Bishop began approaching him as well.

A morbid smile spread across Geran's determined face. Kaldon, taking a defensive stance, braced his sword to block whatever came.

Like a bolt from the sky, an arrow shot past him, penetrating the Dark Bishop's back. The body dropped to the ground. Quickly looking to see where the arrow came from, his breath stopped, and emotion arose. Anneya was alive. She wasted no time rushing into the fight.

Locrian and Shar followed behind her. Shar targeted the twelve soldiers, her dark curls bouncing as she ran right at them. Locrian and Anneya rushed the Dark Paladin.

Kaldon, Tolek, Locrian, and Anneya all surrounded Geran. For the first time, there was worry in the Dark Paladin's eyes. He let out a straining yell, lifting both swords. Before he could continue, Locrian spun his staff. Anneya locked an arrow onto her bow. Kaldon and Tolek wielded their swords.

Geran spun his two blades, but with the four warriors surrounding him, there was nowhere for him to flee. There was nowhere to hide. At the consistent assault from the four sources, he thrust a sword toward Tolek. Tolek dodged in a spin, bringing the hilt of his sword into the Dark Paladin's middle. At the grunt of the General, Locrian swung his staff down upon Geran's head. Anneya fired an arrow as the metal shaft pierced into his leg. The General let out a snarl, dropping to one knee.

Kaldon saw the opportunity. He took it. Being behind Geran, he came in with *Humility*, driving the blade through the General's back.

Geran gasped, wide-eyed. With a final exhale of breath, the Dark Paladin spoke his last words. "The Dominion of Shadow will reign in Agadin," he said in a breathy exhale. "You cannot stop the Shan-Rafa."

Geran collapsed, crumpling face-first into the dirt. The four looked upon the body of the fallen General of the army of Shadow.

Locrian pressed his staff upon the matted back of the defeated Dark Paladin, saying, "I know better than to fear the threats of a dead man."

Chapter Thirty-Nine

The Weight of Responsibility

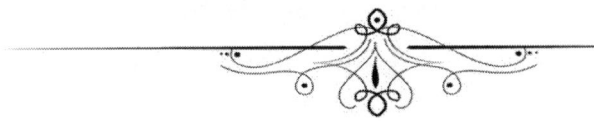

"Today we achieved a profound victory," Locrian said. "The Dark Paladin's army is beyond repair. Many of these warriors will head back to Gorath now that their leader has fallen. The death of the General will spark a memorial ceremony lasting several days. A Paladin's demise is no small occurrence."

There was an exodus of men and women fleeing over the bodies littered everywhere. Without their leader guiding them, their vision and drive were lost. They would journey through valleys and forests, back to wherever home was to them. Kreel ran loose throughout mountain and forest, no longer under the control of the Nahmen. The Mountains of D'aal were infested with them.

Locrian and Tolek stepped to the side in hushed discussion. Shar rummaged through the weapons of fallen soldiers, seeing if anything was worth taking. Behind the heap of fallen soldiers, the

Sovereign's tent still stood—a reminder of what Kaldon failed to accomplish. Letting out a steady sigh, regret seared him. The Dark Paladin may have been killed; however, he missed his chance to slay the Shan-Rafa.

Anneya grabbed his arm, pulling him aside. "I need to tell you something," she said.

Diverting his attention from the Sovereign's tent, he looked at Anneya. Thankfulness rushed through him that she was alive.

"What is it?" he asked, furrowing his brow.

She looked from side to side, making sure no one heard her. "Kaldon, I saw something on my mission with Locrian and Shar, something that changed me."

"What do you mean, *changed* you?" he asked.

She cleared her throat. "There was a Dark Bishop. I could see the hold of the Dominion of Shadow in his eyes. I was certain he was going to kill me."

Kaldon shifted as he stood at the thought of someone harming Anneya.

She paused deep in thought, then continued. "When Locrian spoke to him, he spoke with an authority I didn't know existed. It cut through the man's mania, straight to his heart. He broke down, weeping. When he rose from his tears, he seemed to be changed—new, even. I have no way of knowing for sure; however, I am nearly certain that he turned from the way of Shadow."

Kaldon listened, not knowing it was possible for someone to turn from the Shadow. "What does this mean?"

She pulled him closer, speaking in a softer tone. "It means that many of the men and women serving the Sovereign are at their core, good people. Sure, there are some, like Geran, who have allowed themselves to be fully corrupted, but others are in bondage to the lies of the Sovereign. They need to be brought back from their insanity. This man had a son and a daughter."

Kaldon heard emotion in her tone.

He stroked his chin in thought. "This is why Tymas Droll needs to be stopped. He is a prominent bridge to the Dominion of Shadow invading Agadin. He has brainwashed too many with his heresies. The people of Agadin need to be awakened."

Kaldon looked back at the shaded, ominous tent. "I need to stop him."

Anneya reached out grabbing his hand. Her thumb rubbing over his knuckles. Looking up into his emerald eyes, she said, "I will help you."

He smiled. "It will not be easy. Many have been corrupted."

"I know. For the sake of life itself, he must fall," she said.

Looking over, he saw Tolek. The Paladin ran a cloth over the blade of his sword, freeing it of the crimson stains of blood.

"Tolek," Kaldon said loudly.

The Paladin looked up.

"I failed you. I failed Agadin," Kaldon said in honesty.

A confused look stretched across the Paladin's face. "Failed? What are you talking about? This is a day of victory."

Kaldon looked away, not making eye contact with Tolek. "I failed to defeat Tymas Droll. He is still alive."

"Is it true what Geran said? That the Sovereign of Shadow is a Shan-Rafa?" Tolek asked pointedly.

Kaldon looked down in frustration. "Yes. It is true. I watched him heal a fatal wound right before my eyes."

Tolek nodded. "Then you had no chance of defeating him. I'm not sure a Shan-Rafa is even capable of being killed with a blade. They are far too skilled at healing. They heal as quickly as they are cut. Legend says they are indestructible. We need to prove this *legend* is wrong."

"I could have done something. I should have," Kaldon said as his hand rested upon the hilt of his sword. "Now Tymas Droll is in the Peak of Lore. He disappeared into thin air, by the power of a Nahmen. Lives are in peril."

"Rest, Kaldon," Locrian said, overhearing the conversation. "Geran has been defeated. His army is defused. This is something to celebrate."

Tolek still ran a cloth over *Integrity* as he spoke. "Besides, Droll isn't a threat to the Lore, even with the four Kreel he has with him. There are far too many Bishops, Blades, and Knights for one man to pose any threat, Shan-Rafa or not. My sense is he is looking for something."

"What could he be looking for?" Kaldon asked curiously.

Locrian spoke up. "We have no clue. Tymas wanted to make the Peak of Lore his trophy and failed. I now fear it wasn't his primary goal."

Chills drifted over Kaldon's skin. What could be so valuable to the Sovereign to risk forty thousand soldiers?

"All that aside, you need to understand something," Tolek stated. "You cannot blame yourself for the Sovereign living. No one has ever accomplished anything of significance without failure along the way. And you, my friend, have proven that you are called to do remarkable things."

Looking around, Kaldon saw everyone watching him.

"Kaldon, I saw you heal yourself. You glowed with the Kingdom of Light," Tolek said candidly. "I can heal, but I have never seen anyone shine as brightly as you did while summoning the Kingdom. It strained my eyes. I could hardly look at you."

Locrian approached Kaldon. "Tolek told me of what you did. Considering your lack of training, you should not have been able to defeat one Dark Bishop, let alone three."

Looking from face to face, he felt the Legacy hanging around his neck.

The Paladin eyed Kaldon. "I don't understand you. You can heal, yet you know nothing of healing. You see visions, yet you have the instincts of a Paladin. By instinct alone, you know things you should have needed training for. At the same time, you are underdeveloped in some of the most basic lessons."

Shaking his head in wonder, he continued. "I have no clue what you have the potential to be, Kaldon. I suppose time will reveal your destiny, but there is one thing I am certain of."

The group was silent as they awaited the Paladin's next words.

"Get on your knees," Tolek said with authority.

"Excuse me?" Kaldon responded, unsure.

"Get on your knees, Kaldon Thain," Tolek commanded.

Kaldon kneeled before him, resting his knees upon the rock of the Mountains of D'aal.

Kaldon's eyes met Anneya's. Her eyes watered. At the sight of her, so did his.

Tolek drew his sword, *Integrity*. "I do not know who you are called to be, Kaldon Thain, but there is no doubt in my mind that your destiny is to help write the story of Agadin."

Resting the golden blade on Kaldon's shoulder, he went on. "Kaldon Thain, as Paladin and head of the Peak of Lore, I knight you a Protector of Agadin. May Divinity guide you down roads to greatness. You are one who will write history, live out destiny, and leave an eternal imprint upon our land."

Tolek's words were not only heard, they were felt. Their weight was like a hammer slamming into Kaldon, shattering false identity. *Integrity* lifted from his shoulder. Looking up at the Paladin, he saw a sight he did not expect. Instead of holding the hilt of the sword, Tolek had the sword turned around, gripping its blade. The Paladin offered Kaldon the night-black hilt to grab.

"Tolek, this is your sword. I cannot take it," Kaldon said nearly without words.

Tolek shook his head. "I won't lie. I don't understand the full reasoning behind giving you this sword; however, there is no doubt in my mind that it belongs to you. Take up your responsibility as a Protector of Agadin."

Kaldon eyed the ancient blade. "What will be your weapon?"

Confidence blazed through Tolek's eyes. "I am a Paladin. I *am* the weapon."

Kaldon looked at the night-black hilt. He knew that grabbing it was not just a commitment to carry the mighty blade; he was also embracing the mantle of a Protector of Agadin. He wrapped his fingers around the onyx hilt, feeling its touch. His sight scaled the golden blade made of incorruptible metal. The hilt was not soft or comfortable. It was rough, reminding him that the cost he would pay to wield such a weapon was high. The sword was heavy with duty; weighty with responsibility.

Integrity found its home in his hands.

Suddenly, Locrian shuddered as his eyes grew wide with concern. "Great Divinity, no," the Seer said in a dreadful tone. The wonder of the moment was robbed by the Seer's remark.

"Locrian, what's wrong? Did you have a vision?" Anneya asked.

Locrian spoke softly. "Yes, I did. I don't understand its meaning. All I know is that I just felt grave concern come upon me for the rest of our group. Have any of you heard from Alden, Mikiel, Troy, or Bernice?"

"No, we haven't seen them since they left for their mission," Tolek replied.

Kaldon rose to his feet. "They succeeded in their mission. They must be fine," he said.

The Seer looked at each of the members standing before him. "It is true. They succeeded in their mission; however, something is dreadfully wrong."

Chapter Forty

Through Forest and Pain

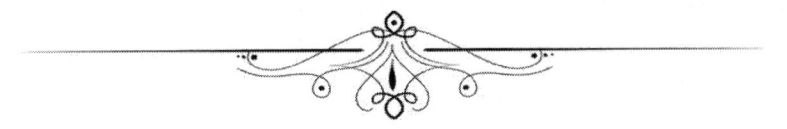

Mikiel ran.

He ran as fast as he could into the black forest. Looking up, he saw no light. Thick-jagged tree branches arched over him. No light shone in.

He didn't know how long it would take him to exit the Mountains of D'aal. All he knew was that he needed to keep going; away from the group, away from the Peak of Lore. There was no turning back. Bernice and Troy hunted him.

The young man panted, exhausted. His legs were burning, his stomach cramping from the exertion. Clutching his blood-stained dagger, his legs kept pumping, pushing him deeper into the gloomy forest.

Jumping over fallen wood and rushing past lines of trees, he thought back to the moment. He did so ever since he began running.

The morning was hazy. Dew covered the sprouting grass as it began to peek through the snow. Bernice and Troy were a ways off, asleep, after a straining night hunting Nahmen. They had completed their mission.

Various trees were spread out around an outcrop of rock. There sat Alden the Seer, sitting on the hard stone, watching the rise of the sun.

"You have finally come, Mikiel," the old Seer said, with his back turned to the young man.

"You knew I would come, old man?" he asked, caught off guard by the fact that the Seer knew it was him.

"Oh yes," Alden muttered. "I saw it in a vision."

"Of course you did," Mikiel's face soured. "Just like you saw my mother's death."

The Seer breathed a heavy breath, a tired breath. He simply looked onward.

Mikiel pulled the dagger out from his travelling clothes; it rustled the silence of morning.

"If you saw me in a vision, then you know what I am here for," he said through gritted teeth. "You will pay for my mother's death, old man."

"I am aware why you are here. You have come to give me eternal peace."

"Aren't you afraid?" Mikiel asked.

The old Seer turned around to face him. His face was draped in apathy, careless of fate. "No, I am not."

Mikiel grew agitated at Alden's indifference.

Alden continued, "I am not strong enough to fight you. Do what you have come to do quickly."

Mikiel slowly walked up to the Seer.

As he neared, the Seer stood, looking into the young man's eyes. He peered into his soul.

"What is it you see in me, old man? Do you have a final prophecy before death takes you?" Mikiel sneered.

Breathing steadily, he gazed into Mikiel. He said, "I see a man who has lost sight of himself. I see that once you heard of your mother's death, you sank so deep into pain that you gave up hope. That was the moment you embraced the Shadow. You are lost."

Tears glazed over Mikiel's eyes. "You are right, Seer. I am lost."

"Then why not turn back? It is not too late for you," Alden said, gripping his wooden staff with both hands.

Mikiel looked down at his dagger. "There is no turning back from the pain I feel."

Mikiel took in the eyes of the Seer. It was the first time he witnessed a glimpse of fear in the old Seer.

"Old man, I hope you enjoyed your last sunrise."

Mikiel finally stopped running, leaning against the trunk of a tree, panting. He looked at his dagger. Its blade did not shine. It was matted in thick maroon, stained by the blood of the Seer.

His eyes were wetted once again. He'd lost count of how many times he wept since killing the Seer. He had never taken a man's life before.

He thought about how he believed he had a profound purpose in the Great War. He knew more than ever that this was true, though his place was not where he once thought. He always thought he would fight to advance the Kingdom of Light. Now, he knew differently.

Tears dripping onto the blood-caked blade, he knew the Seer's death was not only deserved, but necessary. Looking into the mysterious woods, he knew he needed to go deeper. Deeper into the woods. Deeper into the pain.

He began his pace forward again. As he ran, he made a vow in his heart to fulfill his calling. He would walk in greatness.

He would become a *Dark Roek*.

Chapter Forty-One

Refined Like Gold

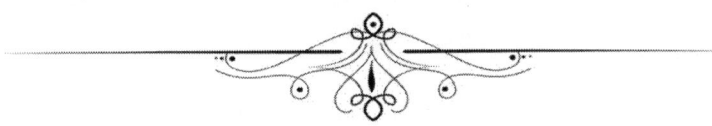

Surveying the towering trees standing before him, Kaldon heard rushing streams in the distance. Feeling the wind around him, he rested on the cool slab of stone.

He sat. He thought.

With the group preparing for their journey back to the Peak of Lore, Kaldon had time to reflect on what had taken place. The Dark Paladin was defeated. The army of Shadow was prevented from overtaking the Peak of Lore. For the first time he could remember, he felt a steady peace. He'd felt peace from the Kingdom of Light before, yet this was not the same. It wasn't external. It swelled up from within him.

He felt *Humility* hanging from his waist; *Integrity* was strapped to his back. Both swords reflected the weight of responsibility he now carried to protect Agadin. Mikiel and the rest of his group were still lost and needed to be found. The Door of the Dominion was still open, and though he didn't understand the full implications of that, he felt its severity. There was much to be done. He stopped himself, knowing it wasn't a moment to overwhelm himself with what still needed to be done. It was a time to take in what had already occurred. It was a day of victory.

Reaching into his cloak, he pulled out the notebook Fen had given him. He was at the final pages of her transcription. Kaldon flipped open the book.

"I saw no hope. The demon dragon seemed impenetrable. I feared the creature would ceaselessly reign over Agadin, causing endless death and destruction. Then it struck me. Such a beast could not be defeated by the elements of Agadin as it was empowered by the Dominion of Shadow. It must bow to the will of the Golden Land.

"From atop the mountain, I stretched forth my hands into the dreary air. I had called the Golden Land to Agadin many times before. I had done so to heal. I saw the Golden Land to understand the River of Time in visions; however, this was like nothing I had ever done before. As my hands reached for the skies, I watched the black clouds part, dividing them in two.

"Then, I saw it. A bronze line pierced the sky. Then, it opened. Above the beast, Marradus, I saw eternity open like a door in the sky. It was the most remarkable sight I ever witnessed. I began to Command Creation; however, I did not command the creation of Agadin. I called forth the elements of eternity.

"Through the deep chasm into eternity that split open the sky, I saw a bolt of lightning. The bolt was so bright, I feared my sight would be lost. I summoned the lightning from the Golden Land into Agadin.

"The lightning bolt from the Golden Land cracked into Agadin's skies, striking Marradus. I watched as the lightning pierced through the beast's onyx scales. The creature roared in lamenting woes. Marradus thrashed through the air, trying to stay in flight.

"The dragon's strength failed. It fell from the sky like an avalanche. Marradus tumbled down the mountain until it crashed upon solid ground, defeated. Agadin was finally safe from the dreadful creature.

"It took me quite some time to descend the mountain to stand before the slain demon. Yet, when I did, I ran my hand over its onyx scales. I then saw

where the lightning bolt from the Golden Land struck the beast. The strike of the bolt left some of the dragon's scales a golden colour. The stained scales were forever marked by the hue of eternity.

"It took me several hours to detach what I could of the dragon's scales. Considering the size, all I could carry was one of the golden scales and a small fragment of one of the onyxes. Their weight made for a staggering journey back.

"I brought the two scales to the most formidable blacksmith in all of Agadin. I would have a weapon fit for one such as myself forged from the scales. The onyx scale was constructed for a sword's hilt. It was as dark as the blackest of nights. The golden scale, its exact opposite, shone endlessly. The colour emanated like the rise of the sun. It was forged as the blade of the sword. A black hilt and gold blade. I had never seen a sword with a golden blade. It was one marked with the very essence of the Golden Land. It was truly a sword fit for a Paragon. I named it Integrity."

- Dawntan Forlorn
The First Paragon

Shaken by the revelation, Kaldon felt the weight of *Integrity* upon his back. There was more written in the book, but he couldn't bring himself to continue. Laying it on the ground, he reached behind his back, pulling forth the sword in awe.

Trembling, he took in the golden blade and night-black hilt. The entire sword was crafted by the scales of Marradus and held the essence of the Kingdom of Light. It was the sword of a Paragon.

Looking into the blade, he saw his reflection. He thought of the occurrences that led him to that very moment. From the sewers of Rundle, he now held the sword of a Paragon.

Earlier in Dawntan's journal, he wrote, "*A Paragon draws from the gifts of the five protectors. A Paragon is all five at once, yet at the same time, is none. A Paragon has the mind of a Philosopher, the vision of a Seer, the compassion of a Shan-Rafa, the skill of a Roek, the courage of a*

Paladin." A Paragon is the sixth Protector of Agadin.

He wondered.

Kaldon rose. Looking to a near rock, he saw the light of sun beaming upon it. Steam rose from the charcoal coloured stone. The stone reminded him of Locrian and his lesson of Commanding Creation.

Kaldon focused intently on the steam that rose from the stone. He gave his attention to the heat.

Heat, become flames of fire, Kaldon thought.

The heat waves rose steadily from the stone, unchanging.

He shifted, refocusing his thoughts.

Heat, become flames of fire, Kaldon spoke in his mind more adamantly.

Nothing happened.

Kaldon remembered Locrian's words. Commanding Creation had little to do with power. It wasn't about strength. It was about authority. Authority was born from unflinchingly knowing who you were. It came from understanding identity.

Holding the golden blade before him, he watched it, mesmerized by the mark of eternal lightning. He looked back at the stone.

Instead of speaking in his mind, Kaldon spoke aloud. "Heat! I command you to become flames of fire!"

Heat waves from the stone quickly thickened, evolving from steam to smoke. The smoke swept high-ward into the air as sparks began cracking from its core. Reds, oranges, and yellows emerged, beginning to tumble through the smoke. Flames stretched forth, taking full form.

The fire flowed through the air like a river. It blazed as it neared Kaldon, wrapping itself around *Integrity*. Flames circled the blade, like a dance upon the ancient sword.

"Kaldon? Are you over here?" The familiar voice came from nearby trees. As he held the flaming sword before his face, he listened to her footsteps.

"Kaldon!" Anneya said, stepping into plain sight, seeing his sword engulfed in fire.

Awestruck, she watched the bewildering sight. "Great Divinity... what is happening?" she whispered.

With assurance moulded in his expression, Kaldon peered over to Anneya. He looked at the woman who was much more to him than simply a Blade.

As fire tumbled upon his sword, the flames blazed in unison with a raging roar inside his soul. His voice was as strong as a mountain; confident, like refined gold.

He said, "I believe I have finally discovered who I am."

Chapter Forty-Two

Slumber's End

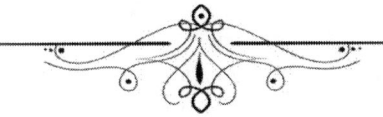

"The bones of Marradus were impossible to destroy. Fire could not burn them. Rock could not crush them. My only option was to hide them. I scattered the bones throughout Agadin, hoping they would never be discovered. The skull of the demon dragon was hidden where it was slain, deep within the isolated mountain.

"I hid the skull as best I could. To do so, not only did I hide the skull, but I hid the mountain. I did what Roeks said was impossible and foolish to even consider. I called forth mountains from the ground. I created them: multitudes of them. The lonely mountain was no longer alone. It was hidden amongst its peers. Distinct chasms were left from where the mountains were called.

"I hid the skull in the very mountain where I would found a facility for training Protectors of Agadin. I would train Paladins, Seers, Philosophers, Roeks, and Shan-Rafas. Deep in the soul of the mountain, the skull slept. Deep within a place I named, 'The Peak of Lore.'"

- Dawntan Forlorn
The First Paragon

"You aren't authorized to be here," Fen said, bravely standing in front of an arched-stone doorway leading deeper into the Depths.

With two Nahmen beside him, Tymas Droll looked upon the guardian of the Depths.

He looked at the walls, covered in extraordinarily rare books. He wished he had time to examine them; however, time was not in his favour. He knew those in the Peak of Lore were likely in a frenzy trying to find the four missing Kreel, his link to transporting into the training facility.

"Oh, Philosopher, I am not here for your precious books. I am here for something far more significant," he explained.

"You aren't taking anything from this library," she said sternly, unmoving.

"I am the Sovereign of Shadow. I will take what I please. If you won't move, I have those who will make you."

Tymas spoke into the ears of one of his Nahmen. "Call my Kreel."

Immediately, four Kreel stepped into the dimly lit chamber of the Depths.

At the sight of the Kreel, she froze, unable to move in the presence of such dreadful beasts. The Kreel stood before her, snarling. With ease, one of them lifted its arm, pushing the Philosopher to the side. Showing no strength for resistance, she crashed into the stone wall, falling to the ground unconscious.

"Should I command the Kreel to eliminate the Philosopher?" one of the Nahmen asked cryptically.

Tymas pondered in thought. "Let's leave her be for now, Nahmen. I am feeling in a rather generous mood today, considering what we are about to find."

The Nahmen obliged in obedience.

Tymas strolled through the doorway leading deeper into the mountain. Following the rocky-stair pathway, he descended into the mountain. He travelled downward for longer than he would have preferred. The facility ran deep; however, he knew a prize awaited him. The path grew darker. No light shone other than the two torches his Nahmen carried. The pathway grew even more cave-like than it already was. It grew dank. Moist. As the Sovereign shuffled over the stone path, he felt water beginning to soak his feet.

Then he saw it. He almost missed it after mistaking it for a colossal boulder.

"Oh, Furion, thank you for guiding me so well," Tymas spoke aloud. His voice echoed throughout the enclosed space.

His eyes took in the magnificent sight. Its teeth, the size of a grown man. Its horns reigning tall. The boned snout that once breathed dreaded flames.

Tymas brushed his fingers along the holes where its reptilian eyes once rested.

"The very last piece to my collection," he whispered to himself, smiling. He had been collecting the bones for several years. Many lives were lost to obtain the ancient relics: the bones of a dragon.

Tymas Droll knew who he was. He knew what he was. He was a Shan-Rafa. All the bones he had spent the last several years accumulating were together in his hometown. Now he would bring the final piece, the skull, back as well; back to Gorath. Then he could perform what only a Shan-Rafa could do.

He would raise the dead.

The Sovereign of Shadow caressed the skull. He stroked it with care. The skull of Marradus.

Through the stale cave air, Tymas whispered into the ear of the long-dead dragon, Marradus.

"My dear one, you were never meant to be confined in a tomb. Let's make a dragon fly again, shall we?"

Story Continues In...

A Journey through Fire

Rise of Shadow • Reign of Light

Volume II

L.R. Knight is the fiction pseudonym of Dr. Luc Niebergall. Luc lives in Alberta, Canada, with his wife of many years. He is the author of many books in multiple genres: teaching, fiction, children's literature, biographies, and history. Luc is recognized as an acclaimed public speaker who teaches around the world. Luc has a father's heart, which is prevalent in his storytelling.

"Stories can speak to the hidden places of our souls. They encourage us to lay aside the complexities of adulthood; to once again embrace childlike wonder."

– Dr. Luc Niebergall

Manufactured by Amazon.ca
Bolton, ON